Dedalus European Classics
General Editor: Timothy Lane

THIS WOMAN,
THIS MAN

GEORGE SAND

THIS WOMAN, THIS MAN

Translated with an
Introduction & Notes by

Graham Anderson

Dedalus

Supported using public funding by
**ARTS COUNCIL
ENGLAND**

Published in the UK by Dedalus Limited
24-26, St Judith's Lane, Sawtry, Cambs, PE28 5XE
info@dedalusbooks.com
www.dedalusbooks.com

ISBN printed book 978 1 912868 81 0
ISBN ebook 978 1 915568 07 6

Dedalus is distributed in the USA & Canada by SCB Distributors
15608 South New Century Drive, Gardena, CA 90248
info@scbdistributors.com   www.scbdistributors.com

Dedalus is distributed in Australia by Peribo Pty Ltd
58, Beaumont Road, Mount Kuring-gai, N.S.W. 2080
info@peribo.com.au   www.peribo.com.au

First published in France in 1859
First published by Dedalus in 2022

Translation & Introduction copyright © Graham Anderson 2022

The right of Graham Anderson to be identified as the translator of this work
has been asserted by him in accordance with the Copyright, Designs and
Patents Act, 1988.

Printed and bound in the UK by Clays Elcograf S.p.A.
Typeset by Marie Lane

A C.I.P. listing for this book is available on request.

THE AUTHOR

Amantine Lucile Aurore Dupin (1804–1876), best known by her pen name George Sand was a novelist, memoirist, and journalist. One of the most popular writers in Europe in her lifetime being more renowned than both Victor Hugo and Honoré de Balzac in England in the 1830s and 1840s, Sand is recognised as one of the most notable writers of the European Romantic era.

In 1880 her children sold the rights to her literary estate for 125,000 francs (equivalent to 36 kg worth of gold, or 1.3 million dollars in 2015). During her lifetime her novels set in the French countryside were her most popular works.

This Woman, This Man (*Elle et Lui*) is not only unlike any of her other novels, but also the most autobiographical work of one of the great female trailblazers in French literature.

THE TRANSLATOR

Graham Anderson was born in London. After reading French and Italian at Cambridge, he worked on the book pages of *City Limits* and reviewed fiction for *The Independent* and *The Sunday Telegraph*. As a translator, he has developed versions of French plays, both classic and contemporary, for the NT and the Gate Theatre, with performances both here and in the USA. Publications include *The Figaro Plays* (Beaumarchais) and *A Flea in Her Ear* (Feydeau).

For Dedalus he has translated *Sappho* by Alphonse Daudet, *Chasing the Dream* and *A Woman's Affair* by Liane de Pougy, *This was the Man* (*Lui*) by Louise Colet and *This Woman, This Man* (*Elle et Lui*) by George Sand. His translations of Grazia Deledda's short story collections *The Queen of Darkness* and *The Christmas Present* will be published by Dedalus in 2023. He is currently translating *Marianna Sirca* by Grazia Deledda for Dedalus.

His own short fiction has won or been shortlisted for three literary prizes. He is married and lives in Oxfordshire.

INTRODUCTION

On 17th June 1833, at a restaurant dinner in Paris organised for his contributors by François Buloz, director of *La Revue des deux mondes*, the novelist George Sand met the poet Alfred de Musset. By the end of the following month, Sand, just turned twenty-nine, and Musset, not yet twenty-three, were lovers. The improbable liaison rapidly developed into a consuming passion on both sides, to the surprise, disapproval and sometimes mirth of those who moved in literary circles. In August of the same year, the couple escaped the prying eyes for a week of romantic solitude in the forest of Fontainebleau. There, Sand witnessed some of the young poet's extremes of behaviour, in particular a hallucinatory episode during a night spent out in the open. In December, the day after the poet's twenty-third birthday, the pair set off on a working tour of Italy. They stopped at Genoa and Florence before arriving in Venice at the turn of the year. Sand had fallen ill in Genoa and was still recovering when they established themselves in an apartment in what is now the Hotel Danieli. Musset's predilection for nocturnal wanderings continued even while his mistress spent the first fortnight of January bed-ridden. The relationship, which had always swung between highs and lows, fierce arguments and impassioned reconciliations, was put under further strain when Musset, in turn, fell ill. He was nursed devotedly by Sand. She secured the professional attendance of a Dr Pietro Pagallo, who diagnosed a kind of typhoid fever. As Musset grew stronger, it became clear that Dr Pagallo had fallen for his patient's charming and distinguished companion. By March, his physical health restored but his emotional health in ruins, Musset abandoned a lost cause and sadly returned to Paris. This however was not the end of the affair, which, after the Pagallo interlude, continued on and off for a further twelve months.

A generation later, in 1859, George Sand published *Elle et Lui*, the present volume. It is the most autobiographical of her works, being a fictionalised account of the notorious affair. Alfred de Musset had died two years earlier, aged 46, weakened by alcoholic excess and a failing heart. His elder brother, Paul de Musset, incensed by her portrayal of the poet and anxious to preserve his reputation, wrote an immediate riposte, *Lui et Elle*. Louise Colet, a woman of letters and once Flaubert's mistress, who had herself formed an attachment with Musset in his later years, produced her own novel, *Lui*, also in 1859. There followed something of a feeding frenzy among contemporary literati, with a hack writer, Gaston Lavalley, publishing a mocking *Eux*, and a series of more or less scathing articles appearing in both the newspapers and the gossip sheets.

There can be little doubt that George Sand was, and deserves still to be considered, a remarkable woman. Although not widely read nowadays in Anglophone countries, her literary output was vast: over a hundred published works, mainly novels, but also including stories, novellas, memoirs, poetry and plays. But over and above these works, Sand's life was a statement of intent and a beacon for generations of women who followed.

She was born in Paris on 1st July 1804, and christened Amande Aurore Lucile. Her father, Maurice Dupin de Francueil, was an officer in Napoleon's revolutionary army, and she spent the fourth year of her young life travelling with him on his campaigns in Spain. Her mother, Sophie Victorine Delaborde, came from different stock: her father was a sometime innkeeper and seller of birdseed. The two were married a month before Aurore's birth, despite the efforts of Maurice Dupin's widowed mother, Madame Dupin de Francueil, to prevent the alliance. Shortly after the couple's return to the family home, the Château de Nohant, in the Berry region, Maurice Dupin died in a riding accident, leaving young Aurore's upbringing and education to be contested between the mother and grandmother.

The spirited – if feckless – mother lived in Paris, abandoning Aurore to her grandmother's care for long stretches. The child's loyalties were miserably torn between the two older women. Eventually she was sent to a convent school run by English nuns in Paris. She emerged after three years, aged sixteen, to be tutored at Nohant. When her grandmother died a year later, Aurore became heiress of the Château de Nohant while still a minor. She was sent to stay with family friends near Melun, where she met and married, in 1822, François Casimir Dudevant, a former soldier like her father and now a lawyer. Their first child, Maurice, was born in 1823, but the marriage proved unhappy. Casimir Dudevant, as the husband, had full control of the Nohant property, but his tastes and sensibilities in no way matched those of his young wife. Their life at Nohant was turbulent: Casimir drank, was rude to the servants, pursued the prettier female ones. Aurore, on her side, formed a friendship with a neighbour, sufficiently closely to cast doubt in local minds on the paternity of her daughter, Solange, born in 1828. By then, husband and wife were sleeping in separate rooms.

Aurore began to chafe for her independence, for the right to manage her own possessions. She had already written a number of private travelogues, and when she met the young novelist Jules Sandeau, her ideas turned towards a life of letters in Paris. She finally made the break in 1830, after coming across her husband's Will and finding in it malicious and disparaging remarks about his wife. Divorce was impossible at the time, and legal separation a long and arduous process (her case was not finally resolved until 1836). Encountering Jules Sandeau again just after *Les Trois Glorieueses*, the three days in July 1830 when the Bourbon monarchy was overthrown by the Parisian uprising, she resolved to join him in the brave new world which seemed to thrive among the young artists and writers of the Latin quarter. They both began to write for the new newspaper *Le Figaro*, combining on a number of projects which ended, in the autumn of 1831, with a jointly written novel, *Rose et Blanche*. This work, a success, was attributed to the authorship of J. Sand. When Aurore produced a novel, *Indiana*, in which Sandeau had no hand, he declined to take any credit and instead, to preserve a sense of continuity, and at the publisher's suggestion, the book was attributed to G. Sand. In choosing George, a male name, in its English spelling, Aurore Dudevant was offering the world, and herself, an intriguing new identity.

A further novel, *Valentine*, published in 1832, advanced her reputation, and improved her financial position. She moved to a better apartment in Paris and the editor of *La Revue des deux mondes* contracted her to write for his journal for an annual fee of 4000 francs. The writer George Sand was launched.

By the time of her infatuation with Musset in the summer of 1833, she had ended her liaison with Sandeau (because of his infidelities), endured a brief and hurtful episode with Prosper Mérimée, begun a deep friendship with the actress Marie Dorval, written what is now perhaps the best remembered of her books, *Lélia* (published in August) and proved to herself that she could both earn a living – the husband still had control of the Nohant estate's revenues, although the property itself belonged to the wife – and find the means to express her ever-growing commitment to the idea of what would now be called women's rights. *Lélia*, a novel which argued that monogamous marriage was an unnatural state and that the opprobrium heaped on women who stepped outside it, whilst men seemed to be granted licence, made a mockery of love, as well as of justice, provoked sharp divisions in a society already in social ferment. By the time of its publication, she was already a distinctive figure in the world of Parisian letters. Having received dispensation from the authorities in Berry to wear men's clothes for the practical purpose of moving more easily about the Nohant countryside, she had access to places and events in the capital where unaccompanied women would not normally be seen. She smoked in public, even (which was worse) when dressed as a woman. And she was known to be in effect, a single mother who had her two young children living with her as often as arrangements with Casimir allowed.

Far from being an angry firebrand it is perhaps worth observing that the people who met her at this time were impressed by the calm serenity of her manner, her hard-working discipline, her apparent self-assurance, her kindly-directed if sometimes forbidding intelligence. Although no great beauty by contemporary standards, she seemed to exercise with her great dark eyes and lustrous black hair a magnetic effect on all who came to know her.

The young Alfred de Musset certainly fell under her spell. Born in Paris in December 1810, the same year as both Chopin, with whom Sand had an equally famous and much longer-lasting relationship, and Louise Colet, author of *Lui*, Musset came from an upper class but by no means rich family. His father worked in a number of positions within the French administration, while his mother, similarly placed socially and financially, managed to sustain a role as a society hostess. Alfred, their younger son, was sent to the distinguished Lycée Henri IV, where he was a classmate of the son of the future constitutional monarch Louis-Philippe. His excellent connections and his precocious literary talents earned him an invitation to join, at only seventeen, the literary salon known as *Le Cénacle*, hosted by Charles Nodier, director of the library of the Arsenal. His first poetry collection, *Contes d'Espagne et d'Italie*, appeared as early as 1829. After abandoning a number of potential career paths, he secured a position as librarian at the French Ministry of the Interior under the July monarchy, and set about an enthusiastic private life as a dandy and haunter of brothels. A rising star, he was already well-known by the time of his meeting George Sand at the restaurant Lointier on

12

17th June 1833.

There could hardly have been two more different characters, with such different experiences of life. From the very outset, those differences both excited the new lovers (Musset moved into Sand's apartment on quai Malaquais at the end of July) and brought them much grief. Musset could not or would not abandon his dissolute habits. The incident in Fontainebleau forest, when Musset believed he had been visited by his own double, was striking enough to be recorded, in different fashions, by Sand, Louise Colet and the poet himself. There is a passage towards the end of Colet's *Lui* in which the character representing Musset describes four or five such uncanny apparitions or premonitions. After four months of turbulent co-habitation, the two lovers embarked in the late autumn of 1833 on their Italian adventure. The overland journey south passed well enough, but Musset proved no sailor and in a foretaste of things to come, the stronger-stomached Sand had to nurse a stricken companion through the sea voyage from Marseilles to Genoa. It is here that, in Sand's novel, the lovers' difficulties come to a head. In Colet's, the short spells in Genoa and Florence are only a prelude to the three months the couple spent in Venice. In this respect, as in many others, Colet's *Lui* follows known events far more closely than Sand's *Elle et Lui*. For Sand, the objective is to capture the atmosphere of a relationship, the shifting layers of feeling which bind lovers together or force them apart. It does not matter that she makes the two lovers artists rather than writers; it does not matter that she makes no mention at all of Venice, concentrating the action on Genoa, Florence and Portovenere, near La Spezia; it does not matter that the third party in what becomes a battle for her favours is presented not as a young Italian doctor but as an older American family friend. The woman's right in any relationship is to be respected, to hold her own views, to belong to nobody but herself. She may give herself to a man, but the giving subtracts nothing from her essential independence of action and thought. It is rather, whether briefly or permanently, an expression of her power to choose.

Musset left Italy dejected, at the end of March 1834. Sand stayed on with Dr Pagallo until August. She returned to Paris, still with Pagallo, in the middle of the month. A desperate Musset sought an interview, which was granted. Each party acknowledged its own faults, but there the reconciliation ended. It was decided they were better apart: Musset retired to the spa of Baden while Sand retreated to Nohant (Pagallo remaining in Paris, something of a fish out of water in this highly-charged drama between two prominent literati). The separation lasted two months. Musset besieged Sand with pleading letters and finally, in October, she yielded. This time it was a dejected Pagallo who returned home. The renewed relationship rapidly ran into the old problems, and a few weeks later it was Musset who broke with Sand. When he persistently refused to respond to her letters she sent him instead a parcel containing a quantity of her famous hair, which she had cut off in a dramatic gesture of appeal. It was at this time that the painter Eugène Delacroix, commissioned by Sand's publisher Buloz, made his first portrait of the writer, showing her in man's clothing with her shortened hair, wearing on her face an expression of deep sadness. The final act came in January 1835, when the bruised pair made a third attempt at getting an impossible relationship to work. Sand was initially triumphant, writing to Musset's friend and confidant Alfred Tattet (who appears in Colet's *Lui* as Alfred Nattier): 'Alfred is my lover again.' But complaints and verbal abuse on his side – he disapproved amongst other things of her strict working regime, which would see her settle at her desk at midnight and write until morning – and hectoring and recrimination on hers (she disapproved equally strongly of his lack of self-discipline), disfigured the mutual passion as catastrophically as before. In early March, George Sand made the definitive break.

Of the two parties, Musset was the more affected. Nothing, for him, was ever quite the same again. In literary terms however, his experience bore significant fruits. A burst of creativity saw Musset produce some of his best work: *Fantasio* (1834), *Les Nuits*, and in 1836, *La Confession d'un enfant du siècle*. The *Confession*, a novel, deals with the Sand affair in the much wider context of the *mal du siècle*, the yearning for an unrealised ideal which characterised the post-1830 era. The character representing Sand was treated with kindness and respect in this work, and Musset's former mistress was not at all displeased by it.

Meanwhile Sand continued her prolific output (it was after all her means of support), writing *Mattea*, *Leone Leoni*, *André*, *Jacques* and the first of her *Lettres d'un voyageur* while still in Venice with Pagallo in the spring and summer of 1834. Her work began to take an increasingly political and socialist turn under the influence of various thinkers: l'abbé Lammenais, the lawyer Michel de Bourges and the philosopher Pierre Leroux. Only after her disappointments following the uprisings of 1848, which saw the fall of Louis-Philippe, and a few years later, the *coup d'Etat* in which the second republic was usurped by the self-proclaimed empire of Louis Napoleon, did her active engagement start to fall away. In the meantime she had broken with her daughter Solange over the latter's marriage to the sculptor Auguste Clésinger, against her mother's wishes. An unhappy period in her life, which coincided with the ending of her long relationship (1838-47) with Frédéric Chopin, found some relief when she met, through her son Maurice, a little-known engraver and playwright called Alexandre Manceau. Although thirteen years her junior, Manceau remained her lover, confidant and secretary from 1852 until his death from tuberculosis in 1865.

Her later years were enriched by a friendship with Gustave Flaubert, to whom she wrote in praise following the publication of his novel *Salammbô* in 1862. A long and warm correspondence ensued, which may seem ironical in the light of Flaubert's earlier association with Louise Colet, who had portrayed Sand in critical terms in her own account of the Musset affair, *Lui*.

George Sand, by now a grand figure – she refused the *legion d'honneur* in 1873 – was to spend increasing periods of time at Nohant, entertaining a wide circle of friends, thinkers and artists, and still producing one or two novels a year. It was there that she died in June 1876, aged seventy-one. (Louise Colet had died in March of the same year.) She remains today a prominent and significant personality, as much for her bold engagement with contemporary issues and for her high-profile love affairs as for her many and varied writings. She was nevertheless, quite possibly, the first truly professional woman writer in nineteenth-century France.

For interested readers, Louise Colet's novel, *Lui*, is also published by Dedalus Books under the title *This Was the Man*, while Musset's *La Confession d'un enfant du siècle* is available in English translations elsewhere.

TO MADEMOISELLE JACQUES

My dear Thérèse – since you permit me not to address you as Mademoiselle – I have an important piece of news from *the world of the arts*, to use the phrase of Bernard, a fellow close to our hearts. Look, that rhymes! Although what I have to tell you contains neither rhyme nor reason.

Just imagine: when I got back home yesterday, having bored you enough with my visit, I found an English Lord waiting for me… well, maybe he's not a Lord; but he's certainly an Englishman, and this is what he said to me, in his mangled French: 'You are a painter?'

'Yes' (I said in English), 'my Lord.'

'You do faces?'

'Yes, my Lord.'

'And hands?'

'Yes, my Lord. Feet too.'

'Good!'

'They're very good!'

'Oh, I am sure! Well then! Will you do a portrait of me?'

'Of you?'

'Why not?'

The *why not* came out in such a good-natured way that

I ceased to take him for an imbecile, especially since the son of Albion is a magnificent specimen. Think of the head of an Antinoüs on the shoulders of… on the shoulders of an Englishman; a head from the best period of classical Greece mounted on the somewhat strangely suited and cravatted exemplar of British 'fashion'.

'Well, my word, you are a fine model, that's for sure, and I'd love to make a study of you for my own purposes; but I can't do your portrait.'

'Why is that?'

'Because I am not a portrait painter.'

'Oh…! Do you have to buy a separate licence in France for each specialism in the arts?'

'No, but the public doesn't like it if we have lots. It wants to know what sort of thing to associate us with, especially when we're young. And if I, standing before you now and clearly very young, were to have the misfortune of doing an excellent portrait of you, it would be very difficult for me to succeed at the next exhibition with anything except portraits. And equally, if I only made a very ordinary portrait of you, the public would forbid me ever to attempt any again: they would decree that I did not possess the necessary qualities for such work and that it was presumptuous of me to chance my arm.'

I told my Englishman plenty more similar nonsense, which I won't bore you with, but which left him wide-eyed. He started to laugh, and it was clear my explanations were inspiring him with the greatest contempt for France, if not for your humble servant.

'To come to the point,' he said, 'the truth is, you don't like portraiture.'

'What! Do you take me for a complete barbarian? No, you must understand that I do not yet dare to attempt portraits, and that it would be inappropriate for me to do so, since one of two things must apply: either it is a specialism which excludes all others, or it is the mark of perfection, the crowning achievement of one's talent, so to speak. Some painters, incapable of actually composing a picture, can copy the living model faithfully and pleasantly enough. They can guarantee a successful career, however little they understand how to present the model in the most favourable way or possess the skill to dress it to its advantage whilst dressing it in fashion. But when one is only a poor painter of historical scenes, very much a beginner and very controversial, as I have the honour to be, one cannot join battle with the professionals. I confess to you that I have never scientifically studied how the folds of a black coat fall and the particularities of a given physiognomy. I am an unfortunate inventor of attitudes, types and expressions. They all have to conform to the idea I have in mind, my subject, the way I envision it if you like. If you were to allow me to dress you in a costume of my choosing and to set you in a composition of my devising… well, there again, you see, it would be pointless, it wouldn't be you. It wouldn't be a portrait you could give to your mistress… still less to your legitimate wife. Neither of them would recognise you. Therefore, don't ask me now to produce what I shall have the skill to do one day, certainly, if by chance I turn into Rubens or Titian, because then I shall have the knowledge to be a poet and creator still, whilst effortlessly and fearlessly capturing reality in all its strength and majesty. Sadly, it is not likely that I shall become anything more than a madman or a beast. Read

Messrs This and That, who have said as much in their articles.'

As you may imagine, Thérèse, I did not say a word of all this to my Englishman: one always elaborates when one puts words in one's own mouth. But of all the things I was able to say by way of excusing my inability to paint portraits, these are the only words which did any good: 'Why on earth don't you ask Mlle Jacques?'

He exclaimed 'Oh!' three times, after which he asked for your address, and off he went without a second thought, leaving me very confused and very cross at not being able to finish my dissertation on portraiture. Because, after all, my good Thérèse, if this fine English animal comes to call on you today, as I think him capable of doing, and if he repeats everything I have just been writing, that is, everything I did not in fact say, on the *manufacturers* and the leading artists, what will you think of your ungrateful friend! That he ranks you amongst the leading artists and judges you incapable of doing anything except nice pretty portraits that everybody likes! Ah, my dear friend, if only you'd heard all the things I told him about you after he'd left…! You know already: you know that, for me, you are not Mlle Jacques who produces those lifelike portraits so much in vogue, but a superior man who has disguised himself as a woman and who, without ever having attended the academy, divines, and knows how to reveal in a head-and-shoulders, the full truth of a body and of a soul, in the manner of the great Renaissance painters. But I fall silent: you don't like to be told what people think of you. You pretend to take it as mere compliments. You are very proud, Thérèse.

I am altogether melancholy today, I don't know why. I lunched so poorly at midday… I never ate so badly before

I had a cook. And then one can't get decent tobacco any more. The state is poisoning us. And then my new boots were delivered and they didn't suit at all… and then it's raining… and then, and then what do I know? For some time now the days have been as long as days with no bread, don't you find? No, you don't find, not you. You don't know this kind of malaise, pleasure which bores, boredom which excites, the nameless affliction I was talking to you about the other evening in that little lilac sitting room where I would like to be now. Because this is a hopeless day for painting, and not being able to paint, it would give me pleasure to weary you with my conversation.

So I shall not see you today! You have your unbearable family there, stealing you for themselves and robbing your most delightful friends of your company! I shall therefore be forced to go out tonight and commit some unspeakable folly…! That is the effect of your kindness towards me, my great and dear friend. It makes me feel so silly and useless when I don't see you that I absolutely have to go off and deaden my sorrows and risk scandalising you. But don't worry, I shan't tell you how I spend my evening.

Your friend and humble servant,
LAURENT   11th May, 183…

**

TO M. LAURENT DE FAUVEL

First, my dear Laurent, if you feel some degree of friendship towards me, I ask you not to commit too often follies that might damage your health. I grant you all the others. Now you will demand an example of such a thing, and there you have me; for embarrassingly, as far as follies go, I know very few which are not harmful. It depends on what you count as follies. If they include those long supper parties you were telling me about the other day, I believe they are killing you and I am very unhappy about them. What are you thinking of, good God, to destroy in such a manner, and so light-heartedly, an existence that is so precious and so beautiful? But you don't want any sermons: I will confine myself to prayer.

As for your Englishman, who is an American, I have just seen him, and since I shall not see you this evening or tomorrow either, perhaps, to my great regret, I have to tell you that you are making a serious error in not wishing to do his portrait. He would have offered you the eyes out of his head, and the eyes out of the head of an American like Dick Palmer amount to a lot of banknotes – which you need, for the very purpose of not committing follies, in other words, not playing poker in the hope of a stroke of luck which never happens to people with imagination, seeing that people with imagination are hopeless gamblers. They always lose, and then have to call on their imagination to pay off their debts, a job which that particular princess does not feel herself suited to, and which she can only undertake at the expense of setting fire to the poor body in which she dwells.

You find me very positive, I expect? Well, that's all the same to me. In any case, if we consider things on a higher plane, none of the reasons you gave your American and me is worth tuppence. You are not capable of producing portraits: yes, that is possible, even certain, if it has to be done in terms of bourgeois success. But M. Palmer was not demanding such a thing at all. You took him for a grocer and you were wrong. He is a man of judgement and taste, he knows his business, and he is enthusiastic about you. Imagine how I received him! He came to me as a last resort, as was very clear to me, and I was grateful to him. And so I consoled him by promising to do everything in my power to persuade you to paint him. We shall discuss the matter therefore, the day after tomorrow, because I arranged for the said Palmer to come here in the evening to help me plead his cause and ensure that he departs with your promise.

On which note, my dear Laurent, try your best to ease the pain of not seeing me for two days. That won't be difficult for you; you know a great many lively spirits, and you have your foot in the door of the smartest sort of society. Whereas I am just a preachy old woman who is very fond of you, who urges you not to go to bed late every night, and who advises you to avoid all excesses and abuses. You do not have the right: talent has its obligations.

Your comrade,
THÉRÈSE JACQUES

***

TO MADEMOISELLE JACQUES

My dear Thérèse, I am leaving in two hours' time for a country house party with the Count of S… and Prince D… youth and beauty will be present, or so I am assured. I promise and I swear to commit no follies and to drink no champagne…

without bitter self-reproach! What else can I do? I would certainly have preferred to wander round your spacious studio, and talk nonsense in your little lilac sitting room. But since you are in retreat with your umpteen provincial cousins, you will certainly not notice my absence the day after tomorrow either: you will have the delightful music of the Anglo-American accent for the whole evening! Ah! He's called Dick, is he, that good M. Palmer? I thought that Dick was the abbreviation for Richard used between intimates! It's true that when it comes to languages, French is the only one I know anything about.

As for the portrait, don't let's discuss it any further. You are far too maternal, my good Thérèse, thinking about my interests to the detriment of your own. Although you have an excellent clientèle, I know that your generosity leaves you some way short of being rich, and that a few extra banknotes will be much better in your hands than in mine. You will use them to make people happy, whereas I, as you say, will only throw them away on a hand of cards.

Besides, I have never felt less in the way of doing any actual painting. For that, two things are necessary, which you have: a reflective mentality and inspiration. I shall never have the first, and *I once had* the second. In consequence, I am disgusted with painting. It's a mad old horseman who's completely worn me out dragging me across country on the skinny crop of his Apocalyptic nag. I can see quite clearly what I lack: for all the good sense you talk, I have not yet lived enough, and I am setting off for three or seven days with Mme Reality, in the shape of several nymphs from the corps de ballet at the Opéra. I very much hope on my return, to be the most accomplished of men of the world, that is to say the most unimpressed and the most open to reason.

> Your friend,
> LAURENT

I

As soon as she read it, Thérèse recognised very clearly the deep frustration and jealousy which had dictated this letter.

"And yet," she said to herself, "he's not in love with me. Oh, definitely not! He'll never be in love with anyone, and with me least of all."

And as she read and pondered, Thérèse feared she might be lying to herself by trying to persuade herself that Laurent was in no danger as far as she was concerned.

"Anyway, how? And what danger?" her thoughts ran on. "Is it possible he's become infatuated with me, and he's suffering because it's not returned? Can an infatuation cause real suffering? I've no idea. I've never felt one!"

But the clock struck five, and Thérèse, putting the letter in her pocket, asked for her hat, sent her housemaid away for the next twenty-four hours, gave her faithful old Catherine a number of specific orders and took a cab. Two hours later, she returned with a thin little woman, who stooped slightly and was so voluminously veiled that even the coachman did not see her face. She shut herself away with this mysterious person, and Catherine served them an especially succulent little dinner. Thérèse looked after and served her companion,

28

who contemplated her with such profound happiness and excitement that she was unable to eat.

For his part, Laurent was getting ready for the trip to the country which he had announced; but when Prince D… came to fetch him in his carriage, Laurent told him an unexpected business matter meant he could not leave Paris for another two hours and he would join him at his country house later on in the evening.

Laurent had no such business however. He had dressed with feverish haste. He had had his hair arranged with fastidious care. And then he had thrown his coat into an armchair, run his hands through the too symmetrically organised curls, with no thought for how he might now look. He strode up and down his studio, sometimes vigorously, sometimes dragging his feet. When Prince D… had gone, extracting multiple promises from him to leave as soon as he could, Laurent ran to the stairs to ask him to wait and to say he'd forget the business matter and come with him; but he did not call him back, and went through to the bedroom, where he threw himself down on the bed.

"Why is she shutting her door on me for two days? There's something behind this! And when she tells me to come on the third day, it's to force me to meet in her home an Englishman or American I don't know! But *she* certainly knows him, this Palmer, whom she refers to by the diminutive of his first name! Then what was the purpose of asking me for her address? Is it all a pretence? Why should she pretend with me? I am not Thérèse's lover, I have no rights over her! Thérèse's lover! I shall certainly never be that! God preserve me! A woman five years older than I am, maybe more! Who knows any woman's age, and especially that one, a woman nobody knows anything about? A past so veiled in mystery must be concealing a significant mistake of some sort, perhaps some well-disguised shame. And on top of that, she is prudish, or pious, or philosophical, who can know? She talks of everything with such impartiality, or tolerance, or detachment... does anyone know what she believes, what she doesn't believe, what she wants, what she loves, or if she's even capable of loving?"'

Mercourt, a young critic and Laurent's friend, called by.

'I know,' he said, 'you're leaving for Montmorency. So I'm just dropping in to ask you for an address, then leaving. Mlle Jacques' address.'

Laurent started.

'And what the devil do you want with Mlle Jacques?' he replied, pretending to look for paper to roll a cigarette.

'Me? Nothing... or rather, yes. I'd very much like to know her; but I only know her by sight and reputation. I need her address for someone who wants his picture painted.'

'You know Mlle Jacques by sight?'

'For God's sake! She's very famous just now, and who hasn't been aware of her? She's made for noticing!'

'You think so?'

'Well, don't you?'

'Me? I've no idea. I like her very much. I'm not competent to judge.'

'You like her very much?'

'Yes, you see, I'm saying so. Which proves I'm not courting her.'

'Do you see her often?'

'Sometimes.'

'So you are her friend… in a serious way?'

'Well, yes! In a way… why do you laugh?'

'Because I don't believe a word of it. No one aged twenty-four is a serious friend of a woman… a young and beautiful one!'

'Hah! She isn't as young and beautiful as you say. She makes a good companion, not unpleasant to look at, that's all. But she belongs to a type I'm not fond of, and I have to forgive her for being blonde. I only like blondes in art.'

'She's not that blonde anyway! Her eyes are a soft black, her hair is neither brown nor fair, and she wears it in an odd style. All the same, it suits her, she looks like a well-meaning sphinx.'

'That's very good! However, tall women are what you like.'

'She isn't all that tall. She's got small feet and small hands. She's a real woman. I've studied her closely, since I'm in love with her.'

'Good heavens, what a ridiculous idea!'

'It can't matter to you, surely, since she's not your type?'

'My dear chap, I'd like her any way she looked. If there were more to it than that, I'd try to be a better person with her than I am. But I wouldn't be in love; I don't go in for love. Consequently, I wouldn't be jealous. Press your case, if you see fit.'

'Me? Yes, if I find an opportunity; but I don't have time to look for one, and fundamentally, I'm like you, Laurent, very happy to be patient, seeing that I'm at the age and in a society where pleasures are not in short supply… but since we're talking of this woman, and you know her, tell me… this is pure curiosity on my part, I insist, if she's a widow or…'

'Or what?'

'I meant, if she's lost a lover or a husband.'

'I've no idea.'

'That can't be true!'

'Word of honour; I've never asked. To me it's quite immaterial!'

'You know what people say?'

'No; and I don't care. What do they say?'

'You see, you do care! They say she was married once, to a rich man with a title.'

'Married…'

'As married as you can get: first by the mayor, then by the priest.'

'Ridiculous! She'd bear his name and his title.'

'Ah, there you are! There's a mystery behind the whole thing. When I have the time, I'll dig about and let you know. They say she has no acknowledged lover, although she lives in a very free and easy way. Besides, you're the one who must know about that sort of thing, surely?'

'I don't know the first thing about it. This is too bad! So you think I spend all my time spying on women or interrogating them? I'm not just some idler like you! I find life short enough as it is simply to get some living and some work done.'

'Living… I make no comment. It seems you get a great deal of living done. As for work… they say you don't work enough. All right, what have you got there? Let me see!'

'No, it's nothing, I haven't got anything started here.'

'Yes you have: that head there… it's very good, my word! Let me have a look, or I'll be rude about you in my next review.'

'Which you're very capable of doing!'

'Yes, if you deserve it. But that head though, it's superb, it's simply a marvel. What's it going to be?'

'How do I know?'

'Shall I tell you?'

'It would be a pleasure.'

'Make it a Sibyl. You can dress it up any way you want, it doesn't commit you to anything.'

'Now that's an idea.'

'And then you don't compromise the person it resembles.'

'You think it resembles someone?'

'For heaven's sake, don't play games. You think I don't recognise her? So, my dear fellow, you've been having me on all the time. Because you deny everything, even the most obvious of facts. You are this person's lover!'

'As the fact that I am now departing for Montmorency proves!' Laurent said frostily, taking his hat.

'It doesn't mean it can't still be true!' Mercourt retorted.

Laurent left the building, and Mercourt, who had gone down with him, saw him climb into a small hired carriage. But Laurent had himself driven to the Bois de Boulogne, where he dined alone in a little café, from which he returned at nightfall, on foot and lost in his reveries.

In those days, the Bois de Boulogne was not what it is today. It was less extensive, more neglected, poorer, more mysterious and more rural: it was a place where your mind could roam.

The Champs-Elysées, less luxurious and less densely populated than nowadays, had newly developed districts where one could still rent little houses with little gardens, all of a very private nature. It was a place where one could both live and work.

It was in one of those miniature houses, white and clean, set amid flowering lilacs and behind a tall hawthorn hedge, its entrance defended by a gate painted green, that Thérèse lived. It was May. The weather was magnificent. How Laurent came to find himself, at nine o'clock, behind this hedge in the empty street yet to be finished, and where street lamps had still to be installed and the pavements were still banks of earth on which nettles and wild grasses grew, was a matter which he himself would have been embarrassed to explain.

The hedge was very thick, and Laurent prowled its length, seeing nothing except a number of leaves faintly gilded by a lamp, which he presumed to be out in the garden, placed on a small table at which he was accustomed to smoke when he spent the evening with Thérèse. So people were smoking in the garden? Or taking tea out there, as sometimes happened? But Thérèse had informed Laurent she was expecting a whole family's worth of provincial relatives, and he could only hear the mysterious whispering of two voices, one of which appeared to be Thérèse's. The other was speaking in very low tones: was it a man's? Laurent listened so hard his ears started ringing, until at last he heard, or thought he heard, these words spoken by Thérèse: 'What does any of that matter? I have only one love on this earth now, and that's you!'

"Well that," Laurent said to himself, hurrying away from the deserted little street and re-emerging on to the noisy thoroughfare of the Champs-Elysées, "sets my mind at rest. She has a lover! And true, she was not obliged to confide as much to me...! Except that she was not obliged to speak on every occasion in a manner that encouraged me to believe she neither belonged nor wanted to belong to anyone. She is no different from any other woman: the need to lie is paramount. Why should that matter to me? All the same I wouldn't have believed it! It even tells me I must have been a bit keen on her without admitting it to myself, since there I was, eaves-dropping on her, the meanest of things to do unless a person's jealous! I can't feel too repentent: it saves me from the considerable misery and deception of feeling desire for a woman who has no more desirable qualities than any other, not even sincerity."

Laurent stopped a passing cab which happened to be free and went to Montmorency. He promised himself he would spend a week there, and not set foot in Thérèse's house for a week after that. However, he remained in the countryside a mere forty-eight hours and on the third evening found himself on Thérèse's doorstep at the very same moment as M. Richard Palmer.

'Ah!' said the American, holding out his hand, 'I am pleased to be seeing you!'

Laurent could not avoid holding out his hand too; but he could not prevent himself from asking M. Palmer why he was so pleased to be seeing him.

The foreigner paid no attention to the artist's fairly impertinent tone.

'I am pleased because I am liking you,' he continued with irresistible warmth, 'and I am liking you because I am admiring you very much!'

'Good gracious, you're here!' a surprised Thérèse said to

Laurent. 'I'd given up hope of seeing you this evening.'

And it seemed to the young man that there was a note of unaccustomed coolness in these simple words.

'Ah,' he replied softly, 'you'd have reconciled yourself to it easily enough! And my arrival seems to have interrupted a delightful evening for two.'

'All the crueller of you to say so,' she said in the same playful tone, 'since you seem to have been trying to bring it about.'

'It was what you intended, since you haven't put your visitor off! Am I to go away?'

'No, stay. I'll bear it as best I can.'

The American, having greeted Thérèse, had opened his wallet and taken out a letter he had been asked to pass on to her. Thérèse skimmed the contents of this letter impassively, without offering a single comment.

'If you wish to reply,' Palmer said, 'I have some things to send to Havana.'

'Thank you,' Thérèse responded, opening the drawer of a small table at her elbow, 'I shall not reply.'

Laurent, who was watching her closely, saw her put the letter with several others, one of which by its form and heading, leapt out at him so to speak. It was the one he had sent Thérèse two days ago. I don't know why he was secretly shocked to see this letter keeping company with the one M. Palmer had just passed on to her.

"I'm just shoved away any old how with the rest of her ousted lovers. It is an honour I have no right to though. I have never spoken to her of love."

Thérèse began to talk about M. Palmer's portrait. Laurent

36

made them work hard to persuade him, noting every fleeting expression on the faces and every tiny inflection in the voices of his interlocutors, at every moment imagining he would detect in them the secret fear of seeing him give way. But there was such good faith in their insistence that he calmed down and chided himself for his suspicions. If Thérèse did have relations with this stranger, living free and alone as she did, seemingly owing nothing to anyone, and never concerned about what people might say of her, did she need the pretext of a portrait to receive frequent and lengthy visits from the object of her affections or her fantasy?

Once he felt reassured, Laurent no longer felt restrained by the shame of revealing his curiosity.

'Are you an American too then?' he asked Thérèse, who was occasionally translating into English for M. Palmer the exchanges he did not completely understand.

'Me?' Thérèse replied. 'Didn't I ever tell you I had the honour of being your compatriot?'

'It's just that you speak English so well!'

'You don't know if I speak English well, since you don't understand it. But I can see what's on your mind, because I know you're curious. You're asking if I met Dick Palmer yesterday or if I've known him for a long time. Well, ask him yourself.'

Palmer did not wait for a question which Laurent would not willingly have asked. He replied that it was not the first time he had come to France and he had known Thérèse when she was very young and living with her people. It was not stated which people. Thérèse habitually claimed that she had never known either her father or her mother.

Mlle Jacques' past was an impenetrable mystery to members of society who went to have their portraits painted by her, and to the small circle of artists she received privately. No one knew where she had come to Paris from, no one knew when, and no one knew who had come with her. She had been known for two or three years only, one of her portraits having been noticed by people of taste and having been suddenly pronounced the work of a master. And thus she had abruptly moved from a meagre and obscure clientèle and existence to a reputation of the first rank and a life of relative comfort. But all this happened without alteration to her taste for tranquillity, her love of independence and the playful austerity of her manners. She never put on airs and never talked about herself except to express her opinions and her feelings, which she did with notable frankness and courage. As for her personal life, she had a way of side-stepping and eluding questions which spared her the necessity of offering any answer. If someone nevertheless insisted, it was her custom to say, after a few vague remarks: 'It's not about me. I have nothing interesting to say and, if I have had any troubles, I can't recall them now, I'm too busy to think about that sort of thing. I'm very happy at the moment, since I have work to do and I love work more than anything else.'

It was by chance, arising out of contacts between artists in the same group, that Laurent had made the acquaintance of Mlle Jacques. Launched into parallel societies as both gentleman and eminent artist, M. Fauvel, at twenty-four, had a practical experience of life many people still lack at forty. By turns it filled him with pride and caused him distress. But he had no experience at all in matters of the heart, for such experience is not acquired through a life of disorder. Thanks to the cynicism he affected, he had thus begun by determining in his own mind that all the men Thérèse treated as friends must be her lovers, and he had been obliged to hear them gradually confirm and prove the purity of their relations with her before he was able to consider her as a person who might have had her passions but was not one to chase after amorous adventures.

From that point on, he had a burning curiosity to know the reason for this anomalous situation: a young woman, beautiful, intelligent, absolutely free and voluntarily unattached. He had seen her more frequently, and little by little almost every day, at first under all manner of pretexts, then in the guise of a friend of no consequence, too much of a gadabout to begin a flirtation with a serious-minded woman, but too much of an idealist, in spite of everything, not to need affection and not to appreciate the value of a disinterested friendship.

And that was true in principle, deep down; but love had slipped into the young man's heart, and we have seen that Laurent was struggling with the invasion of a feeling he still wished to disguise both from Thérèse and himself, all the more so because he was experiencing it for the first time in his life.

'But what I don't see,' he said when he had promised Palmer he would attempt his portrait, 'is why on earth you're so keen to have something that may not turn out to be any good, when you know Mlle Jacques, who would certainly not refuse and whose work is bound to be excellent.'

'She does refuse,' Palmer replied with great candour, 'and I don't know why. I promised my mother, who mistakenly believes I am handsome, a portrait by a master of the art, and she will not think it a good likeness if it is too realistic. That is why I applied to you, as a master of the idealistic. If you refuse me, I shall have the distress of not giving my mother a pleasure she desires, or else the bother of looking elsewhere.'

'That won't take long: there are so many people more capable than I am…!'

'Not in my opinion. But supposing that were so, it is by no means certain they would be available straightaway, and I am in a hurry to send the portrait off. It's for the anniversary of my birth, in four months, and transporting it to America will take about two.'

'In other words, Laurent,' Thérèse added, 'you have to do this portrait in six weeks at the very most; and as I know how much time you need, you would have to start tomorrow. Very well, it's agreed, it's a promise, yes?'

M.Palmer shook Laurent's hand, saying: 'The contract is made then. I make no mention of money; Mlle Jacques will see to those matters, they are not my concern. What time would you like to see me tomorrow?'

The hour fixed, Palmer took his hat, and Laurent felt obliged to do the same out of respect for Thérèse; but Palmer seemed unconcerned about that as well, and took his leave after shaking though not kissing Mlle Jacques' hand.

'Ought I to follow him?' Laurent said.

'It's not necessary,' she replied. 'Everyone who comes to the house in the evenings knows me well. Except that you'll be taking yourself off at ten today. Recently I've forgotten myself, gossiping on with you until nearly midnight, and since I can't sleep after five in the morning, I've been feeling very tired.'

'And you didn't throw me out?'

'No, it never occurred to me.'

'If I was conceited, I'd be very proud about that!'

'But you aren't conceited, thank God. You leave that to stupid people. Now listen: despite the compliment, Master Laurent, I have to scold you. They say you are not working.'

'And it's to force me to work that you put Palmer's portrait like a pistol to my head.'

'Well, why not?'

'You mean well, Thérèse, I know that. You want to make me earn my living in spite of myself.'

'I do not interfere with your means of existence, I do not have that right. I do not have the good fortune… or the misfortune to be your mother; but I am you sister… *in Apollo*, as our classical friend Bernard says, and it is impossible for me not to be upset by your bouts of idleness.'

'But how can you mind about that?' Laurent exclaimed, with a mixture of pleasure and vexation which Thérèse sensed, and which encouraged her to reply frankly.

'Listen, my dear Laurent,' she told him. 'We need to have things clear between us. I feel considerable friendship for you.'

'I'm very proud that you do, but I don't know why…! I'm not fit even to be a friend, Thérèse! I don't believe in friendship between a man and a woman any more than I believe in love.'

'You have already told me so, and what you don't believe is of no consequence to me. For my part I believe in what I feel, and what I feel with regard to you is interest and affection. That's how I am: I cannot have anyone close to me without taking an interest in them and wanting them to be happy. It is my habit to do whatever I can without caring whether they are grateful or not. Now, you are not anyone, you are a man of genius, and what is more, I hope, a man of heart.'

'A man of heart, me? Yes, if you mean by that what the public in general means. I can acquit myself well when it comes to fighting duels, paying my debts and defending the woman I give my arm to, whoever she may be. But if you believe I have a heart in the tender, loving, innocent sense…'

'I know that you like to pretend to be old, worn out and corrupted. Your pretensions have no effect on me at all. It is a fashion that suits the times. With you, it is an affliction, however real or painful, which will pass when you want it to. You are a man of heart precisely because the emptiness in your heart causes you suffering. A woman will come along who will fill it, if she knows her business, and if you let her. But this is not my subject; it is to the artist that I am speaking: the man in you is unhappy only because the artist is not pleased with himself.'

'Well, you're wrong, Thérèse,' Laurent responded sharply. 'It's the opposite of what you say! It is the man inside the artist who is suffering and stifling him. I don't know what to do with myself, do you see? Boredom is killing me. Boredom with what, you're going to say. Boredom with everything! Unlike you, I am not capable of working with calm and concentrated attention for six hours, walking round the garden throwing bread for the sparrows, working again for another four hours and then smiling all evening at a handful of unsolicited callers such as me, for example, whilst waiting until it's time to sleep. My sleep is bad, my walks are full of agitation, my work is feverish. The business of creating disturbs me and makes me shake all over: the business of execution, always too slow for my liking, gives me appalling heart palpitations. When I give birth to an idea that excites me, it is only through tears and by repressing the desire to cry out; and next morning the idea leaves me mortally ashamed and disgusted. If I think of altering it, it's worse, it disappears altogether: better to forget it and wait for another. But the next one comes to me so muddled and vast that my poor being can't contain it. It oppresses me and tortures me until it has taken on achievable proportions, and then the other torture returns, the agony of giving it birth, a real physical suffering which I can't express in words. And that's how my life goes when I allow myself to be dominated by this ogre of an artist which is inside me, from whom the poor man presently before you drags out, one by one, with the forceps of his willpower, scrawny, half-dead mice! Therefore, Thérèse, it is far better that I should live the only way I can live, commit excesses of every sort, and kill that gnawing worm which my colleagues modestly call their inspiration and which I call quite simply my disability.'

'So that's it, then. It's decided,' Thérèse said, smiling. 'Working for you, is the suicide of the intelligence? Well, I don't believe a word of it. If someone told you, tomorrow, you could be Prince D... or the Count of S..., with the millions of the one and the fine horses of the other, you would say, thinking of your despised palette: *Give me back my beloved!*'

'My despised palette? You don't understand me, Thérèse! It is an instrument of glory; I know that perfectly well. And the thing called glory is a kind of esteem accorded to talent, more pure and more special than the esteem accorded to wealth and titles. It follows that it is a great privilege and a great pleasure for me to say to myself: "I am only a minor gentleman of no means, and people like me who don't want to give up their position lead the life of a forest warden who makes his living

43

giving the women who collect up the dead wood a bundle of kindling in return. Well, I have given up my position, I've accepted my station in life, and now, at twenty-four, when I trot my little hired horse amid the throng of Paris' richest and most beautiful people, all mounted on animals worth ten thousand francs, if there's a man of taste among the gawpers sitting along the Champs-Elysées, or a woman of spirit, I'm the one who gets stared at and named, and not the others." You're laughing! Do you find me very vain?'

'No, but very childish, thank God! You won't kill yourself.'

'But I have absolutely no desire to kill myself! I love myself as much as I do anyone, I love myself with all my heart, I assure you! But what I'm saying is that my palette, the instrument of my glory, is the instrument of my torture, since I don't know how to work without suffering. So what I seek in disorder is not the death of my body or my mind, but the wearing out and calming down of my nerves. That's it, Thérèse. What part of that is unreasonable? I can only work at all properly when I'm collapsing with exhaustion.'

'That's true,' said Thérèse, 'I've noticed it, and it surprises me, like some sort of abnormality. But I do fear it's a method of working that could kill you, and I can't imagine how it can do anything else. Wait, answer me this question: did you begin life by embracing work and abstinence, and did you then feel forced to turn to these destructive ways of behaving as the only way of relaxing?'

'No, the opposite. I left school, loving painting, but never believing I would be forced to paint. I thought I was rich. My father died leaving only about thirty thousand francs, which I made a point of getting through as fast as possible so that

I should have at least one year of ease and plenty in my life. When I saw I was broke, I took up the brush; I was torn to shreds and praised to the skies, which these days constitutes the highest form of success; and now, I allow myself, for a few months or a few weeks, luxury and pleasure for as long as the money lasts. When there's nothing left, it's all to the good, because by then I have exhausted my strength and my desires. So I take up my work again with rage, pain and exhilaration, and when the work is finished, the leisured and prodigal life resumes.'

'Have you been living this kind of life for a long time?'

'There's no such thing as a long time at my age! Three years.'

'Well, for your age, three years *is* a long time! And then, you made a bad start. You burnt out your vital spirits before they had properly taken flight. You drank vinegar to prevent yourself from growing. Your head has grown, all the same, and genius has developed inside it in spite of everything. But perhaps your heart has dried up, perhaps you will never be either a complete man or a complete artist.'

These words of Thérèse, spoken with a calm sadness, irritated Laurent.

'So,' he said, getting up, 'you despise me?'

'No,' she replied, holding out a hand, 'I pity you.'

And Laurent saw two big tears spill slowly down Thérèse's cheeks.

These tears provoked in him a powerful reaction: a flood of tears welled in his own eyes and ran down his face. Throwing himself at Thérèse's feet, not like a lover making his declaration but like a child confessing: 'Oh, my poor dear friend!' he cried,

45

taking her hands, 'you're right to pity me, because pity is what I need! I am unhappy you see, so unhappy I am ashamed to say it! This thing I have in my chest, I don't know what it is, in the place where the heart should be, is constantly crying out for something, equally unknown, and I don't know what I should give it to appease it. I love God and I don't believe in him. I love all women, and I despise every one of them! I can tell you that, I can tell you, my comrade and my friend! I sometimes catch myself ready to worship a courtesan, whereas next to an angel I'd probably be colder than marble. My notions about everything are upside down, perhaps my instincts are deviant. What if I told you that already drinking wine doesn't make me merry and full of ideas any more! Yes, I'm the sad sort of drunkard, it appears. I was told that during that riotous house party at Montmorency, the day before yesterday, I declaimed a whole string of tragic things with an emphasis as frightening as it was ridiculous. What do you expect will become of me, Thérèse, if you don't take pity on me?'

'Of course I pity you, my poor child,' Thérèse said, wiping his eyes with her handkerchief. 'But what good can that do?'

'You could be more fond of me, Thérèse! Don't take your hands away! Didn't you say I could be a special sort of friend to you?'

'I said that I was fond of you: you replied that you were unable to believe in the friendship of a woman.'

'Perhaps I would believe in yours. You must have a man's heart, since you have the strength and talent of one. Give me back your friendship.'

'I have not taken it away, and I'm willing to try to be a man for you,' she replied. 'But I wouldn't really know how to go about it. The friendship of a man must have more sternness and authority than I think I'm capable of having. In spite of myself I shall pity you more than I scold you, and you can see it already! I'd promised myself I'd humiliate you today, make you angry with me and with yourself; instead of that, here I am weeping with you, which gets us no further forward.'

'It does, it does!' Laurent cried. 'These tears are good, they have watered the dry places; perhaps my heart will grow again there! Oh, Thérèse! You once told me that I boasted to you about things I should have blushed for, that I was like a prison wall. You forgot only one thing: behind that wall is a prisoner! If I could open that door, you'd see him plainly enough; but the door is locked, the wall is of bronze, and my will, my faith, my ardour, even my promises, cannot break through it. Must I therefore live and die like this? What good will it do me, I ask you, to have daubed the walls of my cell with fantastical pictures if the word *love* is nowhere to be seen in any of it?'

'If I understand you properly,' Thérèse said, pensive, 'you think that your work needs to be warmed by feeling.'

'Don't you think so too? Isn't that what all your reproaches are telling me?'

'Not exactly. It's only that your execution can be too forceful, that's what the critics reproach you for. For my part, I've always treated youthful exuberance with respect, all great artists have had it. And its beauties are enough to dissuade genuine admirers from picking on its faults. Far from finding your work cold and over-emphatic, I can feel its fire and passion; but I was wondering where in you this passion came from, I was looking for its source: I can see it now, it is the soul's capacity to desire. Yes, certainly,' she added, still pensive, as if she were trying to penetrate the veils of her own thinking, 'desire can be a passion.'

'Well! What are you thinking?' Laurent said, following her absorbed gaze.

'I'm wondering whether it's my duty to make war on this turbulent force inside you, and whether, by persuading you to be happy and calm, it might not rob you of the holy fire. On the other hand… I imagine this kind of yearning can't be a situation the mind can endure for long, and that once it has found its vivid expression in its first feverish period, it must either collapse of its own accord or crush us altogether. What do you say? Doesn't each stage of a painter's life have its own force and its own way of showing it? What they call the different *manners* of the masters, aren't they the expression of successive transformations in their own selves? Will you at thirty, find it possible to have reached for the stars and caught nothing? Won't you be forced to focus your efforts on something you can be sure of, whatever that may be? You are at the age of fantasy: but soon will come the age of illumination. Don't you want to make progress?'

'Does it depend on me to force it?'

'Yes, unless you're determined not to keep your faculties in balance. You won't persuade me that self-destruction is the remedy for your fevered state: it's only its fatal consequence.'

'So what do you suggest to calm me down?'

'I don't know: marriage, perhaps.'

'Horror!' cried Laurent with a burst of laughter.

And he added, still laughing and not quite knowing where the qualification came from: 'Unless it's to you, Thérèse. Ah, now that's an idea!'

'Delightful,' she replied, 'but completely impossible.'

Thérèse's response struck Laurent by its calm implacability, and what he had just said as a joke suddenly seemed to him to be a buried dream, as if it had rooted itself in his mind. Such was the composition of that powerful and unhappy mind that all it needed for an idea to plant itself was the word *impossible*, and that was the very word Thérèse had just uttered.

At once a vague impulse to love her swept over him and hardened, and at the same moment his suspicions, his jealousy and his anger returned. Until now he had found the charms of friendship soothing, pleasantly stimulating; he suddenly became bitter and cold.

'Ah! Yes, quite so,' he said, picking up his hat to leave. 'That's the word I keep hearing, whatever I say or do, whether I'm being frivolous or whether it's something serious: *impossible*! It's not an enemy you're familiar with, Thérèse; you love everything so calmly. You have a *lover* or a *friend* who is not jealous, because he knows you are cold, or so very reasonable! It makes me think time must be getting on, and your umpteen *plus one* cousins are perhaps here, outside, waiting for me to leave.'

'What are you saying?' Thérèse asked him, stupefied. 'What sort of ideas are these? Do you suffer fits of madness?'

'Sometimes,' he replied as he went out.

II

The next day Thérèse received from Laurent the following letter:

"My good and dear friend, how did I leave you yesterday? If I said something dreadful, forget it, I didn't know anything about it. I had a dizzy turn, and it didn't clear away once I was outside, because I found myself at my own door, in a carriage, with no memory of having ever climbed aboard.

"It happens to me quite often, my friend: my mouth says one thing when my brain says another. Pity me and forgive me. I am ill, and you were right, the life I lead is detestable.

"What right do I have to question you? In all justice, that was the first time I have done so in the three months you've been allowing me to visit you alone… what is it to me whether you're engaged, married or widowed…? You don't want anyone to know; did I try to find out? Did I ask you…? Oh, listen, Thérèse, there's still a fog in my head this morning, and yet I sense that I'm lying, and I don't want to lie to you. On Friday I had my first fit of curiosity about you, yesterday's one made it the second; but it will be the last, I swear, and to make sure the subject never comes up again, I want to make a clean breast of everything. So, I was outside your door the other day, or rather your garden gate. I looked, I saw nothing; I listened, I heard! Well, why should you care? I don't know his name, I didn't see his face; but I know that you are my sister, my confidante, my consolation, my prop. I know that yesterday I wept at your feet, and that you wiped my tears away with your handkerchief, saying 'What are we to do, what are we to do, my poor child?' I know that, wise, hard-working, calm, respected, since you are a free woman, loved, since you are a contented one, you find the time and the charity to pity me, to know I exist, and to want to make my existence better than it is. Kind Thérèse, anyone who didn't bless you would be an ungrateful beast, and however wretched I am, I am not familiar with ingratitude. When will you want to see me again, Thérèse? It seems to me I have offended you. That would be the last thing I wanted to do. Shall I come to your house tonight? If you say no, oh, my word, I shall plunge into hell!"

Laurent received, with his servant's return, Thérèse's reply. It was short: *Come this evening*. Laurent was neither sly nor conceited, although he often contemplated or was tempted to be both. He was, as has been seen, a creature full of contrasts, whom we describe without explaining, it would not be possible; certain characters escape logical analysis.

Thérèse's reply made him tremble like a child. She had never written to him in that tone. Was she ordering him to come and receive the news of his deserved dismissal? Was she summoning him to a lovers' assignation? Those three words, curt or impassioned: was it indignation that had dictated them or frenzied desire?

M. Palmer arrived, and Laurent, agitated and preoccupied as he was, had to make a start on his portrait. He had promised himself he would interrogate his sitter with consummate subtlety and draw out all Thérèse's secrets. He could not think of a way to open such a conversation, and as the American posed in the most proper manner, as motionless and silent as a statue, the sitting proceeded with barely a word exchanged between them.

Laurent thus had the opportunity to calm down sufficiently to study this stranger's pure and placid physiognomy. Its beauty had a high finish, which on first impressions, gave him the somewhat inanimate appearance that went with regular features. Examining it more closely, one could detect a certain finesse in his smile and fire in his gaze. While Laurent was making these observations, he reflected on his model's age.

'I do beg your pardon,' he suddenly said, 'but I would like to be sure, I must know in fact, whether you are a young man who is slightly fatigued or a mature man who is extraordinarily well preserved. However much I look at you, I don't quite understand what I'm seeing.'

'I am forty years old,' was M. Palmer's simple answer.

'Congratulations!' said Laurent. 'You must be in excellent health then?'

'Perfect!' said Palmer.

And he resumed his easy pose and tranquil smile.

"He's the very picture of a happy lover," the artist told himself, "or of a man who's only ever loved his roast beef." He could not resist the urge to go on and say: 'So have you known Mlle Jacques since she was little?'

'She was fifteen when I saw her for the first time.'

Laurent did not feel brave enough to ask in what year that was. Speaking of Thérèse, he seemed to feel his face going red. What did it really matter to him how old Thérèse was? It was her story he would have liked to learn.

Thérèse appeared to be not yet thirty; Palmer couldn't have been anything more than a friend to her at that time. And then his voice was loud and his pronouncements resonant. If he had been the one Thérèse was addressing when she said: *You're the only one I love now*, he would have made a reply of some sort, which Laurent would have heard.

Finally, evening came, and the artist, who was habitually imprecise in these matters, arrived earlier than Thérèse's customary time for receiving visitors. He found her in her garden, doing nothing, which was unusual, and walking up and down with an agitated air. As soon as she saw him she went over to him, and taking his hand, with more authority than affection, she said: 'If you are a man of honour, you will tell me everything you heard through this hedge. So then, speak to me, I'm listening.'

She sat down on a bench, and Laurent, irritated by this unfamiliar welcome, tried to deepen her anxiety by making evasive replies. But he was browbeaten by her attitude of displeasure and an expression on her face which he had never seen before. The fear of falling out with her, irrevocably, forced him to tell the simple truth.

'So,' she resumed, 'that's all you heard. I said to someone you couldn't even see: "You are now my only love on earth"?'

'I dreamed it then, Thérèse. I'm ready to believe it, if you tell me to.'

'No, you weren't dreaming. I could have, I must have said

53

that. And what did the person say in reply?'

'Nothing that I heard,' said Laurent, on whom Thérèse's answer had the effect of a cold shower. 'Not even the sound of his voice. Are you reassured?'

'No! I have more questions. Whom do you suppose I was talking to in this way?'

'I don't suppose anything. The only person I'm aware of with whom your relations are unknown is M. Palmer.'

'Ah!' Thérèse cried with a strange air of satisfaction. 'You think it was M. Palmer?'

'Why shouldn't it be him? Is it insulting you to imagine a former relationship suddenly renewed? I know that your relations with all the people I've seen at your house over the last three months are as disinterested on their part and as indifferent on yours, as my own relations with you. M. Palmer is very handsome and there is gallantry in his manners. I like him a lot. I do not have the right or the presumption to ask you for an account of your private feelings. Except that... you'll say I have been spying on you...'

'Yes, indeed,' said Thérèse, who seemed disinclined to deny anything, however trivial. 'Why were you spying on me? I can only put the worst construction on it, although I don't understand what it was about at all. Explain what put this fantastical idea into your head.'

'Thérèse!' the young man responded urgently, resolved to unburden himself fully of his troubles. 'Tell me that you have a lover, and that this lover is Palmer, and I shall truly treasure you, I shall speak to you without art or guile. I shall ask you to pardon an act of folly, and you will never have any cause to reproach me again. Come now, do you want me to be your friend? For all my posturing talk, I feel that I need to be and I'm capable of it. Be open with me, that's all I'm asking.'

'My dear child,' Thérèse replied, 'you talk to me as if I were some flighty sort of woman who's anxious to keep her hooks in you but has a fault to confess. I cannot accept this situation; it is entirely inappropriate. M. Palmer is not and never will be for me anything other than a very worthy friend, with whom I am not in close contact and whom I had not seen for many years. That is what I have to tell you, but nothing more. My secrets, if I have any, do not need to be broadcast, and I ask you not to enquire into them more than I wish. It is therefore not for you to question me, it is for you to give me answers. What were you doing here, four days ago? Why were you spying on me? What is this *fit of madness* that I need to know about and pronounce judgement on?'

'I am not encouraged by the tone you choose to adopt. Why would I make my confession when you are so disdainful and refuse to treat me as a good comrade or have any faith in me?'

'Don't make your confession then,' Thérèse went on, getting to her feet. 'It will prove you don't deserve the respect and consideration I have shown you, and that in seeking to know my secrets, you certainly don't show me any.'

'So,' Laurent said, 'you're sending me away, and it's over between us?'

'It's over, and goodbye,' Thérèse replied sternly.

Laurent left, gripped by an anger that prevented him from saying a word; but he had not gone thirty paces down the street before he returned, telling Catherine he had forgotten a message he had been asked to give her mistress. He found

Thérèse resting in a chair in the little sitting room: the door to the garden had been left open; it seemed that Thérèse, wounded and downcast, remained buried in her thoughts. Her greeting was icy.

'Back again?' she said. 'What did you forget?'

'I forgot to tell you the truth.'

'I no longer wish to hear it.'

'Although you were asking me for it!'

'I thought you could have told me without being asked.'

'I could have, I should have; I was wrong not to. Be honest, Thérèse, do you really believe it possible for a man of my age to see you and not to be in love with you?'

'In love?' Thérèse said, frowning. 'So when you told me you couldn't possibly be in love with any woman, you were making fun of me?'

'No, certainly not, I said what I was thinking.'

'And then you found you were wrong, and now you're in love. Are you quite sure?'

'Oh, for God's sake, don't get cross! It's not as sure as all that. Notions of love filtered through my head, through my senses, if you like. Are you so inexperienced as to have judged the thing impossible?'

'I am old enough to be experienced,' Thérèse replied, 'but I have lived alone for a long time. I do not have experience of certain situations. Does that surprise you? But that is how it is. I am very simple, although I have been deceived… as everyone has! You told me a hundred times you respected me too highly to view me as a woman, on the grounds that you loved women only in the coarsest of ways. I therefore believed I was safe from being offended by any desire on your part, and

56

of all the things I valued in you, your sincerity on this point is what I valued the most. I took a close interest in your affairs with a sense of freedom that was all the greater after we said to each other, laughing at it, do you remember, but serious deep down: "Between two people, one of them an idealist, the other practical, lies the Baltic Sea."'

'I said it in good faith, and I confidently began to walk along my shore, without ever thinking of crossing. But it turned out that, on my side, the ice wouldn't hold. Is it my fault if I'm twenty-four and you're beautiful?'

'Am I still beautiful? I was hoping I wasn't!'

'I've no idea, I didn't think so at first, and then one fine day, that's how you appeared to me. You weren't trying to be, on your side, I know that. But I wasn't trying either when I felt its seductive effect; so much not trying, that I refused to allow it and distracted myself. I rendered unto Satan what belongs to Satan, that is to say my poor soul, and I brought here to Caesar only what belongs to Caesar, my respect and my silence. But for a week or ten days now this ill-advised emotion has returned to haunt my dreams. It dissipates when I am with you. Word of honour, Thérèse, when I see you, when you speak to me, I am calm. I don't remember that I ever cried out against you in a moment of madness I myself can't begin to understand. When I talk about you, I say that you are not young, or that I don't like the colour of your hair. I proclaim that you are my great comrade-in-arms, that is to say my brother, and I feel loyal saying it. And then, along come these unaccountable wafts of springtime, invading the winter of my stupid heart, and I imagine it's you who blow them there. It is you, truly, Thérèse, with your veneration of what you call authentic love! It makes one think, whether one likes it or not!'

'I believe you are deceiving yourself. I never talk about love.'

'Yes, I know. You have a distinct prejudice against the subject. You've read somewhere that to talk about love was as good as giving or receiving it. But your silence is extremely eloquent, your reluctance only excites the natural urges and your excessive caution is devilishly attractive!'

'In that case, let's stop seeing each other,' Thérèse said.

'Why? It needn't trouble you that I've had a few sleepless nights, since it's in your power to make me as calm and content as I was before.'

'What do I have to do to achieve that?'

'What I was asking you to do: tell me you are committed to someone. I will accept it as a fact, and as I'm very proud, I'll be cured, as if a fairy had waved her magic wand.'

'And what if I tell you I'm not committed to anyone, because I no longer wish to love anyone, will that not do?'

'No, I will be smug enough to believe you might change your mind.'

Thérèse couldn't help laughing at the gracefully apologetic tone of Laurent's remark.

'Well,' she told him, 'be cured, and give me again the friendship I was proud to have, instead of a love that would make me blush. I love someone.'

'That's not enough, Thérèse: you have to say you're committed.'

'Otherwise you'll think that someone is you, won't you? Very well then! I have a lover. Are you satisfied?'

'Completely. And there, you see, I kiss your hand in

gratitude for your frankness. Be even kinder, and tell me it's Palmer!'

'I can't do that, I'd be lying.'

'In that case… I'm all confused!'

'It's no one you know, it's a person who doesn't live anywhere near…'

'Who comes here sometimes, however?'

'It would seem so, since you caught me saying something…'

'Thank you, thank you, Thérèse! Now I've got solid ground under my feet; I know who you are and I know who I am, and to tell the truth, I think I like you all the more this way, you're a woman and no longer a sphinx. Oh, if only you'd spoken before!'

'This passion has really been wreaking havoc with you then?' Thérèse said teasingly.

'Ah, well, maybe! I'll tell you in ten years' time, Thérèse, and we'll laugh about it together.'

'Let's agree to that; good night.'

Laurent went home to bed very calm and thoroughly disillusioned. He had really suffered on Thérèse's account. He had desired her passionately, without daring to give her any inkling of it. It was certainly not a healthy passion. Vanity had been as much a part of it as curiosity. This woman, of whom all her friends said: "Who is it she loves? I would have liked it to be me, but it isn't anyone", had appeared before him as an ideal to be seized. His imagination had been fired, his pride had been challenged by the fear, by the virtual certainty, of failing. But this young man was not driven solely by self-esteem. He had in him the urge, vivid and dominant at times, towards the solid, the good and the true.

He was an angel, and if not a fallen one like so many others, at least a misled and sickly one. The need to love gnawed at his heart, and a hundred times a day he asked himself with fright if he hadn't already allowed his way of life to take too much toll on him, and if he still had the strength to be happy.

He woke up calm and sad. He was already missing his chimera, his lovely sphinx, who read his soul with indulgent attention, who admired him, scolded him, encouraged and pitied him by turns, without ever revealing anything of her own story, but leaving him free to imagine treasure troves of affection, devotion, perhaps sensual bliss! At least, that was how it suited Laurent to interpret Thérèse's silence about herself, and a certain smile, as mysterious as the Mona Lisa's, which flickered on her lips and at the corner of her eye when he blasphemed in front of her. In those moments, she seemed to be saying to herself: "I could easily describe what paradise is in comparison with this impoverished hell; but that poor simpleton wouldn't understand me."

Once the mystery of her heart had been revealed, Thérèse initially lost all her prestige in Laurent's eyes. Now she was only a woman like all the rest. He was even tempted to diminish her in her own, and although she would never have allowed him to interrogate her, he felt tempted to accuse her of hypocrisy and prudery. But once she declared herself committed to someone, he no longer regretted having stood respectfully back, and he no longer wished for anything from her, not even her friendship, which he would have no difficulty, he thought, in finding elsewhere.

This situation lasted two or three days, during which

Laurent prepared several excuses, if by chance Thérèse were to ask him to account for spending all this time away from her. On the fourth day, Laurent felt overcome by an indescribable sense of disgust. The tarts and courtesans left him nauseous; none of his friends had the patient and sensitive kindness of Thérèse when she noticed his unhappiness, tried to distract him, sought with him its cause and the remedy, in short, when she took care of him. She alone knew what to say to him, and seemed to understand that the destiny of an artist such as him was not a matter of small importance, or a matter on which an elevated spirit was entitled to declare that, if he was unhappy, then too bad for him.

He rushed to her house so hastily that he forgot what he meant to say to excuse himself; but Thérèse showed neither displeasure nor surprise at his absence, and spared him any need to lie by asking no questions. He was piqued by this, and realised he was more jealous of her than he had been before.

"She'll have been seeing her lover," he thought. "She'll have forgotten me."

However he allowed none of his frustration to show, and from then on controlled himself so carefully that Thérèse was deceived.

Several weeks went by in, for him, alternating states of rage, coldness and tenderness. Nothing in the world was as necessary to him and as beneficial as the friendship of this woman, nothing was so bitter and so wounding as not being able to make any claim on her love. The confession he had demanded, far from curing him as he had imagined, had made his suffering worse. It was a jealousy he could no longer close his eyes to, since it now had a definite and avowed cause. How could he have believed that once the cause was known, the impulse to try to destroy it would vanish?

And yet he made no attempt to supplant the invisible and fortunate rival. His pride, excessive where Thérèse was concerned, would not allow it. On his own, he hated him, denigrated him in the privacy of his thoughts, attributing all manner of absurdities to this phantom, insulting him and challenging him ten times a day.

And then he lost his taste for suffering, took refuge once more in excess and extravagance, achieved forgetfulness for a moment and fell back into extreme states of sadness, went to spend two hours at Thérèse's house, happy to see her, to breathe the air she breathed and to contradict her for the pleasure of hearing her scolding, caressing voice.

In the end, he came to hate her for failing to guess at his torment; he despised her for remaining faithful to this lover who could not be anything more than a mediocre type, since she never felt the need to mention him. He would walk away from her house, swearing to leave a long interval before he saw her again, and he would have reappeared an hour later if he could have had any hope of being received.

Thérèse, for whom Laurent's love had been for the briefest instant visible, no longer suspected it, so well did he play his role. She was genuinely fond of this unhappy child. An enthusiastic artist beneath her calm and thoughtful air, she had raised an altar, as she said, *to what he might have been*, and there still remained in her a sense of pity, expressed in her spoiling of him, alongside an unbroken respect for his suffering and misdirected genius.

If she had been fully certain it could not excite in him any evil desires, she would have fondled him as one might a son, and there were moments when she held herself in check as the instinct to address him, more intimately, as *tu* rose to her lips.

Was there love in this maternal feeling? Unknown to Thérèse, there certainly was; but a truly chaste woman, and one who has lived far more through work than through the passions, can almost indefinitely conceal from herself a love which she has resolutely forbidden. Thérèse was confident that there was never a question of her own satisfaction in this attachment, in which she did all the work. Laurent found a sense of calm and well-being when he visited her, and she found that she experienced, through the act of giving, these same feelings herself. She knew very well that he was incapable of loving her in the way she understood the term, and had therefore been hurt and horrified by the momentary madness he had confessed to. That crisis now over, she congratulated herself on finding, in an innocent lie, the means to prevent any repetition. And as Laurent, every time he started to feel any strong emotion, was swift to emphasise the unbridgeable ice barrier of *the Baltic Sea*, she was no longer afraid and grew used to living unburned in the middle of the fire.

All these sufferings of the two friends and all these dangers were hidden and left simmering below the surface of a cheerful mockery which is the habitual manner, the indelible characteristic, as it were, of French artists. It is a kind of second nature, for which strangers from the North reproach us, and for which the serious-minded English in particular hold us in some scorn. It is this approach to delicate relationships, however, which gives them their charm, and which often preserves us from committing follies or stupidities. To seek the ridiculous aspect of things is to discover their weaknesses and their illogicalities. When matters of the soul itself are in play, to make fun of the perils is to ready oneself to brave them, just as our soldiers do when they face the fire laughing and singing. To mock a friend is often to save him from a weakness of character which our pity might have encouraged him to indulge. Finally, to mock oneself is to preserve oneself from the silly intoxication of exaggerated self-regard. I have noticed that people who never joke are full of puerile and unbearable vanity.

Laurent's gaiety was spiced with colour and wit, like his talent, and all the more natural for being original. Thérèse had less evident wit, in the sense that she was by nature a dreamer and not given to loquacity; but that was exactly why she needed the playfulness of others: then her own gradually emerged, and her quieter gaiety was not without charm.

The result of their keeping up this perpetual state of good humour was that love, a subject about which Thérèse never joked and did not like to hear others joke in front of her, never entered their conversations, or even let its echo be heard.

One fine morning, M. Palmer's portrait was declared finished, and Thérèse handed to Laurent, on her friend's behalf, a handsome sum which the young man promised to set aside for medical emergencies or any other unexpected and unavoidable expense.

Laurent had made friends with Palmer in the course of painting his portrait. He had discovered him to be what he was: upright, fair, generous, intelligent and educated. Palmer was a rich bourgeois whose inherited fortuned derived from commerce. He had served his time in the business himself, travelling to far flung parts in his youth. At thirty he had had the good sense to consider himself rich enough and to wish to live for higher things. He no longer travelled therefore, except for pleasure, and after having seen, he said, many curious things and many extraordinary countries, he took pleasure in seeing beautiful things and in studying countries whose civilisations were of genuine interest.

Without being particularly well-versed in the arts, he had a sure feeling for them, and his notions in all matters were as sound as his instincts. His grasp of the French language reflected his timidity, so that at the beginning of any conversation he could be almost unintelligible and laughably inaccurate; but when he felt at ease, one could tell that he knew the language and needed only longer practice or more confidence to speak it very well.

Laurent had studied this man with a good deal of anxiety and curiosity to begin with. When it became clear to him, demonstrably, given the evidence, that he was not Mlle Jacques' lover, he came to appreciate him and develop for him a sort of friendship which resembled, distantly it was true, the friendship he felt for Thérèse. Palmer was something of a philosopher, but tolerant, a little rigid with regard to himself and very charitable towards others. In ideas if not in character, he resembled Thérèse, and nearly always found himself in agreement with her on every point. At times, Laurent still felt jealous of what he termed, in musical fashion, their *unison*, and since it was merely an intellectual jealousy, he did not dare complain of it to Thérèse.

'Your description misses the mark,' she said. 'Palmer is too calm and too perfect for me. I have a little more fire than him, and I sing in a slightly higher pitch. In relation to him, I am the note which augments his major third.'

'While I, in that case, am just a false note,' Laurent said.

'No,' Thérèse said, 'with you I modify myself and come down a step to form a minor third.'

'You mean you come down a semi-tone with me?'

'And I find myself half an interval closer to you than I am to Palmer.'

III

One day, at Palmer's request, Laurent went to the Hôtel Meurice, where he was staying, to check that the portrait had been properly framed and packed. The lid was sealed in their presence and Palmer himself wrote on it, with a paint brush, his mother's name and address; then as the commissionaires were lifting up the packing case to send it off, Palmer shook the artist by the hand and said: 'I owe to you the great pleasure my good mother will have, and I thank you again. Now, can you spare me a moment? I'd like to have a little talk. I've something to tell you.'

They went through into a sitting room, where Laurent saw a number of trunks.

'I'm leaving tomorrow for Italy,' the American told him, offering him some excellent cigars and a candle, although he did not smoke himself, 'and I don't want to go without speaking to you on a delicate matter, so delicate that if you interrupt me I shall never find the right words to say it all in French.'

'I promise I'll be as silent as the grave,' Laurent said with a smile, taken aback and rather alarmed at this preamble.

Palmer went on: 'You love Mlle Jacques, and I believe

67

she loves you. Perhaps you are her lover; if you are not, it is clear to me you will be. Ah! You promised not to say anything. Don't say anything, I am asking nothing of you. I believe you to be worthy of the honour I attribute to you. But I fear you do not know Mlle Jacques sufficiently well, or understand that if having your love is a privilege for her, then so for you is having hers. I fear this because of the questions you have asked me about her, and because of certain things that have been said concerning her, in the presence of both of us, and which I could see affected you more than they did me. That proves to me that you know nothing; I do know, and I wish to tell you everything, in order that your attachment to Mlle Jacques should be based on the esteem and respect she deserves.'

'Wait, Palmer!' cried Laurent, who was dying to hear but was overcome by an honourable scruple. 'Are you about to tell me Mlle Jacques' story with her permission or by her order?'

'Neither,' Palmer replied. 'Thérèse will never discuss her past history.'

'In that case, don't speak! I only want to know what she wants me to know.'

'Good, very good!' Palmer replied, shaking his hand. 'But what if the story I have to tell you removes any possible doubts surrounding her…?'

'Why does she hide it then?'

'Out of thoughtfulness for others.'

'All right, speak on!' said Laurent, who was on tenterhooks.

'I shall name no names,' Palmer resumed. 'I shall only tell you that, in a large town in France, there was a rich banker who seduced a charming girl who was his own daughter's governess. From this brief union he had an illegitimate child, a girl, who was born twenty-eight years ago, according to the calendar, on the feast day of Saint-Jacques. This child, listed in the municipal records as being of unknown parentage, was given the simple surname Jacques. This child is Thérèse.

'The governess was provided with a sum of money and married five years later to one of his employees, a respectable man who suspected nothing, the whole affair having been shrouded in utmost secrecy. The child was brought up in the country. Her father had taken charge of her. She was then placed in a convent, where she received a very fine education, was treated with much care and love. Her mother saw her regularly in those first few years. But when she was married, her husband began to entertain suspicions, and resigning from his post with the bank, he took his wife away to Belgium, where he found work for himself and made his fortune. The poor mother had to stifle her tears and obey.

'This woman still lives at a considerable distance from her daughter: she has other children, her conduct since her marriage has been irreproachable; but she has never been happy. Her husband, who loves her, allows her little freedom. And he remains a jealous man, which in her eyes, is a deserved punishment for her error and her lie.

'One might think that age would have brought about her confession and his forgiveness. That is what would have happened in a novel; but nothing is less logical than real life, and the household remains as troubled as it was at the outset, the husband full of love, but anxious and rough-mannered, the wife repentant, but silent and oppressed.

'Thérèse therefore found herself in difficult circumstances: she was unable to receive support, advice, help or consolation from her mother. The mother however, loves her even more for the necessity of having to see her daughter in secret, unknown to anyone, whenever she manages to come to Paris on her own for two or three days, as happened recently. And it is only in the last few years that she has been able to invent pretexts of some sort and obtain permission like this. Thérèse adores her mother, and will never admit to anything that would compromise her. That's why you will never hear her allow a word of blame about the conduct of other women to go unchallenged. You may have thought she was thereby seeking tacit indulgence for her own way of life. Nothing of the kind. Thérèse has nothing to seek forgiveness for; but she forgives her mother everything: that is the history of their relations.

'Now, I have to tell you the history of the Countess of *** That, I believe, is what you say in French when you don't want to name people. This countess, who never bore her title or her husband's name, is Thérèse again.'

'So she's married then? She isn't a widow?'

'Patience! She is married, and she isn't. You will see.'

'Thérèse was fifteen when her father the banker became a widower and thus free; for his legitimate children were all established by then. He was an excellent man, and despite the error I have described and which I do not excuse, it was impossible not to like him. He was a spirited and generous man; we were great friends. He confided in me; I learned the story of Thérèse's birth, and he took me with him on a number of visits he made to the convent where he had settled her. She was attractive, learned, friendly, sensitive. I believe he rather hoped I would decide to ask for her hand in marriage; but my heart was already given at that time; otherwise... but I

70

couldn't think of it.

'He then asked me for information about a young Portuguese nobleman who used to visit him, who owned extensive properties in Havana and who was very handsome. I had met this man in Paris but I didn't really know him, and I refrained from giving any opinion. He was a very attractive-looking fellow, but for my part, I would never have trusted that face. It was to this Count of *** that Thérèse was married a year later.

'I had to go to Russia; when I came back the banker had died of an apoplectic stroke, and Thérèse was married, married to this stranger, this madman – I don't want to say to this scoundrel, since she might have loved him, even after she discovered his crime: this man was already married in the colonies at the time when he had the extraordinary audacity to ask for and to marry Thérèse.

'Do not ask me how Thérèse's father, an intelligent and experienced man, could have allowed himself to be duped in this fashion. I can only repeat what my own experience has taught me all too often: that half the time, everything that happens in this world is a direct contradiction of what it seems ought to happen.

'In the last few months of his life, the banker had made a number of other false steps, which might make one suspect that his mind had already lost its sharpness. He had given Thérèse a legacy instead of handing her a dowry cash in hand. This legacy was declared void when the legitimate inheritors made their claims, and Thérèse, who adored her father, would not have wanted to appeal even if there had been any chance of success. She therefore found herself financially ruined at the very moment she was about to become a mother, and it was just then too, that she found on her doorstep an indignant woman ready to demand her rights and make a fuss. She was the first, and only legitimate, wife of her husband.

'Thérèse displayed a rare steadiness of heart: she succeeded in calming down this unfortunate woman and persuading her not to take the matter before the courts; she persuaded the Count to take his wife back and to return with her to Havana. Because of the circumstances of Thérèse's birth and the secrecy in which her father wished to surround the evidence of his fondness for her, her marriage had taken place privately, and abroad; in addition the young couple had continued to live abroad since then. Even their life together was shrouded in mystery. The count, obviously fearful of being unmasked if he reappeared in society, caused Thérèse to believe his one desire in life was to have her at his side at all times and to enjoy no company other than her own; and the young wife, trusting in love, and romantically inclined, found it perfectly natural that her husband should travel with her under a false name to avoid having to see people of no importance.

'Thus, when Thérèse discovered the full horror of the situation, it was not impossible that the whole thing would be buried in silence. She consulted a discreet expert in law, and having had confirmation that her marriage was void, but that it would nevertheless take a court hearing to dissolve it if she ever wished to exercise her freedom, she immediately took an irrevocable decision. She decided it was better to be neither free nor married than to besmirch the reputation of her child's father by prompting a scandal and the consequent ignominious condemnation. The child was in any event illegitimate; but it was better that he should have no name and remain ignorant of his origins than have to claim a tarnished name and dishonour his father in the process.

'Thérèse still loved this wretched man! She told me so herself, and he too loved her, with a diabolical passion. There were heartrending battles, indescribable scenes. Thérèse fought with an energy beyond her years, and I don't mean beyond her sex: a woman, when she has to act heroically, doesn't do things by halves.

'In the end she won: she kept her child, expelled the guilty party from her life and saw him depart accompanied by her rival, who although consumed with jealousy, was so overwhelmed by her magnanimity that she virtually kissed her feet when she finally left.

'Thérèse moved away, changing both name and country, passing herself off as a widow, determined to be forgotten by the few people who had known her. She began, though grieving, to live wholeheartedly for her son. This child was so dear to her that she thought he would be her consolation for everything; but this last happiness was not to last for long.

'As the Count had a fortune, and no child by his first wife, Thérèse had been forced to accept, at the first wife's behest in fact, a reasonable sum in order to bring her son up suitably. But hardly had the Count escorted his wife back to Havana than he abandoned her once again, escaped, returned to Europe and went to throw himself at Thérèse's feet, begging her to flee with him and the child to the far ends of the earth.

'Thérèse was relentless: she had spent many hours in reflection and prayer. Her soul had hardened, she no longer loved the count. And it was for her son's sake that she did not

wish such a man to become the master of her life. She had lost
the right to be happy but not the right to her self-respect. She
rejected him, without reproaches, but without weakness. The
Count threatened to leave her without resources: she replied
that she was not afraid to work for her living.

'The miserable fool then took it into his head to do
something appalling, either to bring Thérèse to heel or to
take revenge on her for resisting him. He seized the child
and disappeared. Thérèse pursued him; but he had covered
his departure so cunningly that she ran in the wrong direction
and failed to catch up with him. It was then that I met her, in
England, where she had taken up lodgings at an inn, half dead
from despair and fatigue, at her wits' end, and so devastated by
misfortune that I barely recognised her.

'I persuaded her to rest and to let me act on her behalf.
My enquiries were successful in the worst possible way. The
Count had travelled back to the Americas again. The child had
died there of exhaustion on arriving.

'When I had to bring the unfortunate woman the shocking
news, I was myself shocked by the calm way she received it.
For a week she was like a dead woman walking. Finally she
wept, and I saw that she was saved. I was obliged to leave
her; she told me she wanted to settle where she was. I was
worried she did not have the means; she told me her mother
left her short of nothing, and I was deceived. I learned later
that her mother would have been prevented from providing
any assistance: the way her household worked, she hadn't a
centime at her disposal that she didn't have to account for.
Besides, she was quite unaware of her daughter's misfortunes.
Thérèse, who wrote to her in secret, had concealed all this

from her to spare her further misery.

'Thérèse lived in England by giving lessons in French, drawing and music, for she had many talents and had the courage to put them to use to avoid having to depend on anyone's pity.

'After a year she came back to France and established herself in Paris, where she had never been before and where no one knew her. She was only twenty at the time; she had been married at sixteen. All her prettiness had gone, and it took eight years of rest and resignation to restore her health and the gentle cheerfulness of old.

'I only saw her again at rare intervals throughout all that time, since I'm always travelling. But I always found her a model of dignity and pride: she worked with indomitable courage and concealed her poverty by a miracle of order and cleanliness. She never complained about God or any person and never wished to speak of the past. Sometimes she would covertly caress or fondle children, but always moved away as soon as anyone looked in her direction, not wishing, no doubt, anyone to see her emotion.

'It had been three years since I last saw her, and when I came to ask you to do my portrait, I was trying to find out her address, which I was going to ask you for when you started talking about her. Since I'd only arrived the day before, I didn't yet know that she had finally had some success, and a degree of financial comfort and fame with it. It was when I found her like this that I realised her once broken soul could still live, love… suffer or be happy. Try to make sure she is, my dear Laurent, she has certainly deserved it! And if you're not certain you won't make her suffer, blow your brains out tonight rather than enter her house again. That's all I had to say to you.'

'Wait,' Laurent said, very moved. 'This Count of ***, is he still alive?'

'Unfortunately, yes. These men who leave others in the most desperate straits are always quite all right and never come to any harm themselves. They don't ever completely go away either, because this fellow recently had the impertinence to send me a letter for Thérèse: I passed it on to her when you were there, and you saw her give it the welcome it deserved.'

It had been in Laurent's mind, as he listened to M. Palmer's account, that he might marry Thérèse. This story had left him shattered. Palmer's uninflected monotone, his strong accent, and some bizarre ordering of words which we have not thought useful to reproduce, had created in his audience's lively imagination, an impression as strange and as terrible as the fate of Thérèse. This daughter without parents, this mother without a child, this wife without a husband, was she not doomed to extraordinary unhappiness? What sad ideas must have been implanted in her about love and about life! The sphinx reappeared before Laurent's dazzled eyes. Unveiled, Thérèse seemed even more mysterious to him than before: had she ever got over it, or could she ever for a moment do so?

He embraced Palmer effusively, swore that he loved Thérèse and that if he ever had the fortune to be loved by her, then he would remember all his life this special hour and the story he had just heard. Then, after promising Palmer not to give any indication he knew Mlle Jacques' history, he went home and wrote:

"Thérèse, don't believe a word of anything I've said these last two months. Don't believe either what I said to you when you were fearful I might be becoming over-fond of you. I am not over-fond, that's not it at all: I love you passionately. It's absurd, it's insane, it's pitiful; but I, a man who believed I never could or should say or write to a woman the words, *I love you!* now I find them too cold and too restrained for what I'm trying to tell you. I can't live any more with this secret. It is choking me and I can't believe you don't suspect. A hundred times I've wanted to stop seeing you, disappear to some far corner of the earth, forget you. An hour later, I'm at your door. And often, at night, eaten up with jealousy and almost in a rage at myself, I ask God to deliver me from my illness by making this unknown lover turn up, a lover I don't believe in and that you invented to stop me thinking about you. Show me this man in your arms, or love me, Thérèse! If you don't, I see only one other solution, which is to put an end to it by killing myself... it's cowardly and stupid, the banal and hackneyed threat of every despairing lover, but is it my fault if such a desperation exists and makes everyone who suffers cry out in the same way? And am I mad because I've become a man like all the rest?

"All the things I invented to protect me from this feeling, what good have they done me? And all the things I did to make my poor little self as inoffensive as possible because I wished to be as free as possible?

"Is there something you dislike about my behaviour, Thérèse? Am I conceited, dissipated, when I only exaggerated my sillier activities to give you more confidence in me as a harmless friend? But why do you want me to die without ever having loved, when you are the only one who can show me what love is, and you know it? You have in your soul a treasure, and you smile at the side of a wretch who is dying of hunger and thirst. You throw him a few coppers from time to time; to you that's what's called friendship; it is not even pity, because you must know very well that a drop of water only makes the thirst greater.

"And why do you not love me? Perhaps you have loved someone before who was not as deserving as me. I'm not worth a great deal, true, but I love; and isn't that everything?

"You won't believe any of this, you'll say I'm deceiving myself again, like the last time! No, you won't be able to say that, not without lying to God and to yourself. You can see my torment is too much for me, and now I'm making a ridiculous declaration, me of all people, who fears nothing more in this world than being mocked by you!

"Thérèse, don't believe that I have been corrupted. You know very well that at bottom my soul remains pure, and that from the abyss I'd flung myself into I have always, in spite of myself, called out towards the heavens. You know very well that when I am at your side I am as chaste as a small child, and you were not afraid on occasions to take my head between your hands, as if you were going to kiss my forehead. And you used to say: 'Naughty head! You'd deserve it if someone broke you!' And yet, instead of crushing it like a serpent's head, you used to try to imbue it with the pure and cauterising breath of your own spirit. Well, you have been only too successful! And, now that you have lit the fire on the altar, you turn away and you tell me: 'Find someone else to keep it burning for you! Get married, fall in love with a beautiful young girl, sweet-natured and devoted; have children, have ambitions for them, have order, have domestic content, anything you like, except me!'

"And what I say, Thérèse, is: it's you I love with a passion, and not myself. Since I have known you, you have striven to make me believe happiness is possible and to give me the taste for it. If I have not become entirely self-centred, like a spoilt child, it's hardly because you didn't give me the opportunity. Well, I'm worth more than that! I am not asking if your love would bring me happiness. I only know that it would bring life, and, good or bad, it is this life, or else death, that I have to have."

IV

Thérèse was deeply disconcerted by this letter. It fell on her like a thunderbolt. Her understanding of love was so different from Laurent's that she imagined, especially on rereading the expressions he used, that what she felt was not love in the romantic sense at all. There was no heady excitement in Thérèse's heart, or if there was, it had seeped in drop by drop, so slowly she had been unaware of it and believed she was as much in control of herself as on the first day. The word passion revolted her.

"Passions, me?" she said to herself. "So he thinks I don't know what they are, that I want to go back to drinking from the poisoned cup! What have I done, after showing him all that care and tenderness, to prompt him to thank me by offering me despair, fever and death…? But then," she thought, "it isn't his fault, unhappy soul! He doesn't know what he wants, or what he's asking. He's looking for love as if it was the philosopher's stone, something that can't be had, which only makes people believe in it twice as hard. He thinks I have it in my possession and I'm enjoying not letting him have it! Everything he thinks is always touched with a little madness. How can I calm him down and rescue him from a fantasy which is making him miserable?

"It's my fault, he's partly right in saying that. I've been trying to steer him away from a life of excesses and I've made him too used to this purer and simpler kind of attachment; but he's a man, and finds our mutual affection incomplete. Why has he been deceiving me? Why has he been letting me believe he was happy just being here with me? What shall I do to make amends for the silly mistakes of inexperience? I've never had the brash presumptions of my sex, or not enough. I didn't know that any woman, however tired of life she may be, however tepid her manner, can still trouble a man's brain. I should have considered myself seductive and dangerous, as he once told me I was, and I ought to have realised he was only masking his feelings to keep me calm. Is there something wrong with me then – it surely can't be a crime – if I don't have any flirtatious instincts?"

And then Thérèse, searching her memories, recalled how reserved and suspicious her instincts had always been, to protect herself from the desires of men she found displeasing. With Laurent that had not been the case, because his friendliness had won her esteem, because she could not believe he wanted to deceive her, and also, it must be said, because she liked him better than anyone else. She paced up and down, alone in her studio, prey to a powerful sense of disquiet, sometimes glancing at the fatal letter she had left on a table, as if not knowing what to do with it, unable to decide whether to open it again or destroy it, sometimes glancing towards her interrupted work on the easel. She had been working well, and with pleasure, when that letter had arrived, or rather that doubt and disquiet, that surprise and fear. It was like a mirage which raised once again on her unclouded and peaceful horizon all

81

the spectres of her past miseries. Every word written on that paper was like a hymn of death already heard in her previous life, like a prophecy of new miseries to come.

She tried to soothe her mind by returning to her painting. It was her one great remedy for all the minor agitations of everyday life; but that day it was powerless: the fright this passion filled her with invaded the purest and most private sanctuary of her present life.

"Two sources of happiness disrupted or destroyed," she told herself, throwing down her paintbrush and staring at the letter: "work and friendship."

The rest of the day passed without her coming to any conclusion. Only one thing was clear in her mind: the resolve to say no. But she wanted it to be a no which was not the kind of instant retort flung back by offended women who fear they might succumb unless they barricade the door as fast as possible. How to deliver this irrevocable *no*, which must leave no hope and yet not stamp with a red-hot iron the sweet memory of their friendship, was for her a difficult and painful problem. The memory in question was her own love; when one has to bury a person one has loved dearly, it is a grievous matter to reconcile oneself to throwing a white shroud over that face and to slipping that person into the communal grave. One would like to embalm them in a private tomb, which one would come to contemplate from time to time, offering a prayer for the soul of the one therein.

When darkness fell, she had still not found a way to refuse him without causing him too much suffering. Catherine, who noticed she was merely picking at her dinner, asked her anxiously if she was ill.

'No,' she replied, 'I am preoccupied.'

'Ah, you're working too hard!' the kindly old woman said. 'You don't think enough about living.'

Thérèse raised a finger; it was a gesture Catherine knew and it meant: "Don't talk about it."

Thérèse set aside an hour in the evenings when she received her small number of friends, but the only one to take advantage for some time had been Laurent. Although the door remained open to anyone who wished to drop in, he came alone, either because the others were away (it was the season for country visits and vacations), or because they had sensed in Thérèse a certain preoccupation, an involuntary and ill-disguised wish to talk exclusively with M. de Fauvel.

Laurent used to arrive at eight, and Thérèse looked at the clock, saying to herself: 'I haven't replied. He won't come today.'

A terrible void opened in her heart when she added: 'He mustn't ever come again.'

How was she to occupy herself on this endless evening, which she usually spent chatting with her young friend, whilst making a few light sketches or attending to some small womanly tasks whilst he smoked, nonchalantly sprawled on the divan's cushions? She wondered about escaping a tiresome situation by going to find a friend she knew in Saint-Germain, and who accompanied her sometimes on theatre visits; but this person went to bed early, and it would be too late by the time Thérèse arrived. It was such a long way, and cabs in those days went so slowly!

Besides, it would be necessary to dress suitably, and Thérèse, who lived in slippers, like artists who work with total concentration and hate any impediment, was reluctant to put on her visiting clothes. Should she grab a shawl and a veil, send for a hired carriage and have herself taken for a slow drive along the deserted byways of the Bois de Boulogne? Thérèse had done something similar with Laurent on occasion, when the stifling summer evenings made them feel the need to seek a little coolness under the trees. They were the sort of outings which would seriously have compromised her with anyone else; but he kept such mutual pleasures religiously secret; and they both enjoyed the eccentricity of these mysterious private trips, which concealed no mystery. She recalled them now, as if they were already far in the past and told herself, sighing at the thought that they would not happen again: 'That was the good time! It couldn't start again, either for him, suffering, or for me, now I know.'

At nine o'clock, she finally made an attempt to answer Laurent; but a ring on the bell made her jump. It was him! She stood up to go and tell Catherine to say she had gone out. Catherine came in: it was just a letter from him. In spite of herself, Thérèse experienced a flicker of regret that he hadn't come himself. The letter contained merely these few words:

"Farewell, Thérèse, you do not love me, and I... I love you like a child!"

These brief lines caused Thérèse to tremble from head to foot. The only passion she had never sought to exclude from her heart was a mother's love. That wound, although seemingly healed, was as permanently bleeding as every unassuaged love.

'Like a child!' she repeated, clutching the letter in hands shaking from who knows what inner turmoil. 'He loves me like a child! What made him say that, my God! Does he know the terrible effect that has on me? *Farewell!* My son knew all about *farewells*, but it is a word he never cried out when they stole him away. I would have heard him! And I'll never hear him again.'

Her nerves already overstretched, and with this new emotion surging from the most painful of sources, Thérèse burst into tears.

'Did you call me?' Catherine asked her, entering the room. 'But goodness! What's the matter? You're crying again, just like the old days!'

'Nothing, nothing. Leave me alone,' Thérèse replied. 'If anyone comes to see me, say I've gone to the theatre. I want to be alone. I'm ill.'

Catherine left the room, but through the garden. She had seen Laurent walking furtively beside the hedge.

'Don't sulk like that,' she told him. 'I don't know why my mistress is crying, but it can only be your fault, you cause her a lot of trouble. She doesn't want to see you. Come and apologise to her!'

For all her respect and devotion to Thérèse, Catherine was convinced Laurent was her lover.

'Crying?' he exclaimed. 'Oh, my God! Why is she crying?'

And he crossed the garden in three strides to go and fall at the feet of Thérèse, who was sobbing in the little sitting room, head in her hands.

Laurent would have been filled with joy at seeing her like

this if he had been the rogue he sometimes pretended to be; but his heart, at bottom, was admirably good, and the surreptitious influence of Thérèse brought him closer to his true nature. The tears that covered her face therefore caused him real and profound pain. He begged her on his knees to forget this further folly on his part and to let her own gentle good sense bring balm to this crisis.

'I only want whatever you want,' he told her, 'and since you are weeping for our dead friendship, I swear to bring it back to life rather than to bring you new grief. But listen, my sweet, good Thérèse, my cherished sister, we have to be open with each other, because I don't have the strength to go on hiding things! I want you to have the courage to accept my love as an unfortunate discovery you've made, and as a disease you're kind enough to cure me of by your patience and pity. I will try my hardest to help, you have my word! I won't ask you for so much as a kiss, and I believe it won't cost me as much as you may fear, because I don't yet know if physical desire plays any part in all this. No, in truth, I don't think it does. How could that be, after the life I've led, and am still free to lead? It's my soul that's thirsty; why would that frighten you? Give me a little of your heart and take all of mine. Accept being loved by me, and don't tell me again you find it offensive, because the reason for my despair is seeing you despise me too much to permit me, even in my dreams, to have aspirations… it lowers me so much in my own eyes that it makes me want to kill the person unfortunate enough to be morally repugnant to you. Raise me up instead from the swamp I had fallen into, by telling me to atone for my bad life and become worthy of you. Yes, leave me some hope, however feeble; it will make me a different man. You'll see, you'll see, Thérèse! Just the idea of working to make me seem better in your eyes is already giving me new strength, I can feel it. Don't take that away from me. What will become of me if you reject me? I'll go down step by step and lose all the progress I've made since knowing you. All the fruits of our special friendship will be lost for me. You will have tried to cure a sick person and you will have produced a corpse! And then what about yourself, so noble, so good? Will you be pleased with your work? Won't you reproach yourself for not having brought it to a better end? Be my sister of charity, one who doesn't limit her care to bandaging an injured man but strives to reconcile his soul with heaven. Come, Thérèse, don't withdraw your loyal hand, don't turn your head away, so beautiful when it's sad. I won't get off my knees until you have given me, if not permission to love you, at least your pardon for doing so!'

Thérèse had to take this outpouring seriously, for Laurent was in good faith. To reject him too precipitously would have amounted to admitting her affection for him was only too keen: a woman who shows fear is already defeated. So she put on a brave face, and perhaps she truly felt it, for she believed herself strong enough still. And besides, his very weakness came to her aid. To break with him now would be to provoke some dreadful emotions which it was better to appease, whilst seeking a way to loosen the bond with due skill and prudence. It could be a question of several days. Laurent was so volatile and switched so rapidly from one extreme to the other!

So they both calmed down, helping each other to forget the storm, and even forcing themselves to laugh at it, in order to reassure each other about the future. But whatever they did, their situation was fundamentally altered, and their intimacy had taken a giant step forward. The fear of losing each other had brought them closer together, and even while they both swore that nothing was changed between them regarding their friendship, all their words and all their ideas were shot through with a certain languidness of soul, a sort of tender weariness which signalled already, submission to love!

Catherine, bringing in tea, completed the process of bringing them together again, as she put it, by her innocent and motherly concerns.

'You'd do better,' she told Thérèse, 'to eat a chicken wing than to scour your stomach with this tea! Do you know,' she said to Laurent, pointing to her mistress, 'she hasn't touched her dinner?'

'Well, quick, bring her some supper!' Laurent cried. 'Don't say no, Thérèse, you must eat! What would become of me then if you fell ill?'

And, as Thérèse refused to have anything, for she really wasn't hungry, he pretended, at a sign from Catherine urging him to insist, that he was hungry himself, which was true, since he had forgotten to have his own dinner. Thus prompted, Thérèse took pleasure in offering him some supper, and they ate together for the first time – which in Thérèse's solitary and modest way of life, was not an insignificant thing to do. Eating alone with someone is an important stage towards intimacy. It is the shared satisfaction of a person's material needs, and if one were to look for a higher interpretation, it is an act of communion as the word implies.

Laurent, whose ideas were apt to take a poetic turn even when being light-hearted, humorously compared himself to the prodigal son, for whom Catherine eagerly slew the fatted calf. This fatted calf, appearing in the guise of a slender chicken, naturally encouraged a certain gaiety in the two friends. It offered so little satisfaction to the young man's hunger that Thérèse felt mortified. There were few resources in the district, and Laurent did not want Catherine to go to any extra trouble. They unearthed from the depths of a cupboard a large jar of preserved guava fruit. It was a present from Palmer, whose contents Thérèse had never thought to explore, and which Laurent explored with considerable thoroughness, chattering away the whole time about that excellent fellow Dick, of whom he had been idiotic enough to be jealous, and whom he henceforth loved with all his heart.

'You see, Thérèse,' he said, 'how sorrow makes one unjust! Believe me, children need to be spoiled. The only good children are the ones treated with kindness. Therefore give me lots of guavas, and then more! Harshness is not just bitter gall, it's deadly poison!'

When the tea arrived, Laurent realised he had been eating very selfishly, and that Thérèse, while seeming to be eating, had eaten nothing at all. He chastised himself for his inattentiveness and made his confession; then, sending Catherine away, he wanted to make the tea himself and serve Thérèse. It was the first time in his life he had made himself anyone else's servant, and it gave him a subtle pleasure he found naively surprising.

'Now,' he told Thérèse, on his knees, handing her a cup, 'I understand how one can be a servant and love one's situation. It's just a question of loving one's master.'

With certain people, even the smallest of services comes at

a high price. There was a certain stiffness in Laurent's manners and the way he carried himself, which he never relaxed even with more worldly sorts of women. He behaved towards them with the ceremonious coolness that etiquette required. With Thérèse, who in her modest home played hostess like the amiable woman and cheerful artist she was, he had always been favoured and pampered without having to do anything to reciprocate. To have acted as the man of the house would have been an error of taste and propriety. Suddenly, in the wake of these tears and mutual effusions, and without his noticing it, Laurent found himself accorded a right he had no claim to, and which Thérèse, surprised and affected, was unable to deny him, and he seized on it instinctively. He appeared quite at home, as if he had earned the privilege of looking after the lady of the house, in the manner of a good brother or of an old friend. And Thérèse, not seeing the danger of his taking possession like this, watched him proceed, eyes wide with astonishment, wondering if she hadn't up to now been radically mistaken in taking this tender and devoted boy for a man of aloof and chilly manners.

During the night however, Thérèse gave the situation much thought. But the following morning Laurent sent her some magnificent flowers and exotic sweetmeats. He had given it no thought at all: he did not want to give her space to breathe because he could hardly breathe any more himself. The presents were accompanied by a note, so tender, so gentle and respectful, that she couldn't help being touched. He called himself the happiest of men, there was nothing more he desired, except her forgiveness, and the moment she had pardoned him he was king of the world. He was ready to accept any privation and discipline, provided he was not forbidden to see and to hear his friend. That alone was beyond his powers; the rest of it counted for nothing. He was well aware that Thérèse could not have any love for him, which did not prevent him from saying, ten lines further down the page: "And is our sacred love not indissoluble?"

And so Laurent continued, saying first one thing then the opposite, switching between true and false a hundred times a day, with a candour by which no one was more duped than himself. He smothered Thérèse with exquisite attentions, striving with all his heart to persuade her of the chaste nature of their relations, whilst assaulting her at every moment with exalted words of adoration. When he saw her upset, he sought to distract her; when he saw her sad, he sought to raise her spirits, when he saw her severe, he sought to soften her heart towards him. And little by little, without her becoming aware of it, he brought her to the point where she had no will and no existence of her own.

There is nothing quite so perilous as these close relationships in which both parties agree to avoid harsh words, and when neither of them secretly finds the other physically unattractive. Artists, thanks to their independent way of living and their occupations, which often oblige them to abandon social conventions, are more exposed to these dangers than those who live ordered and practical lives. They must therefore be forgiven for having more sudden enthusiasms and more powerful impressions. Public opinion feels it owes them that much, for it is generally more indulgent towards those who necessarily sail through storms than towards those who know only flat calm. And then the world expects artists to have the fire of inspiration, and it is only right and necessary that this fire, which blazes for the pleasure and satisfaction of the public, should eventually consume the artists themselves. Then they become objects of pity, and the good bourgeois, learning of their disasters and catastrophes, returns to the bosom of his family in the evening and says to his excellent and worthy companion in life: 'You know, that poor girl who used to sing so well, she's died of grief. And that famous poet who used to say such beautiful things, he's committed suicide. It's a terrible shame, little wife… those people all end badly. We're the happy people; us, the simple ones…'

And the good bourgeois is right.

For a long time however, Thérèse had lived, if not as a good bourgeoise, because you need a family for that, and God had refused her one, then at least as an industrious toiler, setting to work early in the morning and neither chasing pleasures nor sinking into idle stupor at the end of the day. She had unbroken aspirations towards a stable and domesticated life; she liked order, and far from displaying the childish contempt that some artists flaunted for what they called in those days the grocer-class, she bitterly regretted not having married into that safe and steady society, where, in place of talent and fame, she would have found affection and security. But one does not choose one's destiny, since the foolish and the ambitious are not the only incautious people at whom destiny aims its thunderbolts.

V

If Thérèse had a weak spot for Laurent, it was not in the mocking and licentious sense the phrase has acquired in relation to love. It was through an act of her will, after nights of painful meditation, that she told him: 'I want what you want, because we have arrived at a point where the fault about to be committed is the inevitable reparation for a series of faults already committed. I have been a contributor to your unhappiness by not having the selfish prudence to stay away from you. It is better that I take responsibility for myself, by remaining your companion and your consolation, at the cost of my own repose and pride… listen,' she added, gripping his hand between hers with all the strength she possessed, 'never take this hand away, and whatever happens, do not forget that before becoming your mistress I was *your friend*. Your honour and courage are at stake in this. I said to myself as soon as this passion of yours took hold: we loved each other too well as we were, for us not to love each other less well any other way. But that happiness could not last for me, since you no longer share it. And also, for you, our relationship has been an equal mixture of pain and joy, and now pain has risen to the top. All I ask, if you should ever tire of my love as you have tired of my friendship, is to remember this: I am not falling into your arms in some bout of wild delirium; I give myself to you because I feel my heart swell with a sentiment more tender and more durable than any surge of physical gratification. I am not superior to other women, and I do not assume the right to consider myself invulnerable; but I love you so fiercely and so purely that I would never have lapsed like this if you could have been saved by my strength alone. At first you thought my strength was good for you, it showed you how to find your own and how to cleanse yourself of an evil past. Now you're convinced of the opposite; so firmly that today the opposite is what is indeed happening. You're turning bitter, and it seems if I resist, you're ready to hate me and return to a life of excess, uttering blasphemies even against our poor friendship. So, then! For you I offer God the sacrifice of my life. If your character or your past must bring me suffering, so be it. I shall be sufficiently recompensed if I save you from destroying yourself, which you were in the process of doing when I met you. If I don't succeed, at least I will have made the attempt, and God will forgive me for my futile devotion, for he will know how sincere I was!'

Laurent was a paragon of enthusiasm, gratitude and faith in the first few days of this union. He rose above himself, his ideas developed an almost religious turn. He blessed his mistress for bringing him at last into the knowledge of true love, that noble and faithful state: he had dreamed of it so long, and believed himself forever barred from it through his sins. She was dipping him once more, he said, in the water of his baptism, she was expunging in him even the memory of the bad days. It was a kind of adoration, of ecstasy, of worship.

Thérèse innocently believed it. She abandoned herself to the joy of having given all this happiness and restored all this greatness to an exceptional soul. She forgot all her fears and smiled at them as empty fancies she had taken for sound arguments. They mocked them together; they reproached themselves for not flinging their arms round each other the very first day, so obviously were they made for each other, to understand, cherish and appreciate each other. There was no longer any question of being prudent or delivering sermons. Thérèse became ten years younger. She became more playful and childlike than Laurent himself. She could barely think of enough ways to make his life a bed of roses.

Poor Thérèse! Her intoxication did not last a week.

How is it that those who have abused their youthful powers must suffer the terrible punishment of being rendered incapable of appreciating the sweetness of a harmonious and logical life? Is he really a criminal, the young man who finds himself pitched into the world, with no restraints on him and full of aspirations, convinced of his ability to withstand the siren call of transient delights and pleasures? Is his sin anything more than ignorance? Might he have learnt in the cradle that the exercise of life is inevitably an eternal battle with oneself? There are indeed men like this who are to be pitied and whom it is difficult to condemn, who have perhaps never had a guide, a prudent mother, a serious friend, a sincere woman for their first mistress. They have been gripped from the outset by a kind of vertigo; corruption has seized them in its claws like prey and made brutes out of the ones who had more sensuality than soul, and made madmen out of the ones who struggled, like Laurent, between the mire of reality and the ideal of their dreams.

That was what Thérèse said, to be able to persist in loving that suffering soul; and that was why she endured the wounds we are about to relate.

The seventh day of their happiness was irrevocably the last. The ill-fated number lodged itself forever in Thérèse's memory. A series of fortuitous circumstances had combined to prolong this eternity of joys for a whole week. No one close to Thérèse had come to call, she had no especially pressing work in hand. Laurent was promising to set to work again as soon as he could take possession of his studio, having temporarily surrendered it to the builders for refurbishment. The heat in Paris was crippling; he proposed to Thérèse that they should go and spend forty-eight hours in the country, in the forests. It was the seventh day.

They left on a riverboat and arrived in the evening at a hotel, from where, after dinner, they set out to explore the forest by the light of a magnificent moon. They had hired horses and a guide, who quickly annoyed them with his conceited chatter. They had ridden five or six miles and come to a great mass of rocks which Laurent already knew. He suggested they send back the horses and the guide, and return on foot, even though it would be rather late.

'I don't see why we shouldn't spend the whole night in the forest,' Thérèse said. 'There are no wolves or robbers. Let's stay here as long as you want, and never come back at all, if that's what you feel like.'

They were alone, and it was then that a bizarre, almost fantastic scene occurred; one which must nevertheless be recounted exactly as it happened. They had climbed to the top of the rock and had sat down on a thick carpet of moss, dried out by the summer heat. Laurent stared up at the splendid sky, where the brightness of the moon obscured the stars. Two or three of the largest shone alone above the horizon. Laurent lay on his back and contemplated them.

'I wish I knew,' he said, 'the name of that star just over my head. It seems to be staring at me.'

'That's Vega,' Thérèse replied.

'Do you know the name of every star then, professor?'

'More or less. It's not difficult. In fifteen minutes you could know as much as I do, if you wanted.'

'No, thanks; I definitely prefer not to know; I prefer to give them names of my own.'

'Quite right too.'

'I prefer to wander as I fancy, drawing my own lines up there, making my own groups and patterns. It's better than walking in the footsteps others have chosen. But then, perhaps I'm wrong, Thérèse! You like well-trodden paths, don't you?'

'They're easier on the poor feet. I don't have seven-league boots, like you!'

'You're making fun of me! You know very well you're stronger and a much better walker than I am!'

'That's easy to explain: I don't have wings to fly away on.'

'Just you dare get some and leave me here! But don't let's talk about separating: the word's enough to bring on the rain!'

'What! But who's thinking of that? It's a terrible word, don't repeat it!'

'No, no! Don't let's think of it, don't let's think of it!' he cried, jumping abruptly to his feet.

'What's the matter? Where are you going?' she said.

'I don't know,' he replied. 'Ah! Yes, now I think of it… there's an extraordinary echo round here, and the last time I came, with little… you don't want to know her name, do you? It was a wonderful effect, to hear her, from where we are now, singing over there on that mound opposite.'

Thérèse made no reply. He realised that it was indelicate to inject this untimely memory of one of his undesirable acquaintances into the middle of a romantic vigil with the queen of his heart. Why had it suddenly come back to him? How had the irrelevant name of that excitable virgin sprung to his lips? He was mortified by his clumsiness; but instead of simply admitting so and driving it from her mind with torrents of tender words which he was expert at drawing from his soul when passion inspired him, he did not want the humiliation, and asked Thérèse if she would like to sing for him.

'I couldn't,' she replied gently. 'It's been a long time since I was on a horse, I feel a little breathless.'

'If it's only a little, then try anyway, Thérèse, it would give me such pleasure!'

Thérèse was too proud a woman to let herself be angry. She was simply sorrowful. She turned her head aside and pretended to cough.

'So, then,' he said, laughing, 'you're just a weak woman! And you don't believe in my echo, I can see. I want you to hear it. Stay here. I'll climb that mound myself. I hope you're not scared to stay here on your own for five minutes?'

'No,' Thérèse responded sadly, 'I'm not at all scared.'

To scale the other rock, it was necessary to go down into the little ravine which separated it from theirs; but this ravine was deeper than it looked. When Laurent, after having scrambled half way down, saw how far he still had to go, he stopped, afraid of leaving Thérèse alone for so long, and shouting up to her, he asked her if she hadn't called him back.

'No, absolutely not!' she shouted in return, not wishing to thwart his fanciful idea.

It is impossible to explain what went on in Laurent's head. He took her *absolutely not* as a harsh remark, and began to scramble on down, but less quickly, and turning things over in his mind.

"I've hurt her," he said, "and now she's sulking, the way she did when we used to play brothers and sisters. Is she still going to have these moods now she's my mistress? But why did I hurt her? I was wrong, certainly, but without meaning to be. It's virtually impossible that some fragment of a past memory won't come floating back to mind. And is it going to offend her every time, and mortify me? What does my past matter to her, since she's accepted me for what I am? All the same, I was wrong! Yes, I was wrong; but won't it ever happen to her too, won't she find herself mentioning that strange fellow she loved when she believed she was his wife? Now we're together, she won't be able to help remembering the times when she didn't live with me, and will I consider that a crime?"

Laurent answered himself instantly: "Oh, but yes! I couldn't bear it! So I was very wrong then, and I should have begged her forgiveness straightaway."

But he had already reached that moment of moral fatigue when the soul has run out of enthusiasm, when the simultaneously feeble and ferocious creature which we all are to a greater or lesser extent feels the need to reassert its own identity.

"How many more rounds of self-accusation, promises, cajoling, emotionalism? For heaven's sake!" he told himself. "Can't she be happy and confident for seven days running? It's my fault, I'm prepared to admit; but there's even more on her side for making such a fuss about something so little – and for ruining this beautiful poetic night I'd been planning with her, in one of the loveliest spots in the world. I've been here before with some of my looser sorts of friends and girls, that's true. But is there any place around Paris I could have taken her where I wouldn't have run into similarly awkward memories? One thing's for sure, I don't find them remotely exciting, and it's almost cruel to hold them against me…"

As he formulated in his heart these responses to the reproaches Thérèse was probably directing at him in hers, he arrived at the bottom of the valley, where he felt disturbed and exhausted, as if after a quarrel, and he threw himself on the grass in a fit of weariness and frustration. For seven whole days now he had not been his own man; he felt the need to repossess himself and believe himself alone and untamed for a while.

Thérèse, on her side, was woebegone and frightened at the same time. Why had the word *separate* suddenly risen to his lips like a harsh cry and disturbed the peaceful air they had been breathing together? What was that about? What had provoked it? She sought an answer in vain. Laurent could not have explained it to her himself. Everything which had followed had been excruciatingly cruel; and how exasperated he must have been to have said it, a man of his refined education! But where did this anger come from? Did he carry inside him some serpent which sank its fangs into his heart and drew from him wild and fatal words?

She had watched his progress down the side of the rock until he entered the thick gloom of the ravine. She could no longer see him and was surprised at the time it was taking for him to reappear on the slope of the mound facing her. She was seized with fear: he might have tumbled into some precipice. Her eyes vainly probed the grassy terrain, scattered with great black rocks. She was standing up to try to call him when a cry of inexpressible distress rose up to her, a hoarse, appalling, despairing cry which made her hair stand on end.

She ran like an arrow in the direction it came from. If there had indeed been a precipice, she would have leapt into it without thinking; but it was no more than a steep slope, on whose mossy surface she slipped several times, tearing her dress against the bushes. Nothing could stop her; she arrived, without knowing how, at Laurent's side: she found him standing, distraught, shaken by a convulsive trembling.

'Ah, there you are!' he said, grabbing her by the arm. 'It's a good thing you came! I'd have died here!'

And like Don Juan after the statue has spoken, he added in a harsh and abrupt voice: *'Let's get away from this place!'*

He dragged her on to the path and set off, walking at random, unable to give an account of what had happened to him.

After a quarter of an hour, he became calmer at last, and sat down with her in a clearing. They did not know where they were, the ground was strewn with flat rocks which resembled tombs, between which juniper trees sprang up haphazardly, looking in the dark like cypresses.

'My God!' Laurent suddenly said. 'Are we in a cemetery

then? Why have you brought me here?'

'It's just wild growth,' she replied. 'We've walked through several patches of it already this evening. If you don't like it, let's get into the shelter of the big trees again.'

'No, let's stay here,' he replied. 'Since chance or fate casts me among these reminders of death, it's as well to face them and drain them of their horror. The place has its charm, like anything else, don't you think, Thérèse? Everything that powerfully stirs the imagination is a grim sort of pleasure to some degree. When a head is to fall on the scaffold, the crowd comes to watch, and it's all quite natural. We don't live on our tender emotions alone: we have to experience horrifying ones to make us feel life's intensity.'

For a few minutes he said more in the same vein, his thoughts having no apparent direction. Thérèse did not dare question him and tried to distract him; it was clear to her that he had suffered some fit of delirium. In the end he regained his composure enough to want and to be able to tell her what had happened.

He'd had a hallucination. Lying on the grass in the ravine, his head had become confused. He had heard the echo, singing all by itself, and the song had been an obscene one. Then as he propped himself up to locate this phenomenon, he had seen someone pass in front of him on the tussocky ground, a man, running, pale, his clothes torn, his hair streaming in the wind.

'I saw him so clearly,' he said, 'that I had time to think and tell myself it was a rambler out late, surprised and chased by robbers, and I even looked for my cane to go and help him. But the cane had got lost in the grass, and this man was coming nearer. When he was very close, I saw that he was drunk, not being chased. As he ran past he sent me a dazed and hideous look, and pulled a horrible face, full of hatred and contempt. Then I was frightened and threw myself face down on the ground, because this man… was me!

'Yes, it was my ghost, Thérèse! Don't be scared, don't think I'm mad, it was a vision. I understood that all right when I found myself alone again in the darkness. I couldn't have made out the features of a human face, I saw this one only in my imagination. But how sharp, how horrible, how terrifying! It was me, twenty years older, my face hollowed out by illness or excess, wild eyed, slack mouthed, and even though almost every vestige of my being had been erased, this phantom had enough vigour left in it to insult and challenge the being that I am now. Then I said to myself: "Oh God! Is this what I shall be then in years to come…?" Some bad memories came back to me tonight, which I voiced without meaning to. Does it show the old man is always there inside me, even though I thought I was rid of him? The spectre of debauchery and excess won't let go of his prey, and he'll come and mock me, even in the arms of Thérèse, and shout at me: *It's too late!*

'So I got up to come and find you, my poor Thérèse. I wanted to ask your pardon for my wretchedness and beg you to protect me. But I don't know how many minutes or centuries I would have gone round in circles, unable to move forward, if you hadn't eventually come. I recognised you straight away, Thérèse: I wasn't scared of you, I felt I was saved.'

It was difficult to know, when Laurent talked like this, if he was relating a thing he had actually experienced, or if he had muddled together in his brain an allegory born of his bitter reflections and an image glimpsed in a state of semi-slumber.

He swore he hadn't fallen asleep on the grass however, and that he had always been aware of where he was and of time passing; but even that was difficult to be sure of. Thérèse had lost sight of him and from her point of view, the passing time had been painfully long.

She asked him if he was subject to these hallucinations.

'Yes,' he said, 'when I'm drunk. But the only thing I've been drunk on this last fortnight you've been mine is love.'

'Fortnight!' said Thérèse, astonished.

'No, less than that,' he went on. 'Don't pick me up on dates: you can see I'm not clear in my head yet. Let's walk, it'll put me right again.'

'You need to rest though: we should think about going back.'

'Well, what are we doing?'

'We're not going in the right direction. Our point of departure is behind us.'

'Do you want me to walk past that cursed rock again?'

'No, but we need to turn off to the right.'

'Exactly the opposite.'

Thérèse insisted; she was not mistaken. Laurent refused to yield, and even lost his temper and spoke to her angrily, as if it were grounds for a quarrel. Thérèse gave way and followed where he wanted to go. She felt broken with emotion and sadness. Laurent had just spoken to her in a tone she would never have adopted with Catherine, even when the excellent old woman annoyed her. She forgave him, because she sensed he was ill; but the state of distressed excitement she saw he was in frightened her all the more.

Thanks to Laurent's obstinacy, they lost their way in the

forest, walked for four hours, and returned only as dawn was breaking. Walking in the thick fine sand of the forest floor is hard work. Thérèse could hardly drag one foot after another, and Laurent, reinvigorated by this strenuous exercise, never thought of slowing his pace for her sake. He strode ahead, always claiming to have discovered the right path, asking her from time to time if she was tired, and not guessing that her "no" was only said to spare him the regret of having been the cause of this misadventure.

The next day Laurent was perfectly normal, as if nothing had happened, although the strange crisis had shaken him considerably. But it is a peculiarity of excessively nervous temperaments that they can recover their equilibrium as if by magic. Thérèse even had occasion to notice, the day after these terrible episodes, that she was the one who felt shattered, whereas he seemed to have acquired a new strength.

She had not slept, expecting to see him overtaken by some serious illness; but he took a bath and felt ready to resume their exploration of the forest. He seemed to have forgotten how upsetting the previous evening had been to their honeymoon. The sadness that had overtaken Thérèse soon vanished. Returning to Paris, she thought nothing had changed between them; but that same evening, Laurent took it into his head to do a sketch of Thérèse and himself, the pair of them wandering through the moonlit forest, he with his wild and distracted look, she with her torn dress and body bent with exhaustion. Artists are so used to sketching each other that Thérèse took his in good part. But although she too had facility and wit at the end of her pencil, not for anything in the world would she have wished to make one of Laurent, and when she saw him making a comic caricature of the nocturnal scene which had been a torture to her, it grieved her. There are certain sorrows of the soul, it seemed to her, that can never have a humorous side.

Laurent, instead of understanding, gave the thing an extra twist of irony. Beneath his own figure he wrote: *Lost in the forest and in his mistress' mind*; and under the figure of Thérèse: *The heart as torn as the dress*. The composition was entitled: *Honeymoon in a Cemetery*. Thérèse forced herself to smile. She praised the drawing, which in spite of its light-heartedness, showed the hand of a master, and made no comment on the sad choice of subject. That was a mistake: she would have done better to insist, as soon as he began, that Laurent should not let his high spirits stamp their heedless boots wherever the whim took him. But she walked on tip-toe herself, for fear he might become ill again and have another fit of delirium if she criticised his lugubrious joke.

Two or three similar incidents alarmed her and made her wonder whether the quiet and orderly life she wanted to give her friend was really the regime best suited to that exceptional temperament. She had told him: 'You will sometimes be bored perhaps; but boredom offers respite from over-stimulation, and when your moral health has fully returned, you will take pleasure in little things and come to know what enjoyment really is.'

Things developed in precisely the opposite direction. Laurent did not admit his boredom, but he found it unbearable, and he gave vent to his feelings through a series of bizarre and bitter mood swings. He had created for himself a life of perpetual highs and lows. The sudden transitions from dreaminess to exhilaration and from relaxed ease to noisy excess had become a kind of normality he could no longer do without. The happiness which he had for several days savoured with delight came to irritate him like the view of the sea in a flat calm.

'You are lucky,' he told Thérèse, 'to wake up every morning with your heart in the same place. Mine disappears while I'm sleeping. It's like the night-cap my nanny used to make me wear when I was a child: sometimes she found it round my feet, sometimes on the floor.'

Thérèse told herself that serenity could not suddenly descend on a troubled soul and that he needed to grow accustomed to it by degrees. To that end, he should not be prevented from returning occasionally to the vigorous life of old: but what could they do to prevent his vigorous activities from staining their ideal, from dealing it a mortal blow? Thérèse could not be jealous of the mistresses Laurent had had, but she did not see how she would ever be able to kiss him on the forehead the morning after one of his orgiastic nights. It was therefore essential, since the work which he had enthusiastically taken up again exacerbated his restlessness rather than calmed it, to find a way, with his consent, to redirect this energy.

The natural way would have been to focus it on their new love. But even in that direction Laurent would grow so excited that he could not be content with reaching anything less than the seventh heaven. Lacking the power to achieve impossible heights, he looked instead towards hell, and his brain, even his face, would sometimes be marked with a diabolical glow.

Thérèse studied his tastes and his fantasies, and was

surprised to find them easy to satisfy. Laurent loved any sort of diversion, the more spontaneous the better. It was not necessary to take him to some world of impossible enchantments, it was enough to take him anywhere and find an amusement he was not expecting. If instead of making him dinner at her house, Thérèse announced, putting on her hat, that they were dining together at a restaurant, and if instead of a particular theatre she had asked him to take her to, she suddenly asked him to take her to a completely different sort of show, he was delighted by this unexpected distraction and took the greatest pleasure in it. On the other hand, whenever they followed a plan of any sort which had been drawn up in advance, he felt ungovernably ill at ease and had to spend the evening denigrating everything. So Thérèse treated him like a convalescent child who is refused nothing, and she tried to pay no attention to any resulting inconvenience for herself.

The first and most serious was the compromising of her reputation. She was said to be, and known to be, a respectable woman. Not everyone was persuaded she had had no other lover before Laurent; in addition, after a woman had put it about that she had once seen her in Italy with the Count of ***, who had a wife in America, she was assumed to have been kept by the man she had in reality married. We have seen how Thérèse preferred to bear this stain than to embark on a scandal-raising case against the unfortunate man she had once loved. But everyone agreed in considering her a prudent and rational woman.

'She keeps up appearances,' they said. 'There have never been any rivalries, or any hints of scandal surrounding her. All her friends respect her and speak well of her. She's a level-headed woman, with no desire to draw attention to herself; which adds to her merit.'

When she was seen out and about on Laurent's arm, people were astonished, and the criticism directed at her was all the more severe for her having avoided any for so long. Laurent was highly rated by the artistic fraternity, but he had very few friends among them. They did not appreciate the way he liked to associate with elegant gentlemen from a different class, and for their part, the friends he had in that society could not comprehend his conversion and did not believe in it. Thérèse's tender and devoted love, therefore, was taken as a wild and passionate whim of the moment. Would a chaste woman have chosen as her lover, amongst all the serious men of her acquaintance, the only one who had led a life of dissolution with all the worst and most licentious women in Paris? And for those who did not wish to condemn Thérèse, Laurent's violent passion appeared to be nothing more than a piece of roguishness successfully brought off, and which he was clever enough to extricate himself from when he was tired of it.

Thus Mlle Jacques lost credit on all sides for the choice she had recently made and which she seemed to want to advertise.

That was certainly not Thérèse's intention. But with Laurent, although he had resolved to treat her with respect, there was really no way of concealing his lifestyle. He could not give up the outside world and there was no choice but to let him return and bury himself in it, or else plunge in herself to rescue him. He was accustomed to see the crowd and be seen by it. When he had lived a whole day in retreat, he felt he had toppled into a cellar and cried out for air and sunlight.

With the loss of her reputation there soon came another sacrifice Thérèse had to make: her domestic security. Until now she had earned enough money through her work to lead a comfortable life; but only on condition of having regular habits, moderation in her expenditure and the same in her other occupations. The spontaneity which so delighted Laurent put her in some difficulties. She hid this from him, not wishing to refuse him the sacrifice of this precious time, which is the artist's principal capital.

But all this was no more than the frame round a much darker picture, over which Thérèse threw a veil so thick that no one suspected how unhappy she was, and so effectively that her friends, scandalised or troubled by her situation, distanced themselves from her, saying: 'It's a rush of blood. We'll wait for her eyes to open; it won't take long!'

It had happened already. Every day there deepened in Thérèse the sad conviction that Laurent had already ceased to love her, or that he loved her so poorly that their union offered as little hope of happiness for him as it did for her. It was in Italy that absolute certainty of that fact was made clear to both of them, and it is their Italian journey that we shall relate.

VI

Laurent had wanted to see Italy for a long time; it had been a dream of his since childhood, and the unexpected sale of a number of works finally put him in a position to realise it. He offered to take Thérèse, proudly showing her his modest fortune, and swearing that if she didn't wish to accompany him he would abandon the expedition. Thérèse knew he would not abandon it without regret and reproaches. So she tried to think of ways to gather some money herself. Her solution was to arrange an advance on work to be done during their trip; and they set off towards the end of autumn.

Laurent had built up a vivid mental image of Italy and anticipated his first sight of the Mediterranean would bring him springtime in December. He had to lose his illusions and endure bitter cold during the crossing from Marseilles to Genoa. Genoa delighted him, and as there was plenty of art to see, which was the main purpose of the voyage for him, he readily agreed they should stay there for a month or two, and rented a furnished apartment.

After a week, Laurent had seen everything, and Thérèse was only just beginning to get organised for her own painting, because it must be said, she could not manage without

111

producing some work. To secure a few thousand francs, she had had to make an agreement with a picture dealer to bring home several copies of hitherto unpublished portraits from which he intended to make engravings. The task was not unpleasurable: a man of taste, the dealer had specified various portraits by Van Dyck, one in Genoa, another in Florence, and so on. Thérèse had made a speciality of copying this particular master; doing so had helped her develop her own talent and earn enough to live on before painting portraits on her own account. But first she had to begin by obtaining permission from the owners of these masterpieces, and diligent as she was, it took a week before she was ready to begin on the Genoa copy.

Laurent felt no disposition to copy anything at all. His individuality was too pronounced and too passionate for that type of study; he gained a benefit of a different kind from viewing great things. That was his right. Nevertheless, more than one of the great masters, face to face with an opportunity like this, would perhaps have taken advantage of it. Laurent was not yet twenty-five and could still learn. That was Thérèse's opinion, who also saw in it an opportunity for him too, to add to his financial resources. If he had deigned to copy a Titian, who was his preferred master, no doubt the same dealer Thérèse had turned to would have purchased it or sold it to an art lover. Laurent found this idea absurd. While he had any money in his pocket he could not conceive of descending from the lofty peaks of art to think about sordid gain. He left Thérèse absorbed before her model, ribbing her a little in advance about the Van Dyck she was going to produce, and hoping to put her off the fearsome task she dared to undertake. Then he started to drift about the town, somewhat concerned about how to spend the six weeks Thérèse had asked him to give her to bring her work to a satisfactory conclusion.

And in truth, there was no time to be lost from her point of view, what with December's short dark days, her restricted materials and the lack of the usual conveniences offered by her own studio, the poor light, a large gallery inadequately heated, if heated at all, and streams of idle onlookers, mostly tourists, who wanted to view the masterpiece and stood in her way, distracting her with their generally preposterous observations. She had already caught a cold, and now, suffering, saddened and more than anything alarmed to see signs of boredom in Laurent's eyes, she returned to the apartment to find him in a bad mood, or to wait until hunger drove him home. He couldn't let two days go by without reproaching her for having accepted such a mind-numbing job, and suggesting she give it up. Did he not have enough money for two, and what was the point of his mistress refusing to share it with him?

Thérèse held firm. She knew that the money would not last long in Laurent's hands, and he might very well find he didn't have enough left to return to Paris when he tired of Italy. She begged him to let her work, and to work himself as he saw fit, but as every artist can and must work when he has his future to advance.

He agreed that she was right, and resolved to settle down to something. He unpacked his boxes, found a suitable spot and motif and made several sketches; but whether it was due to the change of air and habits, or so recent a sight of so many different masterpieces which profoundly stirred his emotions and which he needed time to digest, he felt gripped by a temporary impotence, and fell into one of those depressions he was unable to combat alone. It would have taken some powerful emotion from outside himself: a burst of magnificent music coming from the ceiling, an Arabian steed entering the room through the keyhole, an unknown literary masterpiece suddenly falling into his hands, or better still, a naval battle breaking out in the port of Genoa, an earthquake, any event at all, wonderful or terrible, under whose impulse he might find himself energised and renewed.

Suddenly, in the middle of these vague and turbulent longings, an evil thought entered his head without his inviting it.

"When I think," he said to himself, "about *before*," (that was what he called the time when he was not in love with Thérèse) "the least little foolishness used to get me going again! Today I have many things I used to dream of having: money, meaning six months of liberty and leisure, Italy at my disposal, the sea at my door, and at my side a mistress as tender as a mother, at the same time as being a serious and intelligent friend; and all of this isn't enough to bring my soul to life! Whose fault is it? It's not mine, that's for sure. I've never been spoilt, and I didn't need all this before to keep me happy. When I think that the cheapest bottle of wine went to my head just as efficiently as the noblest vintage; that the funniest little face with provocative eyes and a revealing dress was enough to lift my spirits and persuade me the conquest of such a person would make a regency hero of me! Did I need an ideal such as Thérèse? How on earth can I have persuaded myself that moral and physical beauty were what I needed in love? I was perfectly capable of being happy with *less*; so *more* was bound to overwhelm me, since the better is the enemy of the good. And then, anyway, is there such a thing as beauty

114

when it comes to the senses? Real beauty is whatever pleases. Beauty you've had your fill of is like beauty that never existed. And then again, there's the pleasure of change, and perhaps that's the whole secret of life. To change is to renew yourself; to be able to change is to be free. Is the artist born for slavery, and isn't fidelity observed, or just the promise of it, a form of slavery?"

Laurent allowed his mind to fill with these old sophistries, always new for souls adrift. He soon felt the need to express them to someone, and that someone was Thérèse. It couldn't be helped, since she was the only person Laurent saw!

The evening's conversation always began in much the same fashion: 'What a boring town this is!'

One evening he added: 'It must be very boring being a painting. I wouldn't like to be the model you're copying. That poor beautiful Countess in her black and gold dress, who's been hanging there for two hundred years, well, if her soft eyes haven't already damned her she must be damning herself in heaven to see her image shut up in this miserable country.'

'And yet,' Thérèse responded, 'she still enjoys the privilege of beauty, a success which survives death, made eternal by the hand of a master. She may be dust in her tomb, but she still has lovers. Every day I see young people, insensitive to the merits of the painting as they may be, stand in ecstasy in front of that beauty, which seems to breathe and smile with calm triumph.'

'She resembles you, Thérèse, do you know that? There's a bit of the sphinx about her, and I'm not surprised you admire her mysterious smile. They say that artists always create according to their own natures: it's easy to see why you chose the portraits of Van Dyck for your apprenticeship. His figures are tall, slender, elegant and proud, like your own.'

'Oh, compliments now! Stop there, I can see mockery on the way.'

'No, I'm not laughing at it. You know I don't laugh any more. With you everything has to be taken seriously: I'm following the regulations. I have just one sad observation to make. Your defunct Countess must be thoroughly tired of always looking beautiful in the same way. I've had a thought Thérèse! A fantastical idea. It came from what you were saying just now. Listen.

'A young man, probably one with ambitions as a sculptor, fell in love with a marble figure carved on a tomb, and one day this poor madman opened the lid to see what remained of this beautiful woman in the sarcophagus. And he found... what he was bound to find, the imbecile, a mummy! Then his reason returned, and embracing this skeleton he told it: "I like you better like this; at least you are something which has lived, whereas I was in love with a stone which has never even been aware of itself."'

'I don't understand,' said Thérèse.

'Nor do I,' Laurent said. 'But perhaps in matters of love, the statue is what one erects in one's head, and the mummy is what one gathers to one's heart.'

Another day he made a sketch of Thérèse, catching her face and her attitude, dreamy and sad, in an album which she then leafed through. There she blushed to find a dozen scribbled drawings of women of the most shameless type and in the most impertinent of poses. These were phantoms from the past who had flitted through Laurent's memory and attached themselves, perhaps almost accidentally, to these blank pages. Thérèse, without saying anything, tore out the one which had placed her in this bad company, threw it in the fire, closed the album and replaced it on the table; then she sat by the fireside, rested her foot on the fender and tried to talk about something else.

Laurent did not respond, but he told her: 'You are too proud, my dear! If you had burned all the pages you didn't like, leaving only your own picture in the book, I would have said: "Quite right, well done"; but to remove yourself while leaving the others there means you would never do me the honour of fighting over me.'

'I have fought over you, when the threat came from idleness and waste,' Thérèse replied. 'I'll never fight over you with any of these vestal virgins.'

'Well, that's pride, as I said! It's not love. On my side, I have fought over you when the threat came from saintliness, and I'd fight over you with any of its monkish representatives.'

'Why would you fight over me? Aren't you tired of loving the statue? Isn't the mummy closer to your heart?'

'Ah, you're the sort who remembers every word I've said! My God, what's a word? It can be interpreted any way one wants. You can hang an innocent man with a word. I see I'll have to watch what I say with you. Maybe the wisest thing would be not to have these little conversations with each other at all.'

'Is that where we've got to, my God?' said Thérèse, starting to cry.

That was where they had got to. Laurent was distressed at her tears and sought her pardon for having caused them, but it did no good. The damaging situation continued the following day.

'What do you expect me to do then in this detestable town?' he asked her. 'You want me to work; it's what I wanted too; but I can't! I wasn't born like you with a little steel spring in my brain, so that you only have to push the button for the will to function. I'm a creator, that's what I am! It doesn't matter whether it's great or small, feeble or powerful, it's not the kind of spring that works to order. It's only activated by the breath of God, if it suits him, or by some passing gust of wind. I am incapable of doing anything at all when I am bored or when I'm in a place I don't like.'

'How is it possible for an intelligent man to be bored?' Thérèse said. 'Unless he's deprived of air and daylight in the depths of a dungeon? Is there nothing in this town? You thought it was wonderful the day we arrived. Are there no beautiful things to see, no interesting outings to go on in the area? No good books to study, no intelligent people to talk to?'

'I've had my fill of beautiful things. I don't like going on outings by myself. The best books irritate me when they tell me things I don't believe. As for meeting people... I have some letters of recommendation which you know very well I can't use!'

'No, I don't know that. Why?'

'Because, of course, my society friends have pointed me towards society people, and those sort of people don't live behind their four walls doing nothing, they entertain them-selves. And since that's not your world, Thérèse, since you can't go with me, it would mean my leaving you on your own!'

'In the daytime, since I'm obliged to work where the picture is, in that palace!'

'In the daytime people visit each other and make plans for

118

the evening. The evening is when one enjoys oneself, whatever part of the world one's in; don't you know that?'

'Well, go out in the evenings sometimes if it's necessary. Go to dances, go to *conversazioni*. Don't go gambling, that's all I ask you.'

'And it's the thing I can't promise. In society you have to either sit at cards or sit with the women.'

'You mean every man of the world ruins himself gambling or spends his time flirting?'

'Those who do neither soon grow bored in society or else they bore it themselves. I am not a drawing room chatterer, not me. I'm not yet vacuous enough to force people to listen when I have nothing to say. Come now, Thérèse, do you want me to throw myself into that world, with all its risks and dangers for us?'

'Not yet,' said Thérèse. 'Wait a little. Oh dear, I wasn't prepared to lose you so soon!'

Thérèse's grieving tone and woeful look annoyed Laurent more than usual.

'You know you only have to make the smallest of complaints,' he said, 'to keep me on the course you've set for me, and you abuse your power, my poor Thérèse. Won't you regret it one day, if you see me ill and exasperated?'

'I regret it already, since I bore you,' she replied. 'Do what you want then!'

'So you're abandoning me to my fate? Are you tired of the struggle already? Well, that means that *you're* the one who doesn't love *me* any more!'

'Judging by your tone, you seem to wish that was the case!'

He answered: "No," but a moment later it was yes in every sense. Thérèse was too serious, too proud, too reserved. She would not climb down from her empyrean heights with him. A saucy word to her was an outrage, a trivial memory called down her censure. She was sober in all things and had no understanding of other people's sudden enthusiasms or extravagant fancies. She was the better of the two of them, no doubt about it, and if she needed compliments, he was ready to compliment her; but is that what it was about, between them? Wasn't finding the right way to live together the real issue? She was more cheerful before all this, more fun, more amorously playful with him, and she didn't want to be so any more. Now she was like a sick bird on its perch, feathers ruffled, head between its shoulders and the spark gone from its eye. Her pale, mournful face was frightening at times. In this big gloomy room, all the sadder for its traces of former opulence, she seemed almost like a ghost. On occasion he was even scared of her. Could she not fill this lugubrious space with unaccustomed song and joyous bursts of laughter?

'Let's think: what can we do to prevent this chill of death from settling on our shoulders? Sit at the piano, and play me a waltz. I'm going to waltz, all by myself. Do you know how to waltz? I bet you don't! You only know sad things!'

'Right,' Thérèse said, standing up, 'let's leave tomorrow, and never mind what happens! You'd go mad here. Perhaps it will be worse somewhere else; but I'll stick to my task to the very end.'

At that word, Laurent lost his temper. So it was a task was it that she had set herself? So she was coldly fulfilling a duty? Perhaps she had made a vow to the Blessed Virgin to offer up to Her the sacrifice of her lover? It was the only thing she hadn't yet done, turn into a religious fanatic!

He snatched up his hat with the air of lofty contempt and departed with the flourish his sense of grievance demanded. He left without saying where he was going. It was ten in the evening. Thérèse spent the night in dreadful anguish. He returned at dawn and shut himself in his room, slamming the doors noisily. She did not dare show her face for fear of annoying him and quietly retired to her own room. It was the first time they had gone to sleep without exchanging words of affection and forgiveness.

In the morning, instead of going out to her work, she packed her bags and got everything ready for their departure. He did not wake until three in the afternoon, and asked her with a laugh what she thought she was doing. He had sorted himself out, recovered his good temper. He had been walking all night, alone on the sea shore; he had thought things over, calmed down.

'That great sea out there grumbling away, never stopping, I lost patience with it,' he said cheerfully. 'It made me poetical at first. I compared myself to it. I wanted to throw myself into its great green bosom…! And then I thought the waves were just monotonous and ridiculous, incessantly grumbling about the fact that there were rocks on the shore. If the sea hasn't the strength to destroy them, it should shut up! It should copy me, because I don't want to go on complaining any more. I'm full of good humour this morning; I've decided to work, I'm staying. I've combed my beard with extra care; give me a hug, Thérèse, and don't let's talk of last night's stupid carryings-on. Unpack all these parcels, yes, and get rid of those trunks, quick,

I don't want to see them! They're lined up like a reproach, and I don't deserve that any more.'

This was a long way from the swift and easy submissions of the time when a worried glance from Thérèse was enough to make him bend the knee, and yet it was only three months ago.

A surprise event came to distract them. M. Palmer, arriving in Genoa that morning, came to invite them to dinner. Laurent was delighted with this diversion. Normally rather chilly in his manners with other men, he leapt on the American, greeting him enthusiastically, telling him he must have been sent from heaven. Palmer was more surprised than flattered by this warm welcome. A glance at Thérèse had been sufficient to tell him that happiness did not reign here. Laurent however, made no mention of his boredom, and Thérèse was surprised to hear him sing the praises of the town and its surroundings. He even declared the women delightful. How did he know that?

At eight o'clock he asked for his coat and went out. Palmer wanted to leave too.

'Why don't you stay a little longer,' Laurent said, 'with Thérèse? It would give her pleasure. We're very much on our own here. I'm going out for an hour. Wait for me and we'll have tea together.'

By eleven o'clock, Laurent had not returned. Thérèse was very downcast. She made vain efforts to hide her despair. She was no longer anxious, she felt lost. Palmer saw everything and pretended to see nothing: he kept the conversation going to try to distract her; but since Laurent was still not back, and it would not be proper to wait for him beyond midnight, he took his leave, shaking Thérèse's hand. The handshake conveyed to her, in spite of himself, the message that her courage did not fool him and that he understood the extent of her disaster.

Laurent returned just at that moment and witnessed Thérèse's emotion. As soon as they were alone, he teased her about it in tones intended to suggest any suspicion of jealousy was beneath him.

'Stop it,' she said, 'don't make things painful for me without purpose. Do you think Palmer is paying too much attention to me? Let's leave, I offered you the chance.'

'No, my dear, I'm not quite that absurd. Now that you've got some company and you allow me to go out occasionally on my own account, everything is fine, and I feel in the mood for working.'

'Please God that's so!' Thérèse said. 'For my part, I shall do as you wish, but if you are pleased that I now have company, have the good taste not to speak about it in the manner you've just used, I could not tolerate it.'

'What the devil are you getting so cross about? What did I say that was so hurtful? You're becoming far too gloomily sensitive, my dear friend! What would be so bad about the good Palmer loving you, if he did?'

'The badness would be your leaving me on my own with him, if you thought the things you say.'

'Ah! It would be bad to... abandon you to the danger? It's clear the danger exists, according to you, and that I wasn't wrong!'

'Very well then! We'll spend our evenings together and not receive any visitors. That's fine as far as I'm concerned. Are we agreed?'

'You are a good woman, my dear Thérèse. Forgive me. I shall stay with you and we will see whoever you want. That will be the best and most soothing arrangement.'

Indeed, Laurent appeared to return to something like his old self. He made a start on a handsome study in his work-room and invited Thérèse to come and see it. A number of days went by without further storms. Palmer had not reappeared; but soon Laurent tired of this well-regulated life, and went to find him, reproaching him for abandoning his friends. Scarcely had he arrived to spend the evening with them than Laurent found a pretext to go out and remained absent until midnight.

A week passed in this fashion, then another. Laurent gave one evening in three or four to Thérèse, and what evenings they were! She would have preferred solitude.

Where did he go? She never knew. He did not appear in local society; the cold, damp weather made it impossible to imagine the waters of the bay were any attraction. But often he did go out in a boat, he said, and his clothes, indeed, smelled of tar. He was teaching himself to row and was taking lessons from a coastal fisherman whom he went to meet on the harbour side. He claimed it did him good for his next day's work, to tire himself out because it reduced his nervous over-excitement. Thérèse no longer dared go and find him in his studio. He showed signs of vexation when she asked to see his work. He didn't want to hear her thoughts when he was busy putting his idea down on canvas, and he didn't want her silence either, which he took as a kind of criticism. She was only to see his work when he judged it fit to be seen. In the old days he would never begin anything without explaining his plan; now he treated her as if she were a member of the public, an unwanted onlooker.

Two or three times he remained out all night. Thérèse

could not get used to the worry these prolonged absences caused her. She would have exasperated him if she had shown signs of noticing; but as can be imagined, she watched, and sought to discover the truth. It was impossible for her to follow him in person at night in a town full of sailors and adventurers from every nation. Nothing in the world would have made her lower herself to having him followed by someone. She would quietly enter his room and watch him sleeping. He seemed overwhelmed with fatigue. Perhaps it was a desperate struggle within himself, undertaken to disperse the tumult in his mind through physical exercise.

One night, she noticed that his clothes were muddy and torn, as if the struggle had been a literal one, or as if he had fallen. Alarmed, she went closer and saw blood on his pillow. He had a slight cut on his forehead. He was sleeping so deeply she hoped she could uncover his chest without waking him, to see if he had any other injuries; but he woke up and flew into a rage which for her was the final blow. She tried to run away, he held her back by force, pulled on a dressing gown, locked the outer door; and then, pacing the apartment in great agitation by the feeble illumination of a night light, he finally poured out all the accumulated pain in his soul.

'Enough of this,' he said. 'Let's be frank with each other. We don't love each other any more, we never have! We've been deceiving each other. You wanted to have a lover; perhaps I wasn't the first, or the second, it doesn't matter! You needed a servant, a slave. You thought my bad character, my debts, my boredom, my weariness with this life of excess, my illusions about true love, would put me in your hands, I would never be able to get a grip on myself. To bring such a perilous enterprise to a good conclusion, you would have needed on your side a happier temperament, more patience, more flexibility and above all more sparkle! You have no sparkle at all, Thérèse, I say so without offence. You are all of a piece, monotonous, stubborn and excessively vain about your claimed moderation, which is merely the philosophy of short-sighted people of limited faculties. As for me, I'm mad, unreliable, ungrateful, anything you like; but I'm sincere, I don't calculate, I give myself without a backward glance: it explains why I can feel restored to normal so easily. My moral freedom is something sacred, and I don't permit anyone to take it over. I placed it in your care, I didn't give it to you. It was up to you to use it well and to know how to make me happy. Oh, don't try to say you didn't want me! I know all about women's ploys, the modesty, the conscience-shifting. The day you gave in to me, I understood you were thinking you had me well and truly conquered, and all that feigned resistance, those tears of distress, your invariable forgiving of my conceits, were merely the common art of hanging out the bait and getting the poor fish to bite, dazzled by the artificial fly. I have deceived you, Thérèse, by pretending to be fooled by that fly: it was my right. You wanted adoration in return; I gave you adoration in quantities with no effort and no hypocrisy; you are beautiful and I desired you! But a woman is only a woman, and the lowest of them gives us as much pleasure as the greatest queen. You were simple enough not to know that, and now, you have to turn in again on yourself. You need to realise that monotony does not suit me, I have to be left to follow my instincts, which are not always sublime, but which I can't destroy without destroying myself at the same time... what is bad about any of this, and why should we tear our hair out over it? We have been a couple and we are separating, that's all. There's no need to hate and disparage each other because of it. Avenge yourself by fulfilling poor Palmer's hopes, he's languishing under your spell. His joy will make me glad, and the three of us will remain the best of friends. You will recover your former charms, which you've lost, and the light in your eyes, which are wearing out and growing dull from being on constant watch to find out what I'm up to. And I will become, on my side, the good comrade again that I was before; and we'll forget this nightmare we're going through together… is that agreed? You're not answering? Is it hatred you want? Beware! I have never hated, but I can learn anything, things come to me easily, you know! Listen, I had a tussle with a drunken sailor tonight. He was twice as big and strong as me; I beat him black and blue, and I only received a scratch. Mind out: I could be as vigorous in moral battles, if necessary, as in physical ones; and if it comes to a war of loathing and vengeance, see if I don't flatten the devil in person without leaving a single hair of mine in his paws!'

Laurent, pale, bitter, by turns sarcastic and furious, his hair awry, his shirt ripped and his forehead bleeding, was so frightening to look at and listen to that Thérèse felt all her love turn to disgust. She was so despairing of life at that moment that she never even thought of being afraid. Mute and motionless in the armchair where she had sat down, she let the torrent of blasphemy rage on, and even while telling herself this madman was capable of killing her, she waited, with icy disdain and complete indifference, for the climax of his outburst.

He fell silent when he had no strength left to speak. Then she rose and left the room without having uttered a syllable in reply and without giving him a glance.

VII

Laurent was a better man than his words suggested. All the terrible things he said to Thérèse in the course of that dreadful night were not really what he thought. They were his thoughts of the moment, or rather he spoke without knowing what he thought. After sleeping on it, he remembered nothing, and if anyone had told him, he would have disclaimed it entirely.

But one aspect was true, which was that at the present moment, he was tired of love in this more elevated sense, and longed with all his being for the sorry excitements of the past. It was the punishment for the bad path he had taken on entering life, a very cruel punishment no doubt, one which he understandably railed energetically against as a man who had planned none of it in advance and who had leapt laughing into an abyss from which he imagined he could easily climb when he wanted to. But love is regulated by a code which seems to rest, as social codes do, on that fearsome formulation: *Ignorance of the law is no excuse!* And hard times indeed await the man who is ignorant! The child may well throw himself between the panther's claws, believing he can give her a friendly stroke: she will take no account of such innocence: she will devour him, because it is not for the panther to spare the child. Thus it is with poisons, thus with lightning strikes, thus with vice, all blind agents of the fatal law that man must *know* or *suffer the consequences*.

All that remained in Laurent's memory the morning after this crisis was the consciousness of having had a decisive exchange of views and a vague recollection of her look of resignation.

"Perhaps everything is for the best," he thought, on finding her as calm as when he had left her.

He was nevertheless shocked to see her so pale.

'It's nothing,' she told him mildly. 'This cold is making me very tired, but it's only a cold. It'll take as long as it needs.'

'Well, Thérèse,' he said. 'What have we settled now about our relationship? Have you thought about it? The decision is yours. Are we to leave each other on bad terms, or stay together on a different footing, the friendship we enjoyed *beforehand*?'

'Bad terms? That's not what I feel,' she replied. 'Let's remain friends. Stay here if that's what you want to do. I'm going to finish my work, and I'll be returning to France in a fortnight.'

'But do I have to find another house for the next two weeks? Aren't you afraid people will talk?'

'Do as you think fit. We each have our own set of rooms here, independent of each other; only the sitting room is common: I don't need it; I'll give it to you.'

'No, I want you to keep it. You won't hear me coming and going; I'll never set foot in here if you forbid it.'

'There is nothing I forbid you to do,' Thérèse replied, 'except believe for a single instant that your mistress can forgive you. As for your friend, she is above this particular sphere of disillusionment. She still hopes to be able to be useful to you, and you will always be able to see her when you feel the need for affection.'

She offered him her hand and left to go to work.

Laurent did not understand her. So much self-control was beyond him to explain, a man unfamiliar with passive courage and silent resolutions. He believed she intended to re-establish control over him and draw him back towards love through friendship. He promised himself he would not succumb to any weakening of spirit, and to be more certain, he decided this definitive rupture needed a witness. He went to find Palmer, confided in him the unhappy story of their love and added: 'If you love Thérèse as I believe, my dear friend, make Thérèse love you. I can't be jealous, quite the reverse. Since I have made her thoroughly unhappy and you will be just right for her, I'm sure of it, you would be helping me out by dispelling a sense of remorse I have no wish to live with.'

Laurent was surprised by Palmer's silence.

'Am I offending you, speaking as I do?' he asked. 'That is not my intention. I like you very much, I hold you in considerable esteem, respect even, if you like. If you blame my conduct in all this, say so; it will be better than this air of indifference or disdain.'

'I am not indifferent to Thérèse's sorrows, nor to yours,' Palmer replied. 'I'm just sparing you the advice or reproaches which would have been too late anyway. I thought you were made for each other. Now I am persuaded that the greatest and only happiness you can give each other is to separate. As for my personal feelings towards Thérèse, I do not recognise you have any right to question me; and as for the feelings, which according to you, I may be capable of inspiring in her, that is a supposition which, after what you have just told me, you have no right to voice to my face, still less to Thérèse.'

'Quite so,' said Laurent, seemingly casual, 'and the message is clear. I can see that I shall be in the way here now, and I think the best thing I can do is go away so as not to embarrass anyone.'

And indeed he left after frosty farewells to Thérèse, and took himself off at once to Florence with the intention of throwing himself into society or his work, as the whim took him. He found it ineffably sweet to say to himself: "I shall do whatever comes into my head without causing anyone to suffer or worry. The worst of tortures when one is no more wicked than I am is to be forced nevertheless to acknowledge there's a victim. Well, here I am free at last, and any harm I do will only rebound on me!"

Thérèse was doubtless wrong not to let him see how deeply he had wounded her. She had too much courage and pride. Since she had undertaken to cure a hopelessly sick man, she ought not to have recoiled from the harsher remedies and crueller procedures. She ought to have made that overcharged heart bleed profusely, she should have heaped reproaches on his head, given him back insult for insult, misery for misery. Seeing the harm he had done, Laurent might perhaps have learnt better judgement. Perhaps shame and repentance might have saved his soul from the crime of slaying love in cold blood.

But after three months of futile effort, Thérèse was disheartened. Did she really owe such devotion to a man she had never wished to enslave, who had pressed himself on her despite her own griefs and pessimistic expectations, who had clutched at her coattails like a lost child and called out to her: "Take me with you, keep me at your side, or I shall die, here at the roadside…?"

And this child now cursed her for having yielded to his cries and his tears. He accused her of taking advantage of his weakness to steal him away from the pleasures of liberty. He turned his back on her and walked away, filling his lungs with air and saying: "At last, at last!"

"Since he's incurable," she thought, "what good does it do to make him suffer? Didn't I see there was nothing I could do? Didn't he tell me, and almost prove, alas, that I was stifling his genius by trying to cure his fever? When I believed I had succeeded in making him disgusted by his excesses, didn't I see he was all the more avid for them? When I told him: 'Go back into society,' he was afraid I would be jealous and threw himself instead into a secret and even coarser world of dissipation. He came back drunk, with his clothes torn and blood on his face!"

The day Laurent left, Palmer said to Thérèse: 'Well, my friend! What do you want me to do? Should I run after him?'

'No, absolutely not!' she replied.

'I might be able to bring him back!'

'I would be extremely sorry if you did.'

'You don't love him any more then?'

'No, not at all.'

There was a silence, after which Palmer, thoughtful, continued: 'Thérèse, I have a very serious piece of news to tell you. I hesitate, because I'm afraid of delivering another blow, and your emotions are upset enough as they are…'

'I beg your pardon my friend. I am horribly sad but I am completely calm and prepared for anything.'

'Well then! Thérèse, I have to tell you that you are free: the Count of *** is no more.'

'I know,' Thérèse replied. 'I have known for a week.'

'And you didn't tell Laurent?'

'No.'

'Why?'

'Because it would instantly have provoked some sort of reaction. You know how anything unexpected makes him volatile and overexcited. One of two things would have happened: either he would have imagined telling him my new situation meant I wanted to marry him, and the fright at being tied to me would have made his aversion worse; or else he would have seized on the idea of marriage of his own accord, in one of those fits of devotion that overwhelm him. The kind of fit of devotion that lasts… fifteen minutes at most, then gives way to deep despair or wild rage. The unfortunate man is guilty enough in his behaviour towards me; there was no need to throw his fantasy another piece of bait and give him another excuse for betraying my trust.'

'So you no longer have any regard for him?'

'I am not saying that, my dear Palmer. I feel sorry for him; I'm not accusing him. Perhaps another woman will make him happy and good. I was able to do neither. It is probably my fault as much as his. Whatever, it has proved to me clearly enough that we should not have tried and we should not try any longer to love each other.'

'And now, Thérèse, now that you've been given back your freedom, will you not be thinking about taking advantage of it?'

'What advantage is there to take?'

'You can marry again, and know the joys of having a family.'

'My dear Dick, I have loved twice in my life, and you can see where it has got me. It is not in my destiny to be happy. It is too late to look for what I have missed. I am thirty years old.'

'It is because you're thirty that you can't let the chance of love slip by. You have just experienced the full force of a passion and this is exactly the age when it is difficult for women to step aside. It is because you have suffered, because you have not been loved well, that the hunger for happiness, a yearning which cannot be suppressed, will visit you again and will maybe lead you, from one disappointment to another, into situations even worse than the one you have just left.'

'I hope not.'

'Yes, of course you hope; but you're wrong, Thérèse. You must be wary of everything: your age, your heightened sensitivity and the apparent return of tranquillity induced by this moment of dejection and fatigue. Love will seek you out, don't think it won't. You will hardly have time to get used to your freedom before you'll find yourself pursued and pestered. When you held yourself aloof, it kept the hopes of the people around you in check; but now that Laurent has perhaps made it possible for them to treat you with less respect, everyone who considered themselves your friend is going to want to be your lover. You will inspire powerful passions, and some of these men will be clever enough to convince you. In the end…'

'In the end, Palmer, you presume that I am a lost woman because I am an unhappy one! That is very cruel, and makes me all the more painfully aware how far I have fallen!'

Thérèse put her head in her hands and wept bitterly.

Palmer let her weep; seeing that she needed the relief of shedding these tears, he had deliberately provoked them. When he saw she was feeling better, and calm again, he knelt before her.

'Thérèse,' he said, 'I have caused you much pain, but you must forgive me because my intentions are good. Thérèse, I love you, I have always loved you, not with a blind passion, but with all the faith and devotion I am capable of. More than ever, I see in you a noble existence spoiled and broken through the fault of others. You may indeed be a fallen woman in the world's eyes, but not in mine. On the contrary, your love for Laurent proved to me that you were a woman, and I love you better as you are than armed head to toe against every human weakness, as I was convinced you were before. Listen to me, Thérèse. I am a philosopher in my way, by which I mean I believe in reason and toleration more than society's prejudices and the niceties of romantic sentiment. Even if you were to be led dismally astray I will never stop loving you and you will never fall in my esteem, because you are the sort of woman who could only ever be led astray by her own loving heart. But why should you have to suffer any of these disasters anyway? I am perfectly sure that if today you encountered a heart that was devoted, calm, faithful, free of those maladies of the soul which sometimes make great artists and often bad husbands, a father, a brother, a friend, a husband, why not, you would be saved forever from the dangers and misfortunes of the future. Well! Thérèse, I dare to say I am that man. There is nothing brilliant about me to dazzle you with, but I have a sound heart to love you with. I trust you absolutely. As soon as you are happy, you will be grateful; and grateful, you will be faithful and forever restored. Say yes, Thérèse, agree to marry me, and agree straightaway, with no alarm, with no misgivings, with no false delicacy, with no self-doubt. I give you my life and ask nothing from you except to believe in me. I feel I am strong enough not to be disturbed by the tears you shed because of another man's ingratitude. I shall never reproach you for the past, and I take it upon myself to make the future so sweet and so safe for you that no stormy winds will ever pluck you from my bosom.'

Palmer talked for a long time, and with a heart-felt emotion which Thérèse had not known he possessed. She tried to claim herself unworthy of his trust; but to resist on those grounds, according to Palmer, was to dwell on a sense of moral frailty in herself which she must combat. She felt that Palmer was telling the truth, but she also felt he wished to take on his own shoulders a fearsome task.

'No,' she told him, 'I'm not afraid of myself. I can't love Laurent any more and I don't. But what about the world at large, what about your mother, your own country, what people think of you, the honour of your name? I am a fallen woman; you have said so, and I feel it. Ah, Palmer, don't press me like this! It's too terrifying, what you're willing to face for my sake!'

The next day and during the days that followed, Palmer persisted energetically. He did not let Thérèse breathe. From morning to evening, alone with her, he exercised his will with ever greater strength in the attempt to convince her. Palmer was a man of feeling and first impulses; we shall see later whether Thérèse was right to hesitate. What worried her was the precipitous way Palmer was acting, trying to force her to make a decisive step and engage herself to him by a promise.

'You are afraid of giving me time to think,' she told him. 'So you don't have as much confidence in me as you claim.'

'I trust your word,' he replied, 'as the fact that I'm asking you for it proves. But that doesn't mean I must therefore believe you love me, since you won't answer me on that score, and you're right. You don't yet know what to call the friendship you feel. For my part, I know that what I feel is love, and I'm not one of those people who are reluctant to look inside themselves with a clear eye. With me, love is logical. It is a powerful wanting. It can therefore withstand any blows you may cause it to endure when you give yourself to reflections and reveries likely to prevent you, ill as you are now, from seeing your own true interests.'

Thérèse felt almost wounded when Palmer spoke to her of her own interests. She saw too much self-abnegation in Palmer, and could not bear his thinking her capable of accepting without being willing to respond. All at once, she was ashamed of herself in this battle of generosity, in which Palmer surrendered himself entirely without asking anything more than that she accept his name, his fortune, his protection and his life-long affection. He was giving everything, and in sole recompense, he begged her to think of herself.

Thus hope revived in Thérèse's heart. This man whom she had always believed merely pragmatic, and who still affected a naïve pretence of being so, was revealing himself to her in so unexpected a light that her spirit was startled by it and somehow reanimated in the depths of her misery. It was like a ray of sun in the darkness of a night she had assumed must be eternal. At the moment when, unjust in her despair, she was going to curse love, he was forcing her to believe in love and to look on her disaster as an accident for which heaven wished to send her recompense. Palmer, a man of cold and symmetrical beauty, revealed himself at every moment transfigured before the astonished, uncertain and melting gaze of the woman he loved. His timidity, which gave his initial overtures a slight roughness, gave way to a new expansiveness, and although he may have expressed himself with less poetry than Laurent, he was all the more persuasive as a consequence.

Thérèse perceived the genuine ardour behind this rather rough façade of stubbornness, and could not help smiling tenderly to see the passion he expended on the pretence of coldly pursuing his plan of saving her. She felt touched, and allowed him to extract the promise he insisted on.

Out of the blue, she received a letter in a hand she failed to recognise, so altered was the writing. She had difficulty even deciphering the signature. She managed however, with Palmer's assistance, to read these words:

"I played my hand, I lost; I had a mistress, she deceived me, I killed her. I have taken poison. I am dying. Farewell, Thérèse.
Laurent."

'We must go!' said Palmer.

'O my friend, I do love you!' Thérèse replied, throwing herself into his arms. 'I can tell now how right it is you should be loved.'

They left immediately. They took an overnight boat to Livorno, and by evening of the next day were in Florence. They found Laurent at an inn, not dying, but in a fit of cerebral fever so violent that four men could not hold him down. Setting eyes on Thérèse, he recognised her and clung to her, crying out that they wanted to bury him alive. He gripped her so tightly that she fell to the ground, choked. Palmer had to carry her half-fainting from the room; but she returned after a few minutes, and with a perseverance which bordered on the prodigal, she spent twenty days and twenty nights at the bedside of this man whom she no longer loved. He recognised her only well enough to heap coarse insults on her head, and as soon as she left him for a moment, he called for her, saying he would die without her.

He had happily not killed any woman, or taken any poison, and maybe not even lost his money at cards, or done any of the things he had written to Thérèse under the influence of a sudden attack of delirium and illness. He never remembered writing that letter, which she would have been wary of mentioning; he was frightened enough by the loss of his reason, when he was sufficiently recovered to become aware of it. He still had plenty of other sinister dreams, while the fever lasted. He imagined that Thérèse was pouring him poison, that Palmer was handcuffing him. The cruellest and most frequent of his hallucinations was to see a large gold pin which Thérèse withdrew from her hair and slowly drove into his skull. She did indeed have such a pin to hold her hair in place, in the Italian manner. She removed it, but he continued to see it and to feel it.

As her presence seemed more often than not to make

him agitated, Thérèse normally sat behind his bed, with its curtain between them; but whenever he had to be made to drink anything, he flew into a rage and protested he would take nothing unless it was Thérèse who gave it to him.

'She's the only person who has the right to kill me,' he would say. 'I hurt her so badly! She hates me, she must take her revenge! Don't I constantly see her, at the end of my bed, in the arms of her new lover? Come on then, Thérèse, come here, I'm thirsty: let me have the poison.'

Thérèse let him have rest, calm and sleep. After several days of worsening agitation from which the doctors thought he would not recover, recording it as a medical anomaly, Laurent's restlessness suddenly subsided, leaving him inert, broken, drifting in and out of sleep, but saved.

He was so weak that he had to be fed while only semi-conscious, and to be fed in doses small enough to put no strain on his digestion. This meant constant attention and Thérèse regarded it as her duty not to leave his side for a moment. Palmer tried to make her break off to rest by giving her his word of honour he would replace her at the patient's side. But she refused, aware that human strength was not immune to the stealthy ambush of sleep, and that, since a miracle seemed to be operating in her, alerting her to the exact instant when the spoon should be brought to the patient's lips, without her ever being overcome by fatigue, it was she, not some other person, whom God had charged with saving this fragile life.

She it was indeed, and she saved him.

If medical science, however enlightened, is inadequate in desperate cases, it is very often because the treatment is almost impossible to follow with absolute precision. We do not know enough to say with any accuracy how great a degree of disturbance is caused to a life teetering on the edge by any given minute when the patient is in need or is receiving every care. And the miracle that can make the difference between life and death is often calmness, tenacity and timeliness in those looking after him.

Finally, one morning Laurent woke as if from a state of lethargy, appeared surprised to see Thérèse on his right and Palmer on his left, held up a hand towards each of them, and asked where he was and where he had been.

For a long time they kept him in ignorance about the duration and intensity of his illness, for he was taken aback to find himself so thin and so weak. The first time he looked at himself in a mirror, he gave himself a fright. In the first days of his convalescence, he asked for Thérèse.

He was told she was sleeping. He was very surprised at this.

'Has she turned into an Italian then,' he said, 'sleeping in the daytime?'

Thérèse slept for twenty-four hours without waking. Nature resumed its rights as soon as the anxiety was lifted.

Little by little, Laurent learnt of the lengths to which she had taken her devotion, and he saw in her face the signs of a great weariness following on great personal unhappiness. As he was still too weak to do anything, Thérèse sat at his bedside, sometimes reading to him, sometimes playing cards to amuse him, occasionally taking him out for a carriage ride. Palmer was always with them.

Laurent's strength returned with a speed as extraordinary as his whole character. His brain however, was not always entirely lucid. One day he said to Thérèse with a certain irritation, in a moment when he found himself alone with her:

'This is too bad! When is our fine friend Palmer going to give us the pleasure of taking himself off?'

Thérèse saw there was a gap in his memory, and did not answer. He then applied his mind and added:

'You think I'm ungrateful my friend, to speak in that way of a man who has shown me almost as much devotion as you have. But I'm not so vain or so simple after all, that I don't realise he shut himself up in a very disagreeable invalid's room for a month in order not to be separated from you. Come on, Thérèse, can you swear he did it just for my sake?'

Thérèse found this point-blank question hurtful, as well as the affectionate *tu*, which she thought had been deleted from their relationship for ever. She shook her head, and turned the conversation in another direction. Laurent sadly gave way. But he returned to it the next day; and as Thérèse, seeing him strong enough not to need her any more, was preparing to leave, he said to her with genuine surprise:

'But where are we going, Thérèse? Aren't we all right here?'

She had to give him some explanation, for he was insistent.

'My child,' Thérèse told him, 'you are staying here: the doctors say you need another week or two before you can make any sort of journey without danger of a relapse. For my part, I'm returning to France, since I've finished my work in Genoa, and it is not my intention just now, to see the rest of Italy.'

'That's fine, Thérèse, you are free. But if you want to return to France, I am free to want to as well. Can't you wait a week? I'm sure I don't need more than that to be fit to travel.'

There was so much simple candour in his forgetfulness of the wrongs he had done, and he was so childlike in that moment, that Thérèse had to prevent a tear from falling at the memory of this adoption she had undertaken, once so tender, and was now forced to abdicate.

Without realising she had slipped into calling him *tu* again, she told him as kindly and considerately as she could that they must part for a while.

'But why do we have to part?' cried Laurent. 'Don't we love each other any more, then?'

'That would not be possible,' she continued. 'We shall always have our friendship; but we have caused each other a great deal of mutual harm, and your health could not tolerate any additional strain at present. We should let sufficient time go by for all of this to be forgotten.'

'But I *have* forgotten!' Laurent exclaimed, in good faith and so ingenuously it was touching. 'I don't remember any harm you may have done to me! You have always been an angel to me, and since you're an angel, you can't bear any grudges. You have to forgive everything I've done, and take me away, Thérèse! If you leave me here, I'll die of boredom!'

And as Thérèse displayed a firmness he was not expecting, he became morose and told her she was wrong to feign a severity belied by every aspect of her behaviour.

'I'm well aware what you want,' he told her. 'You want repentance, you require me to expiate my faults. Well, can't you see I detest them? And haven't I expiated them sufficiently by going mad for a week and more? You want tears and oaths, like the old days? What would be the good? You wouldn't

144

believe them any more. It's my future behaviour I need to be judged by, and you can see I'm not afraid of the future, since I'm making you my ally. Come now, Thérèse, you're a child too, and you know very well I've often called you one when I saw you pretending to sulk. Do you think you can persuade me you don't love me any more when you've just spent a whole month cloistered here, twenty days and nights of it spent without sleeping, almost without ever leaving my bedroom? Can't I see, from the blue circles round your lovely eyes, that you would have died in harness if it had gone on any longer? You don't do things like that for someone you no longer love!'

Thérèse did not dare utter the fatal word. She was hoping that Palmer would come in and interrupt this conversation and that she would be able to avoid a scene which could be dangerous for the convalescent. It was not possible, he stood in the doorway to bar her exit, then fell at her feet and writhed in despair.

'My God!' she said. 'Can you possibly believe I would be cruel and capricious enough to deny you a word I was able to say? But I am not able to say it, the word would no longer represent the truth. Love is over between us.'

Laurent got back to his feet in a fury. It was beyond his understanding that he could have killed this thing, love, which he had claimed not to believe in.

'Is it Palmer then?' he shouted, smashing a teapot he had poured himself a tisane from, hardly aware of what he was doing. 'So it's him? Tell me, I insist, I want the truth! It'll kill me, I know it will, but I refuse to be deceived!'

'Deceived!' Thérèse said, taking his hands to prevent him from tearing at them with his nails. 'Deceived! What sort of word to use is that? Do I belong to you? Haven't we been strangers to one another since that first time when you walked out in Genoa, and stayed out all night, after telling me I was your torturer and executioner? Hasn't that been the way of it for four months and more? And don't you think that amount of time, spent by you in unforgiveable ways, hasn't been sufficient to make me mistress of my own life again?'

And seeing that Laurent, instead of becoming angrier at her frankness, was growing calmer and was listening to her with the curiosity of one keen to hear more, she continued: 'If you fail to understand the sentiment which brought me to your fevered bedside and which has kept me with you until now to ensure you are fully recovered, giving you the sort of care only a mother would give, it's because you have never understood anything about my heart. This heart, Laurent,' she said, tapping her chest, 'is neither as proud nor as ardent as yours, perhaps; but as you have said yourself many times in the past, it always remains in the same place. What it has loved, it cannot cease to love; but don't deceive yourself: it is not love as you understand it, or the love you made me believe in, and which you are mad enough to expect from it still. Neither my senses nor my head belong to you any more. I have taken back possession of my person and my will. My confidence in you and my enthusiasm for you are not going to return. I can give them to whoever deserves them, to Palmer if I choose, and there is no objection you would have any right to make, since you were the person who went to him one morning and said: "Console Thérèse for me, you would be doing me a service!"'

'It's true… it's true!' Laurent said, wringing his hands. 'I did say that! I'd forgotten, and now I remember!'

'Then don't forget again,' said Thérèse, once more speaking to him gently, seeing him now quieter and calmer. 'And learn this truth: love is too delicate a flower to spring back up when it has been trampled underfoot. Don't look to me for love any more, seek it elsewhere, providing the sad experience you have had of it can open your eyes and alter your character. You will find it the day you are worthy of it. As for me, I would no longer be able to bear your caresses, they would be demeaning. But my sisterly and motherly affection for you will still be there, in spite of you and in spite of everything. This is a different sort of thing, it is pity, I don't hide that from you, and I tell you so precisely to stop you from imagining you can recapture a love which would be humiliating to you as well as to me. If you want this friendship, which is offensive to you at the moment, to become a treasure to you again, it is there if you wish to earn it. Until now, you have not had the opportunity. But here it is, presenting itself. Take it: leave me. And do so without weakness and without bitterness. Show me the calm and compassionate face of a strong-hearted man, instead of this face of a child, who weeps without knowing why.'

'Let me weep, Thérèse,' said Laurent, on his knees. 'Let me wash my fault away with my tears. Let me worship this holy pity within you still, which has survived a shattered love. It does not humiliate me as you believe; I sense that I shall become worthy of it. Do not require me to be calm, you know I can never be that; but believe that I can become good. Ah, Thérèse, I met you too late! Why did you not speak to me earlier the way you have just spoken now? Why do you overwhelm me with your kindness and devotion, poor sister of charity who can no longer restore my happiness? But you are right, Thérèse, I deserved what is happening to me, and you have finally made me understand it. The lesson will not be lost on me, I can answer for that, and if I can ever love any other woman, I will know how a man should love. I shall owe you everything therefore, my sister, the past and the future!'

Laurent was still speaking effusively when Palmer returned. He embraced him warmly, calling him his brother and his saviour, and, gesturing towards Thérèse, he cried:

'Ah, my friend! Do you remember what you said to me at Hôtel Meurice, the last time we saw each other in Paris? "If you don't believe you can make her happy, blow your brains out tonight rather than return to her house!" I should have done so, and I didn't! And now, look at her, she is more changed than I am, poor Thérèse! She was broken in pieces, and yet she came to pluck me from death's hands, when she should have cursed me and abandoned me!'

Laurent's repentance was genuine; Palmer was greatly moved by it. As he yielded to his feelings of remorse, so the artist expressed it with ever more persuasive eloquence, and when Palmer found himself alone with Thérèse once more, he said to her:

'My friend, rest assured, I was not troubled by your devotion to him. I understood! You wanted to cure both soul and body. Victory is yours. He is saved, your poor child! And now, what would you like to do?'

'Leave him for good,' Thérèse replied. 'Or at least, not see him again for several years. If he returns to France, I shall stay in Italy; if he stays in Italy, I shall return to France. I said this much was settled in my mind, didn't I? And because the decision was already taken, I postponed the final farewell for a little longer. I knew very well there would be an inevitable crisis, and I didn't want to leave him on that note, unless it turned out well.'

'Have you thought about this fully, Thérèse?' Palmer said, pensive. 'Are you quite sure you're not weakening at the last moment?'

'Quite sure.'

'That man seems to me to be irresistible in his grief. He would wring pity from a stone, yet all the same, Thérèse, if you give in to him, you're lost, and he's lost too. If you still love him, remember, you can only save him by leaving him!'

'I know,' Thérèse replied. 'But what are you saying, my friend? Are you ill as well? Have you forgotten I committed myself by giving you my word?'

Palmer kissed her hand and smiled. Peace returned to his soul.

Laurent came to tell them, the following day, that he wished to go to Switzerland to complete his recovery. Italy's climate did not suit him: it was true. The doctors advised him not even to linger until the great summer heats arrived.

In any event, it was decided that they would part here in Florence. Thérèse had no plan for herself other than to go wherever Laurent would not be going; but seeing him so exhausted by the previous day's crisis, she had to promise to spend one more week in Florence, in order to prevent him from starting out before he had recovered the necessary strength.

That week was perhaps the best in Laurent's life. Generous, warm, confiding, sincere, he had found a state of soul which he had never experienced, even during the first seven days of his union with Thérèse. He had been conquered, penetrated, altogether invaded, one might say, by feelings of warm-hearted affection. He was the constant companion of his two friends, going for a carriage ride in the *parco delle Cascine* at a time of day when the crowds are absent, eating with them, taking childlike pleasure in travelling out to dine in the countryside, giving his arm to Thérèse and to Palmer in turn, testing his strength in gymnastic exercises with the latter, accompanying them both to the theatre, and getting *Dick the great traveller*, to map out for him the itinerary of his journey to Switzerland. The great question was to determine whether he should go by Milan or Genoa. He eventually decided on this second route, stopping at Pisa and Lucca, and then following the coast either overland or by sea, depending on whether he felt strengthened or weakened by the first stages of the journey.

The day of departure came. Laurent had made all his preparations with a kind of melancholy cheerfulness. Sparkling with witticisms about his travelling costume, his luggage, on the eccentric figure he would cut in a certain waterproof coat which Palmer had forced him to accept and which was at that time a novelty in the clothes trade, on the mangled French of an Italian servant whom Palmer had selected for him and who was the best of fellows. Gratefully and submissively accepting all the advice and little treats Thérèse gave him, his eyes brimmed with tears through his happy laughter.

The night before that last day, he had a slight return of fever. He made light of it. The carriage which was to transport him, in short stages, was at the hotel door. The morning was cool. Thérèse became concerned.

'Go with him as far as La Spezia,' Palmer told her. 'That's

where he'll take the boat, if he finds the carriage too difficult. That's where I'll meet you the day after he leaves. I've just received news of a vital piece of business which is going to keep me here for twenty-four hours.'

Thérèse, surprised by this decision, and his suggestion, refused to leave with Laurent.

'I beg you,' said Palmer, with a degree of sharpness. 'It's impossible for me to go with you!'

'That may be so, my friend, but it isn't necessary for me to go with him.'

'It is,' he said, 'you must.'

Thérèse took Palmer to mean that he considered this test necessary. The idea astonished and alarmed her.

'Can you,' she asked him, 'give me your word of honour that you do really have an important piece of business here?'

'Yes,' he replied. 'You have my word.'

'Well, I'm staying!'

'No, it is essential you go.'

'I don't understand.'

'I will explain later my friend. I believe in you as I believe in God, you can see that for yourself; trust me. Go.'

Thérèse hastily packed a small bag which she tossed into the carriage, and she climbed in beside Laurent, calling to Palmer:

'I have your word of honour you'll be on your way to join me in twenty-four hours.'

VIII

Palmer, who was genuinely obliged to remain in Florence and to send Thérèse away, felt a heavy blow at seeing her depart. The danger he feared however, did not exist. The bond could not be remade. Laurent did not even think of trying to remind Thérèse of the pleasures they had once shared. But, secure in the knowledge that he had not lost her affection, he resolved to try to win back her esteem. He resolved, did we say? No, he made no plan at all, he simply felt the need to raise himself in the eyes of this woman who had attained for him, a state of nobility. If he had begged her at that point, she would have resisted him without difficulty, she would perhaps have despised him. He took care not to, or rather the thought did not occur to him. He had absorbed her lessons too well to commit a fault of that sort. He assumed with faith and enthusiasm the role of the broken-hearted, the submissive and chastised child; so much so that by the end of the journey, Thérèse was wondering if the victim of this fated love was not in fact him.

During those three days together, Thérèse found a new happiness in being with Laurent. She could see a new era of refined feeling opening before them, a route hitherto unexplored, since she had up to now walked this path alone. She savoured the sweetness of loving, without remorse or anxiety or battles, a pale and enfeebled being who now existed, so to speak, as no more than a soul, and whom she could imagine meeting, after this life, in the paradise of pure essences, as we dream of meeting each other after death.

And then she had been deeply hurt and humiliated by him, at odds and irritated with herself. That love, accepted with so much courage and magnanimity, had left her stained, as it would have if it had been the cheapest of dalliances. There had come a moment where she had despised herself for allowing herself to be so grossly deceived. So she felt something was now being reborn in her, and she found it possible to reconcile herself with the past on seeing a flower growing on the tomb of a buried passion, a flower of eager friendship more beautiful than passion, even in its best days.

It was on the tenth of May that they arrived in La Spezia, a picturesque little town, half Genoese, half Florentine, nestled in a deep bay as uniformly blue as the bluest of skies. It was not yet the season for sea-bathing. The whole area was an enchanted solitude, the weather cool and delightful. At the sight of this beautiful and peaceful water, Laurent, a little fatigued by his days in the carriage, decided on the sea route. They enquired about the availability of transport; a small steamboat left for Genoa twice a week. Thérèse was pleased that the next departure was not that same evening. It meant twenty-four hours rest for her convalescent. She made him reserve a cabin on this boat for the following evening.

Laurent, weak though he still felt, had never been so well. He slept like a log and had the appetite of a child. These first few days of his restoration to health were a period of gentle languor, which stirred in his soul a delicious ferment. The memory of his past life faded like a bad dream. He felt and believed himself to be radically and permanently transformed. In this new regeneration, he no longer had the faculty of suffering. He was leaving Thérèse with a sort of triumphant joy in the middle of his tears. This submission to fate's decrees was in his eyes a voluntary expiation, of which she should take due note. He had not invoked it himself, but he accepted it in the moment when he understood the value of the thing he had scorned. The need for self-sacrifice drove him to tell her that it was her duty to love Palmer, who was the best of friends and the greatest of philosophers. Then he suddenly cried: 'Don't say anything, dear Therèse! Don't talk about him! I don't feel strong enough yet to hear you say you love him. No, be quiet! It would kill me…! But I want you to know that I love him too! What better thing could I tell you?'

Not once in this time did Thérèse pronounce the name of Palmer; and in those moments when Laurent, less heroically, questioned her indirectly, she answered: 'Be quiet. I have a secret which I will tell you later, and which is not what you think. You couldn't guess it, so don't try.'

They spent the last day exploring the gulf of La Spezia in a small boat. They had themselves set ashore from time to time to pick some of the fine aromatic plants which grow in the sand and even in the shallows where the clear water idles. Shade is rare on the handsome shores, where flowering shrubs cover the flanks of the steeply rising headland. The heat becoming noticeable, as soon as they spotted a group of pines, they had themselves rowed over. They had brought their dinner, which they ate just like that, sitting on the grass amid the clumps of lavender and rosemary. The day passed like a dream, which is to say that it passed in a flash and yet contained the sweetest emotions of two living beings.

However, the sun was sinking in the sky, and Laurent was turning sad. He could see in the distance the smoke from the *Ferruccio*, the La Spezia steamer, whose boilers were being fired up in advance of her departure, and the black cloud settled on his soul. Thérèse saw it would be necessary to distract him until the very last moment, and she asked the boatman what else there was to see in the bay.

'There's Palmaria island,' he replied, 'and the *portoro* marble quarry. If you want to see it, you can go on board there as well. The steamer goes that way to take the open sea, because it stops opposite, at Porto-Venere, to pick up passengers and cargo. You'll have plenty of time to embark. I'll see to all that.'

The two friends had themselves taken to Palmaria island.

It is a block of marble towering over the sea and levelling out into a gentle fertile slope on the side facing the bay; on this side are a few dwellings half way up the slope and two villas on the shore. This island is planted like a natural defence at the entrance to the gulf, with a very narrow passage between the island and the little port once consecrated to Venus; hence the name Porto-Venere.

Nothing in the frightful little town justifies this poetic name, but its position on the bare, wave-battered rocks – for the narrow passage between town and island is a funnel for the first real waves coming in from the open sea – is the most picturesque imaginable. It has all the characteristics one would most desire if one were to describe a pirates' nest. The houses, black and miserable, scoured by the salt air, rise in tiers to immeasurable heights on the craggy rock. Not a pane remains unbroken in those tiny windows, which look like anxious eyes scanning the horizon for victims. Not a wall stands with its cement cladding intact, great flaps of it hanging off like storm-ripped sails. Not a single vertical line is to be seen in these buildings leaning one against the other and ready to crumble all together. All of this spreads upwards to the furthest extremity of the promontory, where it abruptly stops, marked only by the truncated remains of an old fort and the spire of a bell-tower, planted like a crow's nest looking out over the immensity. Behind this tableau, which stands out detached against the encompassing sea, rear enormous crags of a livid grey-blue, whose base, made iridescent by the sea's reflections, seems to plunge down into something as indeterminate and impalpable as the colour of the void.

It was from the marble quarry on the island of Palmaria, across the narrow strait, that Laurent and Thérèse contemplated this picturesque effect. The setting sun threw a reddish light on the foreground, giving a uniform appearance to and merging into a single mass the rocks, the old walls and the ruins, to the extent that everything, even the church, seemed to be cut from the same block, whilst the tall rocks of the background were bathed in a glaucous green light.

Laurent was struck by this spectacle, and forgetting everything, embraced it with a painter's eye, in which Thérèse could see gleaming, as in a mirror, all the colours of the fiery sky.

"Thank the Lord!" she thought. "The artist in him is reawakening at last!"

Indeed, since his illness Laurent had not had a single

thought for his art.

The quarry offering no more than the momentary interest of seeing blocks of a fine black marble veined with yellow and gold, Laurent wanted to climb the steepest slope of the island to get the view of the open sea from the top, and he made his way, through a rather unmanageable pine wood, to a lichen-covered ledge, where he suddenly found himself seemingly suspended in space. The rock stood vertically over the sea, which had bitten into its base and was hurling itself against it with a thunderous noise. Laurent, who had not realised the cliff was so abrupt on this side, had such a powerful attack of vertigo that without Thérèse, who had followed him and who managed to get him to lie full length and slide back down, he would have let himself topple into the gulf.

It was then that she saw him wild-eyed and seized with terror, as she had seen him in the forest of ***.

'What is it?' she said. 'Tell me, is this another dream?'

'No! No!' he shouted, getting to his feet and clinging to her as if he took her for some immovable body. 'This isn't another dream, it's reality! It's the sea, the terrible sea which is about to bear me away very shortly! It's the image of the life I am returning to! It's the abyss that's going to open between us! It's the monotonous, relentless, hateful sound of the sea that I'll be listening to at night in Genoa harbour, crashing its blasphemies into my ears! It's that brutish swell I'll be forced to ride out on the boat while it carries me towards an abyss even deeper and less forgiving than the waters' deep! Thérèse, Thérèse, do you know what you're doing, tossing me into the jaws of the monster down there, already opening its hideous maw to devour your poor child?'

'Laurent!' she said, shaking his arm, 'Laurent, do you hear me?'

He seemed to wake into another world on recognising the sound of Thérèse's voice; for when he called out to her, he had believed himself alone. And he turned round in surprise when he saw the tree he was clinging to was nothing other than the trembling and weary arm of his friend.

'I'm sorry! I'm sorry!' he said. 'It's just one last tremor, it's nothing. Let's go!'

And he rushed back down the hillside they had climbed together.

The *Ferruccio* was approaching in full steam from La Spezia at the head of the bay.

'My God, here it comes!' he said. 'Look how fast it's going! If only it could sink before it gets here!'

'Laurent!' said Thérèse sharply.

'Yes, yes, don't worry, my friend, I'm calm now. Don't you know that a look from you is all it takes these days to make me glad to obey? The boat, fine! All over, fine! I am calm, I am contented! Give me your hand, Thérèse. You see, I haven't demanded a single kiss in all the three days we've been alone with each other! The only thing I ask for is this loyal hand. Remember the day you told me: "Never forget that before becoming your mistress, I was your friend!" Well, this is what you were wishing for, I am nothing to you any more, but I am yours for life...!'

He leapt into the boat, thinking that Thérèse would stay on the island's landing stage and the boat would return to collect her when he had boarded the *Ferruccio*; but she jumped in beside him. She wanted to make sure, she told herself, that the servant who was to accompany Laurent, and who had embarked with the luggage at La Spezia, had not forgotten anything his master might need for the voyage.

She took advantage therefore of the little steamer's pausing at Porto-Venere to go on board with Laurent. Vincento, the servant in question, was waiting for them. It will be remembered that he was a trustworthy man chosen by M. Palmer. Thérèse drew him to one side.

'You have your master's money?' she asked him. 'I know he put you in charge of seeing to all the expenses of the voyage. How much did he give you?'

'Two hundred Florentine lire, signora; but I think he has his wallet on him.'

Thérèse had checked the pockets of Laurent's clothes while he was sleeping. She had found the wallet, she knew it was virtually empty. Laurent had spent large sums in Florence; his illness had involved considerable outgoings. He had placed what remained of his little fortune in Palmer's hands, asking him to settle his bills, and he had not bothered to look at them. In matters of money, Laurent was a complete child, and still had no idea of the price of anything abroad, not even what the currencies of the various provinces were worth. It seemed to him the sum he had given Vincento ought to last a long time, but there wasn't enough to reach the frontier for a man who had not the slightest notion of foresight.

Thérèse handed to Vincento all she still possessed at the time, here in Italy. She did not even keep what she needed for herself for a few days, for seeing Laurent approach, she did not have time to take a few gold coins from the roll she quickly slipped the servant, saying: 'Here's what he had in his pockets;

he is very absentminded, and prefers you to look after it.'

And she turned round to shake the artist's hand one last time. There was no remorse behind her deception on this occasion. When she had paid any of his debts before, it had been much to his chagrin and irritation. Now she was a mother to him and nothing more; she was within her rights to act as she did.

Laurent had not seen anything.

'A moment more, Thérèse' he said in a voice choked by tears. 'They'll ring a bell to tell anyone who's not sailing to leave the ship.'

She put her arm in his and went to see his cabin, which was comfortable enough for sleeping in but smelt horribly of fish. Thérèse looked for her perfume bottle, meaning to leave it with him; but she had lost it on the rock of Palmaria.

'Don't worry about it,' he told her, touched by all her kindnesses. 'Give me one of those wild lavenders we picked together back there, on the sands.'

Thérèse had placed these flowers in the bodice of her dress; it would be like leaving him a token of her love. She found something indelicate in the idea, or equivocal at least, and her woman's instinct refused. But as she leant on the steamer's rail she saw, in one of the little boats waiting alongside, a child offering the passengers big bunches of violets. She felt in her pocket, found with joy a last coin and threw it to the young salesman, while he tossed his finest bouquet up to her at the rail. She caught it neatly, and spread the flowers in Laurent's cabin. He understood his friend's exquisite modesty, but he never knew these violets were paid for with the last and only money Thérèse possessed.

160

A young man whose travelling costume and aristocratic bearing made a sharp contrast with those of the passengers, almost all traders in olive oil or locals operating small businesses along the coast, passed by close to Laurent, and glancing at him, said: 'Well! It's you!'

They shook hands with the cold formality of gesture and expression which is the mark of people educated in the manners of society. He was however one of his old hedonistic associates, one of the people Laurent had called, when speaking of them to Thérèse in the days of his boredom, his best, his only friends. He would add, at moments like those: "People of my class!" for he never felt any grievance towards Thérèse without reminding himself that he was a gentleman.

But Laurent was thoroughly altered, and instead of rejoicing at this encounter, he mentally wished to the devil this intruder on his final farewells with Thérèse. M. de Vérac, that was the old friend's name, knew Thérèse from having been introduced to her by Laurent in Paris, and respectfully greeting her, he told her he considered it a stroke of excellent fortune to have run into two travelling companions such as her and Laurent on this poor little *Ferruccio*.

'But I shall not be accompanying you,' she replied. 'I am staying here.'

'What, here? Where? In Porto-Venere?'

'In Italy.'

'Ah! So Fauvel is off to Genoa to run some errands for you, and then coming back tomorrow?'

'No!' Laurent said, impatient at this show of curiosity, which he found intrusive. 'I am going to Switzerland, and Mlle Jacques is not. You are surprised? Well, I have to inform you that Mlle Jacques is leaving me, and I am much grieved by the fact. Do you understand?'

'No!' Vérac said, smiling. 'But I am not obliged to…'

'Indeed you are; you must understand how matters stand,' Laurent went on, with a somewhat haughty insistence in his tone. 'I have deserved what is happening to me, and I bow to it, because Mlle Jacques, without regard to my misdeeds, has nobly acted as a sister and mother to me during a recent illness that threatened my life; I therefore owe her no less gratitude than I do respect and friendship.'

Vérac was very surprised at what he heard. It was a story beyond his experience. Out of discretion, he moved away, after saying to Thérèse that no fine act on her part could come as any surprise. But he observed the farewells of the two friends out of the corner of his eye. Thérèse, on the gangway, jostled and squeezed by the locals, who were all hugging each other in a noisy tumult as the departure bell sounded, placed a maternal kiss on Laurent's forehead. Both of them were crying; then she stepped down into the boat and had herself set ashore on the dark and misshapen slabs of rock that made a stairway up to the entrance to Porto-Venere village.

Laurent was astonished to see her go in that direction instead of returning to La Spezia.

"Oh!" he thought, tears flowing again. "Palmer must be there, waiting for her!"

But ten minutes later, as the *Ferruccio*, having gained the open sea with some effort, turned to round the promontory, Laurent, casting a final glance towards that mournful rock, saw on the platform of the old ruined fort, a silhouette whose head and wind-tossed hair were gilded by the sun: it was the blonde hair and adored figure of Thérèse. She was alone. Laurent held up his two arms in a transport of emotion.

Then he clasped his hands together in a sign of repentance, and his lips murmured two words which the wind whipped away: 'Forgive me! Forgive me!'

M. de Vérac was watching Laurent with amazement, and Laurent, the most sensitive man on earth when it came to inviting ridicule, cared not the slightest that his former companion in pleasure was staring. At that moment, he even took a sort of pride in thus exposing himself.

When the coast had disappeared into the evening mist, Laurent found himself sitting on a bench beside Vérac.

'Well, goodness!' the man said. 'So tell me what's behind these strange events! You've said too much to stop now: all your friends in Paris, in fact all of Paris I could say, since you're a famous man, will want to know how your relationship with Mlle Jacques came to an end. And she's too much in the public eye as well not to excite curiosity. What am I to tell them?'

'Tell them you saw a very sad and very foolish man. What I told you can be said in very few words. Do I need to say them again?'

'So was it you who broke it off first? I'd rather it was, for your sake!'

'Yes, I know what you mean. To be betrayed makes a man ridiculous, to take the initiative is masterful. That's how I thought once upon a time, with you; that was our code. But I've completely changed my ideas on the whole subject since I've loved someone. I have done the betraying, I have been left, I'm in the pit of despair: our former theories, in consequence, did not make sense. If you can find an argument anywhere in the science of life as we used to practise it that will relieve me of my regret and my suffering, then I'll say you're right.'

'I won't look for arguments, dear fellow, suffering isn't susceptible to rationality. I feel sorry for you, since you're all too clearly unhappy. I only wonder if any woman is worth so many tears, and whether Mlle Jacques wouldn't have done better to forgive whatever infidelity it was rather than send you away as miserable as you are now. For a mother, I find her hard and vindictive!'

'That's because you don't know how culpable and stupid I was. Infidelity! If that was all, she would have forgiven me, I'm sure; but insults, criticisms… and worse than that, Vérac! I said the thing no woman who respects herself can forget: *You bore me!*'

'Yes, that's a harsh thing to say, especially when it's true. But what if it wasn't? What if it was just a fit of temper?'

'No! It was a moral decline. I didn't love her any more! Or, in fact, it was worse; I was never able to love her after she committed herself to me. Remember that, Vérac. Laugh if you like, but remember that, for how you conduct your own life in the future. There is a strong possibility that you will wake up one fine morning worn down by false pleasures and violently in love with an honest woman. It can happen to you as easily as it happened to me, because I don't believe you're any more of a rake than I am. Well! When you have overcome this woman's resistance, you will probably find the same thing happening to you as I found. Having got into the bad habit of making love with women you despise, you are condemned to continue needing the kind of unrestrained liberty which is anathema to the higher forms of love. Then you will feel like a wild animal tamed by a child and always on the verge of clawing her to death to break your chains. And one day when you have killed the feeble warder, you will rush off all alone, roaring with joy and shaking your mane; but then, then the beasts of the desert will seem frightening to you, and thanks to having known the cage, you will no longer love liberty quite as much. However little and however reluctantly your heart acquiesced in forming the bond, it will miss it as soon as it has broken it, and it will find itself seized with horror at the reality of solitude, and unable to make the choice between love and the libertine's life. It is a malaise you don't yet know. May God spare you from ever knowing it! And meanwhile, make fun of it all, as I used to do! It won't prevent your day from coming, if debauchery hasn't yet turned you into a corpse!'

M. de Vérac let this torrent of high ideals flow over him with a smile, like a well-sung *cavatina* at the *Théâtre-Italien*. Laurent was sincere, of that there was no doubt; but perhaps his listener was right not to attach too much importance to his despair.

IX

By the time Thérèse had lost sight of the *Ferruccio*, it was dark. She had sent back the boat she had hired and paid for in advance that morning in La Spezia. When the boatman had taken her from the steamer back to Porto-Venere, she had observed he was drunk; she was fearful of returning alone with this man, and expecting to be able to find another boat somewhere along the shore, she had dismissed him.

But when she thought about going back, she suddenly realised she was absolutely without any means whatever. Nothing would have been simpler, admittedly, than returning to the Cross of Malta hotel in La Spezia, where she had arrived the previous day with Laurent, having them pay off the boatman, and then waiting for Palmer to join her. But the idea of not possessing a farthing of her own and being forced to depend on Palmer for tomorrow's breakfast caused her a repugnance which, childish though it might be, she found insurmountable, given the terms she was on with him. To that repugnance was added a pronounced anxiety about the reasons for his recent behaviour towards her. She had noticed the heart-wrenching sadness of his gaze when she had left Florence. She could not help supposing that some obstacle to their marriage had suddenly cropped up, and she could see so many genuine drawbacks for Palmer in this marriage that she thought it her duty not to fight against that obstacle, whatever quarter it came from. Thérèse obeyed an entirely instinctive solution, which was to remain, until she heard otherwise, in Porto-Venere. In the bundle of belongings she had hastily put together, she had brought enough clothes and personal effects to be able to last four or five days wherever she was. As far as valuables went, she had a gold watch and chain, which she could use as security until she had received the fee for her work, which was due to arrive at Genoa in the form of a bank mandate. She had instructed Vincentino to collect her letters from the poste restante in Genoa and send them on to her in La Spezia.

That left her with the question of where to spend the night, and the prospect here in Porto-Venere was not encouraging. Those tall houses which plunge down to the sea's edge on the side facing the channel, are in the town's interior, so closely aligned with the tops of the rocks that in several places one has to stoop to walk under the overhang of their roofs, which project from both sides into the middle of the street. This street, narrow and steep, paved with crude slabs of rock, was half blocked by children, hens and great brass containers placed beneath the irregular angles of the roofs, for the purpose of catching rain water during the night. These containers act as the district's weather forecast: fresh water is so rare here that as soon as a cloud is seen approaching on the wind, the housewives rush to put all possible receptacles outside their door so as to waste no drop of the benison sent from the heavens.

All these doors stood wide open, and as Thérèse walked past them, she suddenly noticed one which seemed a good deal cleaner than the others, and from which emerged a slightly less astringent smell of oil. On the threshold was a poor woman whose gentle and honest face inspired a degree of confidence, and who seemed to anticipate her by addressing a few words to her in Italian or something approximate. Thérèse was thus able to communicate with this good woman, who asked her in an obliging manner if she was looking for someone. She went in, cast a glance round the premises, and asked if she might have the use of a bedroom for the night.

'Yes, certainly, you can have a better room than this, where you'll be more comfortable than at the inn, where you'd hear the sailors singing all night! But I'm not an innkeeper, and if you don't want quarrels to start up, you'll have to say loudly in the street tomorrow that you knew me before you came here.'

'Agreed,' Thérèse said. 'Show me this room.'

She was led up a few steps, and found herself in a large and meanly furnished room which afforded the eye a vast panorama of the sea and the bay; she felt at home in this room at first sight, without really knowing why, unless it was that it felt like a place of retreat from the ties she did not want to be forced to accept. It was from there that she wrote the next day to her mother:

"My dearest beloved, here I am, after twelve hours of rest and peace, and in full possession of my free will for... I don't know how many days, or years! Everything has been thrown into question again, my mind is full of uncertainty, and you shall be the judge of my situation.

"That fatal love which you were so worried about has not been rekindled and will not be. On that point, you can rest easy.

I followed my patient, and I saw him on to his ship yesterday evening. If I have not saved his poor soul, and I hardly dare flatter myself that I have, then at least I have improved it a little, and forced into it for a moment or two some appreciation of the sweeter joys of friendship. If I had cared to take him at his word, he was cured for ever of his tempestuousness; but I could see plainly enough, from his contradictions and his appeals to me, that he had not rid himself of what is elemental to his nature, something I can only define by calling it the love of the non-existent.

"Alas, yes! This child's ideal mistress is something akin to the Venus de Milo animated by the breath of my patron Saint Theresa; or rather he thinks the same woman should be Sappho today and tomorrow Joan of Arc. Woe on me then, for having believed that after investing me in his imagination with all the attributes of Divinity, the scales would not fall from his eyes the very next day! I must be very vain, without realising it, to have been capable of accepting the task of inspiring a whole cult! But no, I wasn't, I swear! I was not thinking of myself; the day I allowed myself to be set on that altar, I said to him: 'Since you absolutely insist on adoring me instead of loving me, which I would much prefer, adore me – alas – only don't smash me to pieces tomorrow!'

"He smashed me! But how can I complain? I knew it would happen, and I had submitted myself to it in advance.

"However, I was weak, indignant and sorry for myself when the dreadful moment came. But courage has the upper hand again now, and God has allowed me to recover faster than I was hoping.

"Now, I need to talk to you about Palmer. You want me

to marry him, he wants it; I do too, or I did! Do I still? What should I say to you, my beloved? I still have scruples, and some fears. Some of this is perhaps his fault. He was not able, or did not wish, to spend with me the last moments I spent with Laurent: he left me on my own with him for three days, three days which I knew would be, and were, without danger on my side. But did Palmer know that, could he guarantee it? Or, which would be worse, did he tell himself he needed to know how matters stood? I can see that on his side it was an unusual and rather romantic display of selflessness, or an unusually high degree of discretion, both of which can only be put down to the finer feelings of a man like him, but it nevertheless made me think.

"I wrote to you about what happened between us; it seemed that he had taken it as his sacred duty to set me on my feet again through marriage, after the violent shocks I had suffered. My own feelings were those of enthusiasm, arising out of gratitude to him, and tenderness, arising out of my admiration for him. I said yes, I promised to be his wife, and I still feel today that I love him as much as I shall be able to love anyone now.

"Yet today I hesitate, because it seems to me he regrets his offer. Am I imagining it? I've no idea; but why wasn't he able to follow me here? When I heard about my poor Laurent's terrible illness, he didn't wait for me to say: 'I'm going to Florence'; he said: 'We're going!' The twenty nights I spent at Laurent's bedside he spent in the room next door, and he never said to me: 'You're killing yourself!' but merely: 'Get a little rest, to help you keep going.' I never saw the faintest shadow of jealousy in him. It seemed that in his eyes I could never do too much to save the ungrateful son whom we had both so to speak adopted. He sensed well enough, this noble heart, that his trust and his generosity were increasing my love for him, and I was infinitely grateful to him for realising it. He was giving me the opportunity to lift myself in my own eyes, and he was making me proud to belong to him.

"Well then, why this whim or this barrier at the last moment? An unforeseen obstacle? Given how strong-willed I know him to be, I scarcely think it can have been an obstacle; it seems more likely that he wanted to test me. I find that humiliating, I admit. Alas, I have become terribly vulnerable since becoming a fallen woman! Isn't that natural? For a man who understands everything, how did he fail to understand that?

"Or else perhaps he has had second thoughts and has finally told himself all the things I was telling him as matters of principle about why I was unsuitable: what would be surprising if he did? I'd always known Palmer for a prudent and rational man. When I discovered hidden depths of feeling in him, I was very surprised. Might he be one of those characters who are inspired by the sight of suffering and who fall passionately in love with victims? It's a natural instinct in strong people, the sublime pity of happy and pure hearts! There have been moments when I have told myself the same thing to account for my own feelings, when I loved Laurent, since it was first and foremost his suffering that drew me to him!

"Everything I'm writing now, my darling, I would not dare tell Richard Palmer however if he were here! I would be afraid my doubts would cause him terrible pain, and I am extremely embarrassed, because these doubts, they are real

171

and I have them in spite of myself, and I am scared, if not for today, then at least for the future. Won't he cover himself in ridicule by marrying a woman he has loved, he says, for ten years, to whom he has never addressed a word and whom he suddenly chooses to approach the day he finds her bleeding and broken under the feet of another man?

"I am here in a dilapidated and magnificent little seaport, where rather passively, I am awaiting word of my fate. Perhaps Palmer is at La Spezia, ten miles from here. That's where we agreed to meet. And I, like a woman sulking, or rather a woman trembling, I can't make up my mind to go and say: 'Here I am!' No, no! If he doubts me, there is no future for us together! The *other man* I forgave five or six outrages a day. This one I could not allow the merest shadow of a suspicion. Is that unjust? No! From now on I want a love of the highest and noblest nature, or no love at all! Did I go out looking for his? He imposed it on me, saying: 'It will be heaven!' The other one rightly said it might be hell, what he could offer me! He did not deceive me. Well, Palmer must not deceive me by deceiving himself; for, after this new error, there would be nothing left for me to do but deny everything, tell myself, like Laurent, that I have lost for ever, through my own fault, the right to believe, and I do not know that I could bear to go on living, knowing that.

"Forgive me, my beloved, all this agitation of mine will make you worried, I'm sure, even though you say you want to know everything! Don't worry, at least, about my health. I feel wonderfully well; before my eyes I have the most beautiful sea, and above my head the most beautiful sky anyone could imagine. I have everything I need, I am staying with some good souls, and perhaps I shall write and tell you tomorrow that all my uncertainties have melted away. Keep loving your Thérèse, who adores you."

Palmer had indeed been in La Spezia since the previous day. He had deliberately arrived just an hour after the *Ferruccio* had left. Finding Thérèse was not at the Cross of Malta, and learning that she must have seen Laurent off from the entrance to the gulf, he awaited her return. At nine o'clock he saw the boatman she had hired that morning, the hotel's boatman, return alone. He was a stout fellow and not accustomed to drinking. He had been *caught out* by a bottle of Cyprus wine that Laurent had given him, after the meal on the grass with Thérèse, and which he had drunk while the two friends were visiting the island of Palmaria. He could clearly remember taking the *signore* and the *signora* on board the *Ferruccio* but had no recollection of having then landed the *signora* at Porto-Venere.

If Palmer had questioned him calmly, he would soon have discovered that the boatman's ideas on this latter point were not very exact; but Palmer, for all his serious and impassive air, was easily spurred to anger and his emotions were running high. He believed that Thérèse had gone with Laurent, gone blushingly, without daring or wishing to confess the truth. He took it as proved, and retired to the hotel, where he passed a dreadful night.

It is not the story of Richard Palmer that we have set ourselves to write. We have called our story *This Woman, This Man*, in other words, Thérèse and Laurent. We shall therefore say of Palmer only what needs to be said of him to explain the events in which he played some part, and we think his character will be sufficiently described by his actions. Let us merely hasten to say in a word or two that Richard Palmer was as ardent as he was romantic, that he took pride in upholding the virtues of the good and the beautiful, but that the strength of his character did not always match the lofty idea he had of it, and that in ceaselessly trying to rise above human nature, he was pursuing an admirable ideal, but one perhaps unachievable in matters of love.

He rose early and went for a walk along the shores of the gulf, thoughts of suicide flitting through his mind, thoughts soon dispersed however, by a sort of contempt for Thérèse. Then the tiredness that follows a disturbed night exerted its own influence and brought him the better counsel of reason. Thérèse was a woman, and he should not have submitted her to a dangerous test. Well! Since that was the way things were, since Thérèse, so high in his esteem, had been vanquished by a deplorable passion after giving sacred promises, no woman was ever to be believed again, and no woman deserved the sacrifice of the life of a gallant man. Palmer's thoughts had arrived at this point when he saw an elegant pinnace, commanded by a naval officer, glide towards the spot where he was standing. The eight oarsmen who propelled the long thin vessel so swiftly and lightly over the calm waters raised their white blades to the vertical with military precision in a mark of respect. The officer stepped ashore and strode towards Richard, whom he had recognised when still some way off.

He was Captain Lawson, commander of the American frigate *Union*, stationed for a year in the gulf. The maritime powers, as is known, send ships out on station for months or years at a time to protect their commercial interests in the various regions of the world.

Lawson was a boyhood friend of Palmer, who had given Thérèse a letter of recommendation for him should she wish to visit the ship while exploring the bay.

Palmer imagined Lawson had news of her, but that was not the case. He had received no letter, he had seen no one connected with Palmer. He took him off to lunch on board and Richard allowed himself to be taken. The *Union* was leaving its station at the end of spring; Palmer toyed with the idea of taking the opportunity to return to America. Everything seemed at an end between him and Thérèse; but he resolved to stay in La Spezia, the prospect of the sea having always exerted a fortifying influence on him in life's difficult moments.

He had been there for three days, spending a good deal more time on the American vessel than at the Cross of Malta, forcing himself to renew his interest in the nautical studies which had occupied the major part of his life, when a young ensign told the story one morning at lunch, half laughing, half sighing, of how he had been lovestruck the previous day; but there was a problem with the object of his passion, on which he would dearly like to have the advice of a man of the world such as M. Palmer.

She was a woman who appeared to be between twenty-five and thirty. He had only seen her sitting in a window, making lace. Coarse cotton lace is made by all the women along the Genoese coast. It was once a branch of commerce exploited by big trading companies, but is still an occupation and cottage industry for women and girls of the area. So the

woman with whom the young ensign was smitten belonged to
the artisan classes, not only because of this line of work but
even more because of the poverty of the dwelling where he
had seen her. The cut of her black dress and the distinction of
her features, however, had thrown him into doubt. Her wavy
hair was neither brown nor blonde, her gaze was distracted, her
complexion pale. She had clearly seen that the young officer
was staring at her, from the inn where he had been taking
shelter from the rain, with great curiosity. She had neither
encouraged him with a glance nor troubled herself to move
away from the window. She had offered him the frustrating
image of indifference personified.

The young sailor went on to say that he had questioned
the landlady of the inn at Port-Venere. This lady had replied
that the stranger had been there for three days, staying with an
old woman of the town who was passing her off as her niece
and who was probably lying, because she was a scheming old
woman who let out a poor room to the detriment of the licensed
and accredited inn, and who was seemingly now meddling
in the business of housing and feeding travellers, but who
must be feeding them very poorly, for she had nothing and
consequently deserved the contempt of established businesses
and discerning travellers.

As a result of this speech, the young ensign found himself
with nothing more urgent to do than to go to the old woman's
house and ask if she had lodging for a friend he was expecting,
hoping, by means of this invention, to get her to talk and to
learn something about his unknown beauty; but the old woman
had been inscrutable, and even incorruptible.

The portrait the sailor painted of this unknown young

woman caught Palmer's attention. It could be that of Thérèse; but what was she doing and why was she hiding herself away in Porto-Venere? No doubt she was not there alone; Laurent must be hidden in some other corner of the town. Palmer turned over in his mind the prospect of disappearing to China to escape having to bear witness to his own misery. However, he took the rational course, which was to find out what exactly was going on.

He promptly had himself taken to Porto-Venere and had no difficulty finding Thérèse there, housed and occupied as described. Explanations were sharp and frank. Both were too sincere to sulk; both were therefore prepared to admit that they had harboured hard feelings about the other, Palmer because Thérèse had not contacted him to say where she was, Thérèse because Palmer had not made greater efforts to find her or found her sooner.

'My friend,' Palmer said, 'your chief reproach seems to be that I abandoned you to a supposed danger. It was a danger that I, for one, never believed in.'

'You were right, and I thank you for that. So why were you sad and almost despairing when you watched me go? And how was it that when you arrived here you weren't able to discover where I was straightaway? Did you presume I'd gone then, and that it was futile to look for me?'

'Listen to me,' Palmer said, avoiding the question, 'and you'll see that I have had some bitter experiences these last few days, which might have made me lose my head. You'll also understand how, having known you when you were very young, and having some notion I might marry you, I missed a happiness I have regretted and dreamed about ever since. At

THIS WOMAN, THIS MAN

the time I was the lover of a woman who led me a merry dance in every possible way. I believed, I once believed, for ten long years, I was duty-bound to set her on her feet again and protect her. In the end her ingratitude and treachery came to a head, and I was able to leave her, forget her, and lead a life of my own choosing again. Well! This woman, whom I believed to be in England, I ran into her again in Florence, just as Laurent was due to leave. Abandoned by a new lover, my successor, she now wanted, and was planning, to get me back again: there had been so many times in the past when I had been generous or weak-willed! She wrote me a letter full of threats and an absurd pretence of jealousy, saying she was coming to abuse and insult you in my presence. I knew her to be a woman who would not hold back at the prospect of making a scandal, I wouldn't for anything in the world have wished you even to be a witness to her in one of her furies. The only way I could persuade her not to appear was to promise to have it out with her that same day. She had taken a room in the very same hotel where we were looking after our patient, and when the carriage for Laurent arrived outside the door, she was there, determined to make a scene. Her evil and ridiculous plan was to shout out, in front of all the people in the hotel and in the street, that I was sharing my new mistress with Laurent de Fauvel. That's why I made you go with him, and why I stayed behind, in order to get rid of this madwoman without compromising you and without subjecting you to having to see or hear her. So don't tell me now, that I intended to put you through a test by leaving you alone with Laurent. I have suffered enough over this, God knows, don't start accusing me! And when I thought you had left with Laurent, all the furies of hell descended on me.'

'And that's what I reproach you for,' Thérèse said.

'Ah! Can you blame me?' Palmer cried. 'I have been so vilely deceived in my life! That wretched woman stirred up a whole world of bitterness and scorn.'

'And that scorn has rebounded on me?'

'Oh, don't say that, Thérèse!'

'Nevertheless I have been betrayed too,' she continued, 'and I believed in you all the same.'

'Don't let's talk about it any more, my friend, I regret having been forced to confide my past life to you. You will think it could colour my future, and that I will be like Laurent and make you pay for the treachery heaped on me. Come on, come on, my dear Thérèse, let's banish these sad thoughts. You are here in the sort of place that would give anyone a sense of dissatisfaction. The boat is waiting for us; come back to La Spezia, where you were settled.'

'No,' Thérèse said, 'I'm staying here.'

'What? What is this, then? Resentment between us?'

'No, no, my dear Dick,' she continued, holding out her hand. 'With you, I never want to feel that. Oh! Help me, please, make our affection for each other a model of sincerity, because for my part, I want to do all a believer's soul can do to make it so. But I didn't know you were a jealous man: you have been, and you acknowledge it. Well, you have to understand that it is not in my power not to suffer cruelly from that jealousy! It's so contrary to what you promised me that I wonder where we are going now, and why, just as I am emerging from a kind of hell, I should enter a purgatory, when all I aspire to is rest and solitude.

'And I don't only fear these tortures which seem to be

looming on my own account. If it was possible in love that one of the two should be happy when the other suffered, the road of devotion would be all marked out and easy to follow. But that is not the case, as you can see: I cannot be in pain for an instant without your feeling it. And so I would necessarily spoil your life, when all I wanted was to make mine harmless, and I'm beginning to cause unhappiness! No, Palmer, believe me; we thought we knew each other and we did not know each other. The thing that charmed me about you was a disposition of mind you no longer have: to trust. Don't you understand that in my debased state, trust was what I needed if I was to love you, that above anything? If I allowed myself to wear the mantle of your affection as a stained and weak woman, assailed by doubts and storms, would you not be in your rights to say to yourself that by marrying you I am making a calculation? Oh, don't say the idea will never occur to you! It will occur in spite of yourself. I know only too well how one suspicion leads to another and what a slippery slope precipitates us from a first disenchantment to a fatal disgust! Well, listen, I for one have drunk enough of that bitter gall; I don't want any more, and I'm not deluding myself, I can't go through what I've suffered again. I told you that the first day, and if you've forgotten it, I have not. Therefore let us set aside this idea of marriage,' she added, 'and remain friends. I am provisionally taking back my word, until I am sure I have your full esteem, as I thought I had it at one time. If you do not wish to submit yourself to a trial, let us separate immediately. As for me, let me emphasise that I do not wish to be in your debt in any way, not even for the smallest service, in my present situation. This situation, I mean, because I want you to know the choice I am making.

I have my board and lodging here on credit, because I have absolutely nothing, I handed all I possessed to Vincentino for Laurent's travel expenses. But it turns out that I can make lace quicker and better than the women of the area, and while I'm waiting for the money I'm owed to be sent from Genoa, I can earn enough here, day by day, to contribute to, if not cover, the frugal food provided by my good hostess. This state of affairs causes me no humiliation and no suffering, and it must continue until my money arrives. At that point I will see what course I need to follow. Until then, return to La Spezia, and come and see me whenever you like; I shall make lace while we talk together.'

Palmer had to submit, and he submitted with good grace. He hoped to regain Thérèse's trust, and he was acutely aware how he had shaken it by his error.

X

A few days later, Thérèse received a letter from Geneva. It was a litany of self-recrimination from Laurent, repeating on paper what he had already said to her face, as if to provide solid proof of his repentance.

"No," he said, "I did not deserve you. I was unworthy of so generous, pure and selfless a love. I exhausted your patience, O my sister, O my mother! The very angels would have grown tired of me! Ah, Thérèse! As I gradually return to health and to life, my memories become clearer, I look into my past as if into a mirror that shows me the spectre of a man I once knew but no longer understand. One thing that's for certain is this miserable creature was demented. Don't you think it's possible, Thérèse, that the terrible illness – whose worst consequences you miraculously spared me – could have been just the culmination of a moral illness already working away in me three or four months earlier? And isn't it possible it was this same illness that deprived me of any awareness of my words and actions? Oh, if that was true, shouldn't you have pardoned me…? But alas, that doesn't make sense. What else is acting badly than a moral sickness? Couldn't the man who kills his father invoke the same excuse? Good and evil: this is the first time the notion has struck me so forcibly. Before I knew you, and made you suffer, my poor beloved, I had never given it a thought. To me, evil was some low-born monster, the apocalyptic beast whose embraces leave their filthy mark on the nefarious dregs of society. Evil, how could it have anything to do with me, who lived the elegant life, who was the beau of Paris, the noble son of the Muses! Oh, imbecile that I was, I imagined, because of my perfumed beard and gloved hands, that my caresses turned licentiousness, the great harlot of every nation, into something pure. I became her fiancé, bound by chains as noble as those that bind convicts in their cells! And you, my poor gentle mistress, I burned on the pyre of my brutal selfishness, and after I had done so, I lifted my head saying: 'It was my right, she belonged to me; there can be no evil in something I have the right to do!' Ah, wretch, wretch that I am, I was a criminal, and I never suspected it! To understand, I had to lose you: you, the only good thing I had, the only person who had ever loved me or been capable of loving the ungrateful and insane child I was! It was only when I saw my guardian angel veil her face and resume her flight towards heaven, that I understood I was for ever alone and abandoned here on earth!"

A long section of this first letter was written in an exalted tone, whose sincerity was confirmed by details from real life and sudden changes of tone, characteristic of Laurent.

"Would you believe, on arriving in Geneva, the first thing I did before thinking of writing to you was to go out and buy a waistcoat? Yes, a summer waistcoat, very pretty, goodness me, and very well cut, which I found in a French tailor's, a happy encounter for a man passing through and anxious to put behind him this city of clockmakers and naturalists. Here I am then, running up and down the streets of Geneva, delighted with my new waistcoat, and stopping outside a bookseller's window where a certain edition of Byron, most tastefully bound, seemed an irresistible temptation. What was I to read on my travels? Theres's one thing I can't stand, it's travel books, unless they are talking about countries I shall never be able to visit. I prefer the poets, who take you travelling in the world of their dreams, and I bought myself this edition. And then I followed in the wake of a very pretty girl in short skirts who had just walked by and whose ankles were masterpieces of the turner's art. I followed, with my thoughts far more on my waistcoat than on her. Suddenly she turned right, and I left, without noticing, and I found myself back at my hotel, where, wanting to put my book away in my trunk, I found the double violets you had scattered round my cabin on the *Ferruccio* when we said our farewells. I had carefully picked them up one by one, and was keeping them like a relic; but now they made me cry like a drainpipe in a flood, and looking at my new waistcoat, which had been the principal event of my morning, I said to myself: 'And that's the child whom that poor woman loved!'"

In another part, he said: "You made me promise to look after my health. You told me: 'Since I was the one who gave it back to you, it partly belongs to me, and I have the right to forbid you to waste it.' Alas, my Thérèse, what do you want me to do with it, this beastly good health which is beginning to have the inebriating effect on me of a fresh young wine? Spring is blossoming, it's the season for love, and I'm very willing; but do I have to? Even you could not succeed in implanting true love, and do you think I shall find a woman capable of achieving a miracle that you could not? Where shall I find this woman, this magician? In polite society? No, definitely not: there you only meet women unwilling to risk or sacrifice anything. They're quite right, undoubtedly, and you could tell them, my poor friend, that the men women sacrifice themselves for are hardly ever worth it. But it's not my fault if I can no more settle to sharing with a husband than with a lover. Love a young damsel? Marry her then? Oh, really, Thérèse, you can't think of that without laughing... or trembling. Me, chained by constraint of law when I can't even be chained by my own will!

"I once had a friend who loved a working class girl and thought he was very happy. I paid court to this faithful girl who supposedly loved him back and I had her for the present of a green budgerigar that her lover refused to give her. She said, innocently: 'Well, it's his dratted fault, he should have given me the budgie!' And since that day I have promised myself never to love a kept woman, in other words a person who wants all the things her lover doesn't give her.

"So when it comes to mistresses, the only possibilities are an adventuress like the women you sometimes meet out on our highways who were all born as princesses but who have suffered some *misfortune*. Too many misfortunes, no thank you! I am not rich enough to fill in the holes of their past!

"A well-known actress? I have often been tempted; but the actress would have to give up appearing before her adoring public, and that particular lover is one I don't feel I have the strength to replace. No, no, Thérèse, I cannot love! I ask too much, and what I ask I am unable to return. I shall therefore have to go back to my old way of life. I prefer it that way, because the image I hold of you will never be tainted by comparison. Why shouldn't my life be organised this way: women for the senses and a mistress for the soul? It has nothing to do with you or with me, Thérèse, that you are not that mistress, that ideal of my dreams, lost, wept over, and dreamed about more than ever. You cannot take offence, I shall never breathe a word about it to you. I will love you in my secret thoughts and no one will ever know, and no other woman will ever be able to say: 'This Thérèse, I have replaced her.'

"My friend, you must grant me a favour you denied me during those last few days we spent together, so sweet and so dear to me: tell me about Palmer. You thought it would cause me further harm. Well, you're wrong! It would have killed me the first time I questioned you about him, when I was so agitated: I was still unwell and a little mad. But when reason returned, when you allowed me to guess the secret – which no one forced you to share – I felt, in the middle of my own pain, that by accepting your happiness I was repairing all my errors. I watched closely how you behaved with each other: I saw that he loved you passionately and yet showed me a fatherly affection. That made a deep impression, you see, Thérèse. I had never conceived of such generosity, such largeness of spirit, in matters of love. Lucky Palmer, how sure of you he is! How well he understands you, and in consequence deserves you! It reminded me of the time I said to you: 'Love Palmer, you'll be doing me a favour!' Oh, what despicable sentiments swirled in my soul then! I wanted to be released from your love, which seemed an unending source of remorse, and yet, if you had told me at the time: 'Very well, I love him...!' might I have killed you?

"And he, that good and great-hearted man, loved you already, and he was not afraid to declare his devotion when you still perhaps loved me! In the same circumstances, I would never have dared risk it. I had too much of that fine self-regard we men of the world are proud to cultivate. It is a clever invention of idiots, designed to prevent us from trying to achieve happiness if it involves any risk or danger to ourselves. And the same self-regard deprives us of the wit to cling on when that happiness is slipping through our fingers.

"Yes, I want to make full confession, my poor friend. When I said to you: *Love Palmer*, I sometimes believed you loved him already, and that is what finally drove me away from you. In those last few weeks there were plenty of times when I was ready to throw myself at your feet. I was stopped by this idea: 'It's too late, she loves another man. I wanted her to love him, but she shouldn't have wanted to as well. Therefore, she is unworthy of me!'

"That's how I reasoned in my folly, and yet, I'm sure of this now: if I had knelt before you in sincere appeal, then even though you were beginning to fall in love with Dick, you would have given him up for me. You would have become once more the martyr I was forcing you to be. So all in all I did the right thing, didn't I, in running away? That's what I felt when I left you! Yes, Thérèse, that's what gave me the strength to rush off to Florence without a word. I felt I was slowly murdering you day by day, and the only way to repair my wrongs was to leave you alone in the company of a man who genuinely loved you.

"That is also what sustained my courage in La Spezia, all through that day when I could still have tried to obtain a pardon; but that hateful idea never entered my head; on that you have my word, my friend. I don't know if you had told that boatman never to let us out of his sight; but it would have been pointless if you had! I would rather have thrown myself into the sea than wish to betray the trust Palmer was showing me by leaving us together.

"Tell him then, tell him directly, that I truly do love you, as far as I am capable of loving. Tell him that he is as responsible as you are for my having tried, condemned and executed myself the way I did. It has caused me immense suffering, God knows, to achieve this suicide of the man I used to be! But I am proud of myself now. All my former friends would judge me a fool or a coward for not having tried to kill my rival in a duel, and then abandon, spitting in her face, the woman who had betrayed me! Yes, Thérèse, that's how I would probably have judged another man's conduct myself, and yet I held to it, with you and Palmer, as resolutely as I did joyfully. It's because I am not a brute, thank God! I am not worth much, but I understand the little that I *am* worth, and I do justice by it.

"So talk to me about Palmer, and don't be afraid I'll be hurt; far from it, I will find it a consolation in my darker hours. It will be a strength as well, for your poor child is still very weak, and when he begins to think about what he could have been for you and what he is now, his head still reels. But tell me that you are happy and I will say to myself proudly: 'I could have broken in on that happiness, disputed it, perhaps destroyed it: I did not do so. It is therefore in some small part my work, and I have the right, now, to Thérèse's friendship.'"

Thérèse sent an affectionate reply to her poor child. For such was the title under which he was henceforth buried, and as it were embalmed, in the sanctuary of the past...

Thérèse loved Palmer, or at least she wished or believed that she loved him. It did not seem to her she could ever regret the passing of the period in her life when she woke up every morning, as she put it, looking round to see if the house was about to collapse on her head.

And yet something was missing, and an unaccountable sadness had overtaken her since she had been living on the grey-blue rock of Porto-Venere. It was like being detached from life, which was not without its charm at times, but there was a mournful and demoralised element which was not in her character and which she could not explain to herself.

She found it impossible to do what Laurent asked in relation to Palmer: she sent him a few lines, briefly eulogising the man and sending, on his behalf, affectionate greetings; but she could not take the further step of admitting him to their intimacy. She shrank from letting him know her real situation, that is to say, from confiding in him the promises on which she had not yet pronounced, even to herself, her final word. And even if her mind had been made up, would it not have been too soon to say to Laurent: "You are still suffering, hard luck, I'm getting married!"?

It took two weeks for the money she was expecting to arrive. For two weeks she made lace with a perseverance which was the despair of Palmer. When she finally found herself in possession of a number of bank notes, she paid her hostess handsomely and allowed herself to go out with Palmer on trips around the gulf; but she wanted to remain in Porto-Venere for some while longer, without being able to explain quite why she insisted still on that gloomy and wretched dwelling.

There are certain moral situations which one can feel but which elude definition. It was to her mother that Thérèse was able, in her letters, to talk more expansively:

"I am still here," she wrote in July, "in spite of the all-consuming heat. I have attached myself like a limpet to this rock where no tree has ever been able to consider growing but where strong and energising winds blow. The climate is hard but healthy, and the continuous view of the sea, which I would once have found it impossible to live with, has come to be in some way necessary. The inland regions behind me, which I can get to in less than two hours by boat, were magnificent in spring. If you go further, beyond the head of the bay and two or three leagues from the coast, you come across some very strange formations. There is a particular region where the terrain had been much disturbed by who knows what ancient earthquakes and now presents quite bizarre features. It's a succession of hills of red sand covered in pines and heathers, rising one behind the other and offering you natural and quite wide paths to walk along on their crests. But then these paths suddenly plunge down into deep abysses, leaving you distinctly embarrassed about how to proceed. If you retrace your steps and make a mistake among the network of little tracks made by the feet of the herds, you end up at another ravine, and Palmer and I have sometimes remained for hours on one of these wooded hill tops without finding the path that brought us there. From these summits one looks down at the vast expanse of cultivated land, divided here and there in an almost regular pattern by strange features, and beyond this expanse stretches the blue expanse of the sea. In that direction, it seems the horizon has no limits. Over to the north and the east stand the Alps, whose crests, boldly delineated, were still snow-covered when I arrived here.

"But those early days of May, when whole tracts were covered in flowering rock roses and white heather with their fresh and delicate scent, are long past. It was a paradise on earth then: these woods were full of laburnums, Judas trees and scented broom, sparkling like gold against the dark foliage of the myrtles. Now everything is burnt, the pine smell has turned bitter, the fields of lupins, so colourful and perfumed before, are just truncated stems, as black as if a fire had raged through them; and with the harvests gathered, the land smokes in the noonday sun, and you have to rise very early in the morning if you want to wander abroad without discomfort. Well, since it takes at least four hours, partly by boat, partly on foot, to get to the wooded regions, the return journey is not pleasant, and all the heights immediately surrounding the gulf, wonderful to look at with their imposing shapes, are so bare that Porto-Venere and the island of Palmaria are still the places to be if you want to breathe with any ease.

"And then there's a plague in La Spezia, in the form of the mosquitoes bred by the stagnant waters of a small lake nearby and of the great expanse of marshes over which the sea and agriculture are fighting a constant battle. Here, it's not the inland waters that trouble us; we have only rock and sea, and no insects therefore, not a blade of grass; but we have amazing clouds of gold and purple, magnificent storms and the most solemn calms! The sea is a painting which changes in colour and feeling every minute of the day and night. There are inlets here full of sounds more varied than you could ever imagine; every sob of despair, every diabolical curse meets and mingles here, and at night, from my little window, I can hear voices from the abyss sometimes braying out in nameless bacchanalia, sometimes singing wild hymns that are fearsome even in their gentlest mood.

"Well, I love all this now! Yes I do, despite the fact that my tastes have always been for the rural, for little hidden-away spots of green tranquillity. Was it that fateful love affair that made me accustomed to, and even need, storms and uproar? It could be! We women are such strange creatures! I have to confess my darling, it took several days before I could get used to doing without my source of torture, I didn't know what to do with myself, with no one to serve and care for any more. Palmer should have been just a little bit badly behaved. But look how unfair it is: as soon as he appeared to be so, I was revolted; and now that he has become angelically good again, I don't know who to blame for the terrible emptiness that comes over me at times. Alas, yes, that's how it feels…! Should I tell you? No, it would be better not to know it myself, or, if I know, not to trouble you with my odd ideas. I only wanted to tell you about this place where I'm staying, my excursions, my occupations, my sad room under the rooftops, or rather looking out over the rooftops. I like being alone here, I like the fact that no one knows me, I like being forgotten by the world, having no duties, no clients, no business matters, no other work to do except what pleases me. I get the small children to pose for me, I amuse myself composing groups. But that kind of thing isn't going to satisfy you, and if I don't say anything about my feelings and intentions, you will be even more anxious. Well! I can tell you that I am fully resolved to marry Palmer and I love him. But I have not yet been able to make up my mind to say when such a marriage will take place. I fear, for him and for myself, what would come after a permanent union of that kind. I am past the age of illusions, and after a life such as mine, I feel I have a century of experience, and consequently, terrors! I thought my parting from Laurent was absolute, and indeed it was in Genoa, the day he told me I was his plague, the death sentence on his genius and fame. Now, I don't feel quite so detached from him; since his illness, his repentance, and the letters he has been writing these last two months, adorable and full of sweetness and self-abnegation, I feel I am still connected by a strong sense of duty to this unhappy child, and I would not wish to hurt him by abandoning him completely. Yet that is what could happen after I am married to Palmer. There has been one episode of jealousy already, and once he has the right to say to me: *I command...!* I fear there could be others. I do not love Laurent any more, I swear, my darling; I would rather die than feel any love for him; but the day Palmer tries to break the friendship, which I still feel in the aftermath of our unhappy passion, perhaps I shall no longer love Palmer.

"I have told him all this. He understands, because he likes to consider himself a great philosopher, and he clings to the belief that what seems fair and good today will never seem any different to his eyes. I believe so as well, and yet I am asking him to allow the calm and contented situation we find ourselves in at present to continue undisturbed, to let the days accumulate round it. I have my moments of spleen, it is true; but Palmer is not by nature very perspicacious and I can hide them from him. I can be wearing what Laurent used to call my sick bird's face without his taking fright. If any future trouble is limited to this – that I can have irritated nerves and a gloomy mind without his noticing or being affected by it – then we shall be able to live together as happily as is possible. If he began to probe my distracted gaze too closely or tried to penetrate the veil of my private thoughts, or subject me to the sort of cruel intrusions that Laurent did with such childish glee whenever my morale was low, I don't think I have the strength left to battle against it, and I'd rather be killed on the spot, it would be over quicker."

At about the same time, Thérèse received from Laurent a letter so full of ardour that it worried her. It was infused no longer with the joys of friendship, but of love. The silence Thérèse had maintained over her relations with Palmer had rekindled in the artist the hope of being together with her again. He could no longer live without her; he had made vain efforts to return to his life of pleasures. Disgust had gripped him by the throat.

"Ah, Thérèse!" he told her. "I used to accuse you of loving me too chastely and of being more fitted for the convent than for love. How could I have uttered such blasphemies? Ever since I have been trying to return to the world of vice, I have felt I am the one becoming chaste as a child, and the women I see tell me I might as well be a monk. No, no, I will never forget those elements of what we had between us that went far beyond love, that mother-like gentleness which could cradle me in its tender, placid smile for hours on end, those expansions of the heart, those stretchings of the intelligence, that two-handed

194

poem of which, effortlessly, we were both the authors and the characters. Thérèse, if you are not Palmer's, you can only be mine! Is there anyone else with whom you will ever rediscover those fierce emotions, that deep tenderness? Were all our times bad ones, after all? Were there not some beautiful ones? And besides, is it happiness you seek, you, the epitome of the devoted woman? Can you live without suffering for someone, and did you not sometimes call me, when you forgave me my follies, your dear burden, your necessary torment? Remember, remember, Thérèse! You have suffered and you are alive. I…? I have made you suffer and I am dying! Have I not made sufficient atonement? My soul has been in agony for three months…!"

Then came reproaches. Thérèse had said too much or too little. Her expressions of friendship were too effusive if it was merely friendship, too cold and too prudent if it was love. She should have the courage to let him live or let him die.

The response Thérèse resolved on was to tell him that she loved Palmer, and that she meant to love him always, without however, mentioning the planned marriage which she could not decide in her own mind to regard as a definite arrangement. She softened as much as she could the blow to Laurent's pride that such a declaration must deliver.

"Rest assured," she told him, "that it was not as you claimed, to punish you that I have given my heart and my life to another. No, the day I responded to Palmer's affections you were fully pardoned, as proved by the fact that I rushed to Florence with him. Do you believe, my poor child, that in caring for you as I did throughout your illness I was really only there as a sister of charity? No, no, it was not duty which kept me tied at your bedside, it was a mother's tenderness. Doesn't a mother always forgive? Well, that is how it will always be, don't you see? Any time, without failing in my obligations to Palmer, that I can be of use to you, take care of you and console you, you will find me there. It is because Palmer does not oppose me in this that I have been able to love him, and that I do love him. If I had left your arms only to embrace your enemy, I would have been horrified at myself; but it was the opposite. It was in the making of our oaths to one another, to watch over you always and never abandon you, that our hands were joined."

Thérèse showed this letter to Palmer, who was profoundly moved and wished to write to Laurent on his own account, to confirm those same promises of unwavering solicitude and true affection.

There was a delay before Laurent replied. He had embarked on a fantasy which he saw vanishing for good. He took it very badly at first; but he determined he must shake off this grief, which he did not feel strong enough to bear. There worked in him one of those sudden and complete reversals which were at times the plague, at times the salvation of his life, and he wrote to Thérèse:

"Blessings on you, my adored sister. I am happy; I am proud to have your faithful friendship, and to have Palmer's moves me to tears. Why did you not speak out earlier, wicked woman? I would not have suffered so much. What did I need in the end? To know you were happy, nothing more. It's because I thought you were alone and sad that I came and knelt at your feet to say: 'Well, since you're suffering, let's suffer together! I want to share your sadness, your emptiness, your solitude.' Wasn't it my duty and my right? But you are happy, Thérèse, and therefore so am I! I bless you for having told me. I am at last delivered from the remorse that has gnawed at my heart! I want to walk with head held high, fill my lungs with good clean air and tell myself I have not soiled and ruined the life of the best of friends. Ah! I'm full of pride to feel this kind of generous joy inside me, instead of the awful jealousy that tormented me before!

"My dear Thérèse, my dear Palmer, you are my two guardian angels. You have brought me happiness. Thanks to you, I finally feel that I was born for something better than the life I have been living. I am born again, I feel heaven's breath descend into my lungs, greedy for a purer atmosphere. My whole being is transformed. I am going to love!

"Yes, I am going to love, I love already…! I love a pure and beautiful child who as yet knows nothing of it and when I am with her I take mysterious pleasure in withholding the secret of my heart, and in seeming and making myself be as innocent, as gay, as childish as she is herself. Oh, aren't they wonderful, those first days of a new and growing feeling! Isn't there something sublime and terrifying in the idea: I am going to give myself away, that is, I am going to give myself, tomorrow, perhaps this evening, I shall no longer belong to myself?

"Rejoice, my Thérèse, at this outcome of the sad and foolish youth of your poor child. Tell yourself that this renewal of a creature who seemed lost and who, instead of crawling in the mire, is opening his wings like a bird, is the work of your love, of your gentleness, of your patience, of your anger, of your rigour, of your forgiveness and your friendship! Yes, all those were the necessary episodes of an intimate drama in which I was defeated before being led to open my eyes. I am your creation, your son, your labour and your reward, your martyrdom and your crown. Bless me, my friends, both of you, and pray for me, I am going to love!"

All the rest of the letter went like this. On receiving this hymn of joy and gratitude, Thérèse felt her own happiness complete and assured for the first time. She held her hands out to Palmer and said: 'Well then! Where and when are we getting married?'

XI

It was decided that the marriage should take place in America. It would be the culmination of Palmer's joy to introduce Thérèse to his mother and to receive the nuptial blessing under her gaze. The mother of Thérèse was unable to promise herself the happiness of being present even if the marriage were to take place in France. Her chagrin was balanced by the joy she felt to see her daughter allied to a man of rational temperament and devoted to her. She could not bear Laurent, and had always trembled at the thought that Thérèse might fall once more under his yoke.

The *Union* was making its preparations for departure. Captain Lawson offered to take Palmer and his fiancée. A festive spirit prevailed on board at the prospect of making the voyage in the company of the much-loved couple. The young ensign atoned for his impertinent scheme by behaving towards them with the utmost respect and showing the highest regard for Thérèse.

Having made all her preparations for embarkation on the eighteenth of August, Thérèse received a letter from her mother, who begged her to come first to Paris, if even for only twenty-four hours. She had to go there herself on family business. Who knew when Thérèse might return from America? The poor mother found no happiness with her other children, who influenced by a challenging and peevish father, maintained a chilly independence in their relations with her. And also, she adored Thérèse, the only one to have been a truly loving daughter and devoted friend. She wanted to bless her and embrace her, perhaps for the last time, for she felt old in advance of her years, ill and weary from a life that offered her only insecurity and narrowness.

Palmer was more put out by this letter than he was willing to admit. Although he had always claimed to be perfectly happy and confident about the lasting friendship between him and Laurent, he had never been able to suppress his worries about the feelings new contact with Laurent might reawaken in her. He was not aware of them, when he proclaimed the contrary; but they infiltrated his consciousness when the gun on the American vessel sent echoing round the gulf of La Spezia its repeated boom of farewell all through that eighteenth day of August.

Every one of those detonations made him shiver, and as the last rang out, he wrung his hands so nervously the knuckles cracked.

Thérèse was greatly surprised. She had thought no further about Palmer's anxieties since the serious talk they had had at the beginning of their stay here.

'Good heavens, what is it?' she exclaimed, watching Palmer closely. 'Have you had some dreadful premonition?'

'Yes, that's what it is!' Palmer replied hastily. 'A premonition… about Lawson, my childhood friend. I don't know why… yes, yes, it's a premonition!'

'You think something bad will happen while he's at sea?'

'Maybe? Who knows? At least you won't be at risk, thank goodness, since we're going to Paris.'

'The *Union* is calling at Brest and staying there for a fortnight. That's where we'll be going to embark?'

'Yes, yes, I expect so, if there's no disaster in the meantime.'

And Palmer remained sad and afflicted, with Thérèse unable to guess what was going on inside him. How could she have guessed? Laurent was in Baden, taking the waters, as Palmer well knew, and Laurent was also taken up with possible plans to marry, as he had written.

They departed the following day by post-chaise, and without lingering at any of their stops, they returned to France via Turin and the Mont Cenis pass.

It was an extraordinarily unhappy journey. Palmer saw signs of misfortune everywhere; he confessed to superstitious feelings and frailties of spirit which had never formed any part of his character. Normally so calm, his needs so easily attended to, he lapsed into unprecedented bouts of anger, against the drivers, the roads, the customs officials, the passers-by. Thérèse had never seen him like this. She could not help but tell him so. His reply was brief and inconsequential, but the expression on his face was so black and his annoyance so obvious that she became frightened of him, and hence of the future.

An implacable destiny attends some lives. While Thérèse and Palmer were re-entering France by the Mont Cenis pass, Laurent was re-entering through Geneva. He arrived in Paris four hours ahead of them, his mind taken up by a pressing worry. He had at last discovered that, in order to send him on his travels for a few months, Thérèse had given away, in Italy, all the money she then possessed, and he had learnt (for everything emerges sooner or later), from a person who passed through La Spezia at that time, that Mlle Jacques was living in Porto-Venere in a state of extreme embarrassment, and was making lace in order to pay rent of six pounds a month.

Humiliated and repentant, irritated and appalled, he wanted to know Thérèse's situation, how things now stood with her. He knew her to be too proud to be willing to accept anything from Palmer, and he told himself, plausibly enough, that if she had not been paid for her work in Genoa, then she must have had her Paris furniture sold off.

He made his way to the Champs-Elysées at once, fearful of finding strangers installed in that dear little house, which he never approached but with a violently beating heart. As there was no porter, he had to ring at the garden gate, not knowing what sort of person might emerge to answer. He did not know of Thérèse's imminent marriage, he did not even know that she was free to marry. A parting letter from her on that very subject had arrived in Baden the day after he left.

He was overjoyed to see the door opened by the elderly Catherine. He flung his arms round her in relief. But the next instant his spirits sank when he saw the look of consternation on that good woman's face.

'What are you doing here?' she said to him crossly. 'You know that mademoiselle is coming home today then? Can't you leave her in peace? Have you come to make her unhappy again? I was told you had separated, and I was glad; because although I may have liked you before, I hated you. It was clear to me you were the cause of her embarrassments and difficulties. Come along, come along, you can't stand about here waiting for her, unless you're bent on killing her altogether!'

'You say she's coming home today!' Laurent exclaimed, several times over.

It was the only part of the old servant's rebuke he heard. He went into Thérèse's studio, into the little lilac sitting room and even into the bedroom, lifting the grey sheets that Catherine had spread over everything to protect the furniture. He looked at them one by one, all those strange and curious little pieces, art objects, items showing her taste, which Thérèse had bought with the fruits of her labour: none was missing. Nothing appeared changed in Thérèse's situation, her Paris life, and Laurent repeated in some bewilderment, staring at Catherine who was following his every move with a suspicious air: 'She's coming home today?'

In saying that he loved a beautiful girl with a love as pure and fair as the creature herself, Laurent had been overstating matters. He had believed he was telling the truth when he wrote to Thérèse in the exalted tones he indulged in when writing to her about himself, and which made such a strange contrast with the cold and mocking tone he believed it his duty to adopt in society. The declaration which he was to have made to the young object of his fantasies he had not made. A bird or a cloud passing in the sky one evening had been enough to dismantle the fragile edifice of happiness and expansion which had arisen one morning in that childlike and poetic imagination. The fear of being ridiculous had seized hold of him, or else the fear of being cured of his invincible and fatal passion for Thérèse.

He stood there, not answering Catherine, who having

much to do to prepare for the arrival of her dear mistress, decided to leave him be. Laurent was in the grip of an extreme agitation. He was wondering why Thérèse was returning to Paris without having told him. Was she coming back secretly with Palmer, or had she done the same as Laurent? Had she made him a proclamation of a happiness that did not yet exist, and the very idea of which had already evaporated? Didn't this sudden and mysterious return conceal a rupture with Dick? The idea simultaneously delighted and horrified Laurent. A thousand different ideas and emotions battled in his head and in his nerves. There was a moment when reality seemed to disintegrate and he convinced himself these pieces of furniture covered in grey sheets were tombs in a cemetery. The idea of death had always horrified him and in spite of himself he thought about it all the time. He could see it in some form or other all around him. He felt he was surrounded by funeral shrouds, and started with fright, calling out:

'Who is dead then? Is it Thérèse? Is it Palmer? I can see it, I can sense it, someone is dead, someone connected with this place I've just returned to…!'

" No," he replied, speaking to himself, "it's you. The only time you were ever really alive was in this house, and now you come back to it limp, abandoned, forgotten like a corpse!"

Catherine entered again without his noticing, lifted off the covers, dusted the furniture, flung wide the closed windows and shutters, and placed flowers in the tall Chinese vases standing on the gilt side tables. Then she came over to him and said:

'Well! What's this? What are you doing here?'

Laurent emerged from his dream, and looking distractedly

around him, saw the flowers multiplied in the mirrors, the Boule furniture gleaming in the sunlight, a whole scene set for celebration, which had replaced, as if by magic, the morbid atmosphere of absence so redolent of death.

His hallucination took a different path.

'What am I doing here?' he said, smiling sombrely. 'Yes, what *am* I doing here? It is a festive occasion here today in Thérèse's house, it is a day of happiness and forgetting. This is a lover's assignation that the mistress of the house is preparing, and the person she is expecting is clearly not me, a dead man! What is a corpse doing in a bridal bedroom? And what is she going to say when she sees me here? She will say what you say, poor old woman, she will say: "Go away! Your place is in a coffin!"'

Laurent spoke as if in a fever. Catherine took pity on him. "He's mad," she thought, "he's always been mad."

And as she was thinking what she might say to send him away as gently as possible, she heard a carriage drawing up in the street. In her joy at seeing Thérèse again, she forgot Laurent and ran to greet her.

Palmer was at the door with Thérèse; but being anxious to change out of his dusty travelling clothes and not wishing to leave to Thérèse the tedious task of unloading the post-chaise at her own house, he climbed straight back in and gave orders to be taken to the Hôtel Meurice, telling Thérèse he would return with her trunks in two hours and come and dine with her.

Thérèse embraced her good Catherine, and while asking her how she had been during her absence, walked eagerly towards the house. She entered with that curiosity one instinctively feels, impatient or anxious or joyful, to set eyes again on the place where one has lived for any length of time. She entered so eagerly that Catherine did not have a moment to tell her that Laurent was there; and she caught him, pale, absorbed and as if turned to stone, sitting on the sofa in her salon. He had not heard the carriage, or the busy sounds of doors opening either. He was still deep in his gloomy reveries when he saw her standing before him. He gave a terrible cry, sprang up to embrace her and fell gasping, almost fainting, at her feet.

They had to remove his cravat and give him ether to inhale; he choked, and his heartbeats were so violent his whole body was shaken as if by electrical impulses. Thérèse, frightened to see him like this, thought he had fallen ill again. Youthful vigour was soon restored to him however, and she noticed how he had regained a little weight. He swore a hundred times his health had never been better, and that he was happy to see her as beautiful again and her eye as limpid again as in the first days of their love. He knelt before her and kissed her feet in token of his respect and his adoration. His outpourings were so effusive that Thérèse was troubled by them and believed it her duty to remind him as quickly as possible of her imminent departure and imminent marriage to Palmer.

'What? What is this? What are you saying?' Laurent exclaimed, as pale as if a thunderbolt had landed at his feet. 'Departure! Marriage…! How? Why? Am I still dreaming? Did you really say those words?'

'Yes,' she replied, 'I'm saying them now. I wrote them in a letter to you. Did you not receive it?'

'Departure! Marriage!' Laurent repeated. 'But you said

before it was impossible. You must remember! What about those times I wanted to protect you from people attacking your reputation by giving you my own name, my very life? And you, you said: "Never, never, while that man is alive!" Has he died then? Or do you love Palmer in a way you never loved me, since you're prepared to overcome for his sake scruples I considered well-founded, and to face down a terrible scandal that seems inevitable to me?'

'Count *** is no more, and I am free.'

Laurent was so stunned by this revelation that he forgot all his good intentions as a disinterested and fraternal friend. What Thérèse had foreseen in Genoa became reality in the most extraordinarily painful of ways. Laurent saw before him an exalted vision of the happiness he could have known by becoming Thérèse's husband, and he shed rivers of tears which no words of reason or remonstration could stop, his troubled and despairing soul heedless to anything but its misery. His grief was so violently expressed and his tears so genuine that Thérèse could not help but be affected by the pathetic and distressing scene. She had never been able to witness Laurent's sufferings without feeling herself all the pity a scolding but vanquished mother feels. She tried in vain to restrain her own tears. They were not tears of regret; she had no illusions about Laurent's reaction, which was nothing more than a reaction; but it worked on her nerves, and the nerves of a woman such as Thérèse were the very fibres of her heart, twisted now by a suffering she could not explain to herself.

She finally succeeded in calming him down, and by speaking to him gently and affectionately, in getting him to accept her marriage as the wisest and best solution for her and for himself. Laurent eventually agreed, with a sad smile.

'Yes, of course,' he said. 'I would have made an abominable husband, and *he*, he will make you happy! Heaven owed you some reward and recompense. You are quite right to thank heaven for this outcome, and to feel it rescues us both, you from a miserable life and me from a remorse worse than even in the old days. It's because it's all so true, so wise, so logical and so well-arranged that I am so unhappy!'

And he began to sob again.

Palmer returned without anyone hearing him arrive. There was a sense of dread in him, and although nothing in his actions was premeditated, he approached the house like a jealous man about to confront a challenge, not ringing the bell and walking carefully so that the parquet flooring did not creak.

He stopped at the sitting room door and recognised the voice of Laurent.

"Ah! I knew it!" he said to himself, plucking at the glove he had been about to set on the handle, apparently to give himself time to reflect before entering.

He thought he ought to knock.

'Come in!' Thérèse called sharply, surprised that anyone should do her the insult of knocking at the door of her sitting room.

Seeing that it was Palmer, she grew pale. What he had just done spoke more eloquently than any number of words: he suspected her.

Palmer saw this sudden pallor and was unable to grasp its real cause. He also saw that Thérèse had been crying; and the sight of Laurent's racked features was enough to disturb his own emotions. The first glance the two men involuntarily exchanged was a glance of hatred and provocation; then they both took a step forward, uncertain whether to shake hands or strangle each other.

In that moment, Laurent was the better and more sincere of the two, for he had spontaneous impulses which redeemed his faults. He opened his arms and folded Palmer in an enthusiastic embrace, without concealing his tears, which began to flow again.

'But what is all this?' Palmer asked him, looking at Thérèse.

'I don't know,' she responded firmly. 'I have just said we were leaving in order to get married. He is overwhelmed with grief. He apparently thinks we are going to forget him. Tell him, Palmer, that near or far, we shall always love him.'

'He's a spoilt child!' Palmer continued. 'He ought to know that my given word is unbreakable, and that I want your happiness above all else. So shall we now have to take him with us to America to stop him from being miserable and making you cry, Thérèse?'

There was something ambivalent about the tone in which these words were spoken. They contained the accents of a fatherly friendship, shot through with a deep and unconquerable bitterness.

Thérèse understood. She asked for her shawl and hat, saying to Palmer:

'We're going to dine out, at a restaurant. Catherine was only expecting me, and there isn't enough in the house to make dinner for two.'

'You mean dinner for three,' Palmer said, still half bitter, half affectionate.

'But no, I'm not dining with you,' Laurent replied, at last realising what Palmer was thinking. 'I must leave you; I'll come back to say goodbye. What day are you leaving?'

'In four days' time,' said Thérèse.

'At least!' said Palmer, looking at her in a strange manner. 'But that's no reason why the three of us shouldn't have dinner together today. Laurent, do me the pleasure. We shall go to the *Frères-Provençaux*, and afterwards we can go for a ride in the Bois de Boulogne. It will remind us of Florence and the *parco delle Cascine*. Come now, I would consider it a favour.'

'I am otherwise engaged,' Laurent said.

'Well, disengage yourself!' Palmer continued. 'There are pens and paper there. Write, write, please!'

Palmer spoke in so decisive a tone that it spared Laurent further hesitation. It seemed to him like an echo of his customary amiable directness. Thérèse had wanted him to refuse, and she could have made him understand so with a look; but Palmer's gaze was on her all the time, and he appeared to be in a frame of mind where everything was interpreted in the worst possible way.

Laurent was very sincere. When he lied, he was the first to be convinced. He believed himself strong enough to carry off this delicate situation, and it was his upright and generous intention to restore Palmer to his former state of trust. Unfortunately, when the human spirit, carried up by lofty aspiration, has scaled certain peaks, if it is then seized by dizziness, it does not merely descend, it tumbles precipitously. That is what was happening to Palmer. A man of loyalty and heart more than all others, it had been his ambitious intention to try to override the inner emotions of an altogether too delicate situation. His belief in his capacities deceived him; who could blame him for that? And he threw himself into the abyss, dragging Thérèse and Laurent with him. Who would not pity all three of them? All three had dreamed of scaling the heavens and attaining the serene regions where passions have nothing earthly about them any longer; but that is not given to man: it is already a great deal for him to believe himself for an instant capable of loving without anxiety and suspicion.

Dinner was a morbidly sad affair; although Palmer, who had assumed the duties of host, set his heart on offering his guests the choicest dishes and wines, everything turned to ashes in their mouths; and Laurent, after trying in vain to recapture the sweetly peaceful state of mind he had enjoyed with these two people after his illness in Florence, declined to accompany them to the Bois de Boulogne. Palmer, who had drunk more than he was accustomed to in order to dull his sensitivities, insisted in a manner that caused Thérèse to lose patience with him.

'Wait a moment,' she told him. 'Don't be so obstinate. Laurent is right to refuse. In the Bois de Boulogne, we shall be on public view in your open carriage, and we could meet people who know us. There is no reason why they should understand the exceptional situation the three of us are in, and they could easily imagine very unflattering things on each of our accounts.'

'Well, let's go back to your house,' Palmer said. 'I'll take the carriage out by myself afterwards, I feel the need for some fresh air.'

Laurent slipped away, seeing that it appeared to be a

deliberate plan on Palmer's part to leave him alone together with Thérèse, seemingly so that he could keep watch on them or catch them out. He went home much saddened, telling himself that perhaps Thérèse was not in fact happy, and a little pleased in spite of himself to be able to think that Palmer was not above human nature, as he had imagined, and as Thérèse had portrayed him in her letters.

We will pass rapidly over the week that followed, a week which undermined, hour by hour, the heroic romance envisaged with more or less conviction by the three unfortunate friends. The most disillusioned had been Thérèse, since after many fears and much sensible consideration, she had decided to engage her life in a certain course, and since, whatever injustices Palmer might perpetrate henceforward, she felt duty-bound, and wished to keep her word.

Palmer released her from it all of a sudden, after a number of manifestations of suspicion that were even more insulting for being unvoiced than all Laurent's harsh words had ever been.

One morning, Palmer, having spent the night concealed in Thérèse's garden, was about to withdraw when she appeared by the gate and stopped him.

'Well!' she said. 'You have kept watch for six hours, and I could see you from my room. Are you thoroughly convinced now that no one came to me in the night?'

Thérèse was ruffled, but nevertheless, by provoking the explanation that Palmer consistently refused to give her, she still hoped to give him back his former confidence in her; but he saw matters differently.

'I see, Thérèse,' he told her, 'that you are tired of me, since you demand a confession which would make me despicable in your eyes. It would not have cost you much though, to close them to a weakness of mine which has not done you any real harm. Why do you not let me suffer in silence? Am I the one who has insulted you and heaped bitter sarcasms on your head? Am I the one who has written you volumes of offensive things, who has then come and wept at your feet the next day and made wild promises, only to begin torturing you all over again the day after? Have I ever even asked you a single indiscreet question? Why were you not peacefully sleeping last night, while I was sitting on this bench and not disturbing your rest by shouts and tears? Can you not forgive me for being the victim of a feeling I do perhaps blush at, but which I at least have sufficient pride to wish and to be able to hide? You have forgiven a man who had far less courage for doing far more than that.'

'I have forgiven him nothing, Palmer, since I have left him and have no intention of going back to him. As for that feeling, which you admit to and believe you have kept hidden, I can tell you that it stands out as clear as day for me, and I am its victim more than you are. You should know that I find it deeply humiliating, and that coming from a strong and thoughtful man like you, it is a hundred times more wounding than the offences of a raving child.'

'Yes, yes, that is quite true,' Palmer continued. 'And so now you are offended, through my fault, and will be forever angry with me! Well! Thérèse, everything is over between us. Do for me what you have done for Laurent: let me keep your friendship.'

'You are leaving me then?'

'Yes, Thérèse; but don't forget, when you agreed to commit yourself to me, I laid at your feet my name, my fortune and my esteem. My word is my bond, and I will keep my promise. Let us get married here, without ceremony or celebration; you will accept my name and half my income, and after that…'

'After that?' said Thérèse.

'After that I shall leave, I shall go and embrace my mother… and you will be free!'

'Is that a threat of suicide?'

'No, on my honour! Suicide is an act of cowardice, especially when one has a mother like mine. I shall travel, I shall resume my journey round the world, and you will not hear of me again!'

Thérèse was revolted by such a proposition.

'This would sound like a bad joke to me, Palmer,' she told him, 'if I didn't know you to be a serious man. I like to believe you do not think me the sort of person who could accept the name and the money you offer as a solution to a case of conscience. Never make any such suggestion again, I would be most offended.'

'Thérèse! Thérèse!' Palmer cried desperately, gripping her arm tight enough to bruise it. 'Swear to me, on the memory of the child you lost, that you don't love Laurent any more, and I'll fall at you feet and beg to be pardoned for that injustice.'

Thérèse pulled her bruised arm free and looked at him in silence. She was offended to the depths of her soul by the oath he demanded; she found its terms even more cruel and brutal than the physical injury she had just suffered.

'My child,' she finally exclaimed through her stifled sobs, 'I swear to you, now in heaven, that no man will ever again so demean your poor mother!'

She stood up and went back into her bedroom, where she locked herself in. She felt so absolutely innocent that she could not descend to justifying herself to Palmer, like a guilty woman. And then she foresaw a dreadful future with a man who could nurture such jealousy, a man who had twice provoked the situation he thought would be dangerous for her and then found cause to accuse her when the crime was his own imprudence. She reflected on the terrible life her mother had lived, with a husband jealous of the past; and she told herself rightly that after the unhappiness of enduring a passion like Laurent's, she had been insane to believe in happiness with another man.

Palmer had arguments on his side and enough pride to make it impossible for him either to hope to make Thérèse happy after a scene such as the one which had just taken place. He felt that his jealousy would not go away, and he persisted in believing it well-founded. He wrote to Thérese:

"My friend, forgive me if I have hurt you; but I cannot fail to acknowledge that I was going to lead you into a pit of despair. You love Laurent, you have always loved him in spite of yourself, and perhaps you always will love him. It is your destiny. I wanted to rescue you from it, and you wanted that too. I also acknowledge that in accepting my love you were sincere, and that you did everything you could to respond. On my side, I allowed myself to harbour many illusions; but each day, since Florence, I felt them ebb away. If he had continued to be as graceless and ungrateful as before, my cause would have been saved; but his repentance and his gratitude softened your feelings towards him. I was touched myself, and yet I forced myself to believe I was not under threat. The effort was in vain. From that time on, between the two of you, and because of me, there have been difficulties you have never mentioned to me but which I guessed easily enough. He began to love you as he did before, and you, even though you stoutly defended yourself, you regretted being committed to me. Alas, Thérèse! That is when you should have taken back your word. I was prepared to release you from it. I gave you the freedom to sail from La Spezia with him: why did you not do so?

"Forgive me, I am reproaching you for having suffered greatly in order to make me happy and commit yourself to me. I have struggled too, I assure you! And now, if you still wish to accept my devotion, I am ready to struggle and suffer some more. Consider whether you wish to suffer yourself, and whether, by following me to America, you hope to be cured of this unhappy passion and the threat it poses of an appalling future. I am ready to take you; but let us not speak of Laurent again, I beg you, and do not make me a criminal for having guessed the truth. Let us remain friends, come and live in my mother's house, and if, in a few years, you do not find me unworthy of you, accept my name and a future lived in America, with no thought of ever returning to France.

"I shall stay in Paris for a week while waiting for your answer.

RICHARD."

Thérèse rejected an offer wounding to her pride. She still loved Palmer, and yet she felt so offended to be offered mercy when she had nothing to reproach herself for, that she concealed from him the rending of her soul. She felt in addition that she could resume no sort of connection with him without prolonging a torment he no longer had the strength to hide, and that their life henceforth would be struggle or bitterness at every moment. She left Paris with Catherine, telling no one where she was going, and shut herself away in a little rustic house which she rented, for three months, out in the provinces.

XII

Palmer left for America, bearing away with dignity a deep wound, but unable to admit he had been in error. There was in him a degree of stubbornness which sometimes affected his character, but only to the extent that it helped him accomplish certain actions, not for the purposes of persisting in some painful and truly difficult course. He had believed himself capable of curing Thérèse of her fatal love, and through his earnest faith, high-minded, unwise if you will, he had achieved that miracle. But now he had lost the fruit of his labour at the moment of picking it, because his faith had failed at the final test.

It must also be noted that the worst possible circumstances for establishing a serious relationship are those in which a person tries too soon to possess a heart which has recently been broken. The rosy dawn of such a union may suggest sunny prospects; but retrospective jealousy is an incurable disease and brings on storms that even old age may not disperse.

If Palmer had been a truly strong man, or if his strength had been of a calmer and more reasoning nature, he could have saved Thérèse from the disasters he believed lay ahead for her. Perhaps he ought to have, for she had entrusted herself to him with a sincerity and lack of self-interest worthy of care and respect. But many men who wish to be and seem to be strong are merely energetic, and Palmer was one of those men about whom one might remain mistaken for a considerable time. Such as he was, he certainly deserved all the regrets Thérèse felt. We shall soon see that he was capable of the most noble impulses and the most courageous actions. His error consisted entirely of having believed in the lasting solidity of what was, in him, a spontaneous effort of the will.

At first Laurent did not know about Palmer's departure for America; he was dismayed to find Thérèse had also left, without bidding him farewell. All he had received were these few lines:

"You have been the only person in France to know about my proposed marriage to Palmer. That marriage is now broken off. Protect us all by keeping the whole subject to yourself. I am leaving."

While writing to Laurent these few chilly words, Thérèse felt a kind of bitterness towards him. Was that fateful child not the cause of all the misfortunes and griefs of her life?

She soon felt, however, that this time her vexation was misplaced. Laurent's behaviour with Palmer and herself had been exemplary during that unfortunate week in which everything had come apart. After the emotions of his initial reaction, he had accepted the situation with complete candour, and had done all he could to bear Palmer no ill will. He had not once sought to turn to his own advantage the injustice Palmer inflicted on Thérèse. He had never ceased to speak of him with respect and friendship. Through a strange combination of moral circumstances it was he, this time, who played the more handsome role. And then Thérèse could not help recognising that if Laurent was sometimes horrifying in his wild moods, nothing little or base entered his thinking.

For the three months following Palmer's departure, Laurent continued to prove himself worthy of Thérèse's friendship. He had been able to discover her hideaway and he did nothing to disturb her there. He wrote to make gentle complaint at the cold manner of her farewell, to reproach her for not having taken him into her confidence in her distress, for not having treated him as her brother; was he not "created and put into the world to serve her, console her, avenge her if need be?" Then came questions which Thérèse could not avoid answering. Had Palmer committed any outrage against her person? Did he need to go to him and demand satisfaction?

"Have I been negligent in some way which has wounded you? Have you any reason to reproach me? I do not believe so, my God! If I am the cause of your pain, berate me, and if I have no part in it, tell me I am allowed to weep with you."

Thérèse justified Palmer's behaviour without giving any explanation for it. She forbade Laurent to discuss Palmer with her. In her generous resolve not to leave any stain on her fiancé's memory, she allowed it to be thought that the rupture came from her alone. This had the effect, perhaps, of restoring in Laurent hopes which she had never intended permitting him to harbour; but there are situations where, whatever one does, one makes an unfortunate move, and where any step is a step on the road to perdition.

Laurent's letters were infinitely gentle and affectionate. He wrote without art, without pretension, and often without taste or propriety. He was sometimes full of empathy and good faith, at others trivial and unabashed. With all their faults, his letters seemed dictated by a sense of conviction which made them irresistibly persuasive, and one could feel in every word the fires of youth and the bubbling sap of an artist of genius.

And beyond all this, Laurent began to work again with ardour, determined never again to relapse into a life of disorder. His heart bled at the privations Thérèse had endured in order to provide him with the means to travel, to find clean air and health in Switzerland. He was determined to pay her back as swiftly as he could.

Thérèse soon felt that the affection of her *poor child*, as he always called himself, was something she cherished, and that, if it could continue in this way, it would be the best and purest feeling of her life.

She encouraged him in motherly responses to persevere in this pattern of work he had returned to, he said, for good. These letters were gentle, resigned, imbued with a chaste tenderness; but Laurent saw a mortal sadness breaking through their surface. Thérèse confessed to being mildly unwell, and his mind was filled with ideas of death, which she laughed off with a melancholy that stabbed at his heart. She really was unwell. With no love and no work, a sense of emptiness was all-pervasive. She had brought away with her a small sum of money, the remainder of her Genoese earnings, and she was eking it out with the strictest economy in order to remain away in the country for as long as possible. She had developed a horror of Paris. And then perhaps she had gradually come to feel the desire, though simultaneously fearing it, to see Laurent changed once more, submissive and altered in every respect, as he demonstrated in his letters.

She hoped that he would marry; since he had once shown vague inclinations in that direction, the good thought might occur to him again. She encouraged him towards it. Sometimes he said yes, sometimes no. Thérèse was always on the alert for signs of any revival of the old love in Laurent's letters: he came close to it just a little every time, but now with an exquisite delicacy, and the emotion that dominated these returns to a feeling which had never been entirely extinguished was a mellow affection, a broad sensitivity, a sort of enthusiastic filial piety.

By the arrival of winter, Thérèse, seeing her resources all but gone, was forced to return to Paris, where her clientèle and her duties towards herself waited. She concealed her return from Laurent, not wishing to see him too quickly; but through some unknown powers of divination, he happened along the virtually deserted street where her little house stood. He saw the shutters open and entered, overjoyed. It was a naïve, almost childlike joy, which would have rendered ridiculous and prudish a suspicious and frosty reception. He left Thérèse to her dinner, begging her to call that evening to see a painting he had just finished, saying he absolutely insisted on having her opinion before delivering it. It was sold and paid for; but if she had any suggestions to make, he would work on it a few days more. This was no longer the deplorable period when Thérèse "didn't know what she was talking about," when she "had a portraitist's narrow and literal judgement," when she was "incapable of understanding a work of imagination," and so forth. She was now "his muse and his inspiring power." Without the aid of her divine breath, he could do nothing. With her advice and her encouragement, his talent would fulfil all it promised.

Thérèse set aside the past, and without being enraptured by the present, she believed it not right to deny what one artist never denies another. She took a cab after her dinner and went to Laurent's studio.

She found the studio filled with lamps and the painting magnificently lit. The painting was a fine and beautiful thing. That unusual genius had the ability, whilst not in active practice, to make the rapid progress which those who persevere at their work are not always able to make. There had been, as a result of his travels and his illness, a year's interruption to his work, and it seemed that, by reflection alone, the faults of its initial exuberance had disappeared. At the same time, he had acquired new qualities which one would have imagined were foreign to his nature: correctness in drawing, greater smoothness in the figurative aspects, a charm in the execution, all the things likely to please the public without detracting from its merits in the eyes of fellow artists.

Thérèse was both moved and delighted. She expressed her admiration with enthusiasm. She told him all the things she felt would encourage the noble pride appropriate to genius and help him put behind him the extravagances of the past. She could find no fault with the piece and even forbade him to add a single brush stroke.

Laurent, modest in his manners and in his language, had more pride than Thérèse had credited him with. He found Thérèse's praise, deep down in his heart, utterly exhilarating. He felt very strongly that out of all the people capable of appreciating him, she was the cleverest and the most perceptive. He also felt, rising imperiously in him once more, the old need for her as someone with whom to share an artist's torments and joys, and the hope of becoming a master, that is to say a man, which she alone could bring him in his moments of doubt.

After Thérèse had contemplated the painting for a long time, she turned round to consider a figure Laurent was asking her to look at, saying it would please her even more. But instead of a canvas, Thérèse saw her mother, standing smiling in the doorway of Laurent's bedroom.

Mme C… had come to Paris, not knowing exactly when Thérèse would be returning from the country. On this occasion, a genuinely important matter brought her here: the marriage of her son, and M. C… had himself been here for some time. Thérèse's mother, learning from her daughter that she had renewed her correspondence with Laurent and fearing for the future, had called on him unannounced to say everything a mother can say to a man to prevent him from making her daughter unhappy.

Laurent was eloquent in matters of the heart. He had been able to reassure the poor mother, and he had persuaded her to linger, telling her: 'Thérèse will be here soon. I want to swear to her, in front of you, that I shall always be for her what she wishes me to be, her brother or her husband, but in all cases her slave.'

It was a very pleasant surprise for Thérèse to find her mother there, whom she had not expected to see so soon. They embraced with tears of joy. Laurent led them to a small sitting room filled with flowers, where a luxurious tea was served. Laurent was rich, he had just earned ten thousand francs. He was happy and proud to be able to pay Thérèse back all she had spent on him. He was perfectly lovable that evening; he won the daughter's heart and the mother's trust, and he had, none the less, the delicacy not to whisper a word of love to Thérèse. Far from it: in kissing the hands of both these women, he declared in all sincerity that this was the best day of his life, and that never, even in private with Thérèse, had he felt so happy and so pleased with himself.

It was Mme C... who after a few days was the first to broach with Thérèse the subject of marriage. That poor woman, who had sacrificed everything to outward appearances and who, despite her domestic unhappiness, believed she had done the right thing, could not bear the idea of seeing her daughter abandoned by Palmer, and she thought that Thérèse ought henceforth to re-establish her place in the world by choosing someone else. Laurent was a famous man now and very much in vogue. On the surface there could never have been a more suitable match. The great and youthful artist had remedied his errant ways. Thérèse's influence on him had overcome the greatest crises of his painful transformation. His attachment to her was unbreakable. It had become a duty for the pair of them to reforge a link which had never been completely broken and which, however hard they may subsequently try, never could be.

Laurent found a highly specious argument to excuse his past failings. Thérèse, he said, had spoiled him from the start through too much softness and resignation. If she had shown her offence at his very first display of ingratitude she would have corrected in him the bad habit, contracted in his contacts with bad women, of giving way to his own whims and losses of temper. She would have taught him the respect one owes to a woman who has given herself out of love.

And then, another consideration that Laurent put forward to excuse himself from blame, and which seemed more serious, was this, which he had already hinted at in his letters:

'Probably,' he told her, 'I was ill without realising it the first time I behaved badly. A brain fever is a thing that seems to strike like a bolt from the blue, and yet it is impossible to believe, with a young and healthy man, that there wasn't some terrible crisis in the making, a long time in advance, maybe causing mental disturbance and beyond his willpower to control. Isn't that what happened to me, my poor Thérèse, in the weeks leading up to the illness that nearly killed me? Neither you nor I could work out the reason for it, and as for me, I often woke up in the mornings and thought about what you had gone through the previous day without being able to tell what was real from what was the night's dreams. You know I couldn't work, and I took an unhealthy aversion to the place where we were staying, and I'd already had an extraordinary hallucination in the forest of ***. And you know how when you reproached me gently for certain cruel words and unjust accusations, I used to listen to you with a dazed look on my face, believing it was you who had in fact dreamed all of that. Poor woman! There was *I*, accusing *you* of being mad! It's obvious that I was mad, and can you not forgive wrongs that were involuntary? Compare my behaviour after my illness with my behaviour before! Wasn't it something like a reawakening of my soul? Didn't you suddenly find me as trusting, compliant and devoted as I was sceptical, irascible and selfish before the crisis that brought me back to myself? And since that moment have I given you any cause to reproach me? Didn't I accept your marriage to Palmer as a punishment I well deserved? You saw me dying with grief at the idea of losing you for ever: did I say a word to you against your fiancé? If you had ordered me to run after him and even blow my brains out if that would bring him back, I would have done so. Because my soul and my life are yours! Is that what you still want? Say the word, and if my existence is obstructing you and ruining your life, I am ready to extinguish it. Say the word, Thérèse, and you will never hear again of this unfortunate who has no other purpose on this earth but to live or to die for you.'

The character of Thérèse had weakened under the pressure of this double love, which after all, had been no more than two acts of the same drama. If this first love had not been trampled and broken, Palmer would never have thought of marrying her, and the effort she had made to commit herself to him was perhaps no more than a reaction to the despair. Laurent had never disappeared from her life, since the argument Palmer felt it necessary to deploy to convince her was to harp endlessly on the disastrous liaison he wished to make her forget and which some fatal compulsion made him bring continually to her mind.

And then the return to friendship after their rupture had been for Laurent a genuine return to passion, whereas, for Thérèse, it had been a new phase of devotion, more affectionate and delicate even than love. She had been greatly injured by Palmer's abandoning of her, but had not buckled. She still had strength enough to combat injustice, and it can be said her whole strength lay there. She was not the eternally suffering woman who utters plaintive cries of futile regret and incurable desire. Powerful reactions were at work in her, and her well-developed intelligence naturally assisted her. She had a high idea of moral freedom, and when another person's love and faith left her bankrupt, she had a proper pride in not arguing over the broken pact piece by piece. She even found something satisfying in the idea of giving back, generously and without reproach, both independence and peace to whoever might claim them.

But she had become a good deal less strong than in her earlier youth in this one respect: she had recovered the need to love and to believe, a need sent into long abeyance by an extraordinary personal disaster. For a long time she had imagined she would live as she did, and that art would be her only passion. She had been deceiving herself, and she could no longer carry such illusions into the future. She needed to love, and her greatest misfortune was that she needed to love in a gentle, self-denying manner, to satisfy at all costs the maternal impulse which was seemingly a fated part of her nature and her life. She had acquired the habit of suffering for someone, she needed to suffer still, and if this need, strange perhaps but not unremarked in certain women and even certain men, had not made her as merciful to Palmer as it had to Laurent, it was because Palmer had appeared to her too strong to have any need himself for her devotion. Palmer had thus erred in offering her support and consolation. Thérèse had been unable to see herself as necessary to this man, who wished her to think only of her own concerns.

Laurent, more naïve, had the one particular charm she was fatally attracted to: weakness! He did not mask it from himself, he proclaimed, with effusive frankness and tireless intensity, the touching frailty which accompanied his genius.

Alas, he too was deceiving himself! He was no more genuinely weak than Palmer was genuinely strong. He had his moments, he spoke, always like a child of heaven, and as soon as his weakness had won the day, he rediscovered his strength and made everyone suffer, as do all children whom one adores.

Laurent was doomed to a fateful inevitability. He said so himself in his lucid moments. It seemed that, born from the conjunction of two angels, he had drunk the milk of a fury, and there had remained in his blood a sediment of rage and despair. His was one of those natures, more common than may be thought in human kind and in the two sexes, which with all its sublime ideas and intense emotions, cannot scale the peak of its powers without at once falling into a sort of intellectual epilepsy.

And then, as much as Palmer, he wished to undertake the impossible, namely to claim he could graft happiness on to despair and savour the heavenly joys of a conjugal bliss and sacred friendship erected over the ruins of a recently devastated past. What these two souls, bleeding from the wounds they had received, had needed, was rest: Thérèse cried out for it with the anguish of awful presentiment; but Laurent felt he had lived through ten centuries during the ten months of their separation, and he was becoming ill from an excess of desire rising in his soul, which must have alarmed Thérèse more than any desire of the senses.

It was through the very nature of this desire that she unhappily allowed herself to feel reassured. Laurent seemed to be regenerated to the point of having restored moral love to the prime place it should occupy, and he now found himself alone in Thérèse's company without any of the emotional transports which used formerly to worry her. He was able, for hours at a time, to speak to her with an affection almost sublime in character, the very man, he said, who had long believed himself voiceless, and who could at last feel his genius expand and take wing in loftier regions! He forced himself on Thérèse's future by ceaselessly demonstrating to her that she had a duty to him, a holy task to fulfil: to guard him from the excesses of youth, from the false ambitions of maturity and from the depraved selfishness of old age. He spoke about himself, and always about himself: why not? It was a subject he spoke on so well! Through her, he would be a great artist, a great heart, a great man; she owed him all this, because she had saved his life! And Thérèse, with the fatal simplicity of loving hearts, came to find his arguments irrefutable and to consider as a duty what had begun as an earnest entreaty for forgiveness.

Thérèse thus allowed their fatal bonds to be taken up again; her one happy inspiration was to delay the marriage, wishing to test Laurent's determination on this point, fearing, on his account alone, an irrevocable commitment. If it had been solely up to her, the reckless woman would have plunged headlong into a situation from which there was no return.

Thérèse's first happiness had not lasted *the span of a week*, as a happy song sadly puts it; the second did not last twenty-four hours. Laurent's reactions were sudden and violent, by reason of the sheer intensity of his joys. We say his reactions, Thérèse said his *retractions*, and that was the right word. He obeyed that inexorable need some adolescents feel to kill or destroy a thing they love to the point of passion. These cruel instincts have been noticed in men of very different character,

230

and history has described them as perverse instincts: it would be more accurate to describe them as instincts which have been perverted, either by a mis-functioning of the brain encouraged by the milieu in which these men were born, or by the fact of enjoying an impunity, fatal to reason, which certain positions have guaranteed them from their first steps in life. Young kings have been known to slit the bellies of creatures they seemed to treasure, for the sole pleasure of seeing their entrails quiver. Men of genius are also kings in the realms they inhabit; they are even absolute monarchs, whose very power intoxicates them. There are some who are tortured by the thirst to dominate, and whom the joy of guaranteed domination excites to the point of madness.

Such was Laurent, in whom certainly, two quite distinct men fought each other. It might have been said that two souls, arguing over which should be the one to animate the bodily shell, had embarked on an unremitting struggle to drive each other out. Caught between these opposing forces, the unfortunate creature lost his independence of will, and fell exhausted each day at the foot of the angel or the demon which had gained the victory.

And when he analysed himself, he seemed sometimes to be reading from a book of spells and to be able to give with terrifying and magnificent clarity the key to the mysterious conspiracy which had him in its power.

'Yes,' he said to Thérèse, 'I am a victim of that phenomenon that magicians used to call possession. Two spirits have seized control of me. Is there in reality a good and a bad? No, I do not believe so: the one which frightens you, the sceptical, the violent, the terrible, does bad things only because it cannot be the master of the good, as it would understand it. It would like to be calm, philosophical, playful, tolerant. The other does not wish this to be the way of things. It wants to be the good angel: it wants to be ardent, enthusiastic, exclusive, devoted, and being mocked, denied and wounded by its opposite, it becomes dark and cruel in its turn, with the effect that two angels I carry inside me combine to give birth to a demon.'

And on this extraordinary subject, Laurent spoke and wrote to Thérèse all manner of things, as full of beauty as they were of horror, which appeared to be true and to add new rights to the impunity he seemed to have given himself with regard to her.

Everything Thérèse had feared she might suffer because of Laurent by becoming Palmer's wife, she had to suffer because of Palmer by becoming Laurent's companion once more. A horrible retrospective jealousy, the worst of all, because it is irritated by anything and soothed by nothing, gnawed at the heart of the unfortunate artist and addled his brain. The memory of Palmer became for him a spectre, a vampire. His mind revolved round the obsessive desire that Thérèse should tell him every last detail of her life in Genoa and Porto-Venere, and as she refused, he accused her of having sought, during that whole period, to *deceive* him. Forgetting that at that same period Thérèse had written to him: *I love Palmer*, and a little later had written: *I am marrying him*, he reproached her for having consistently kept him dangling on the cord of hope and desire by which he was attached to her and which she controlled with a knowing and treacherous hand. Thérèse set before his eyes their entire correspondence, and he recognised that she had told him, in the stated places and at the stated times, everything that loyalty required should be said in order to separate him from her. He grew calmer and agreed that she had managed his insufficiently extinguished passion with excessive delicacy, introducing him little by little to the truth according to how well he appeared able to receive it without grief, and also to how far she herself had been able to feel confident about the future towards which Palmer was leading her. He recognised that she had never offered him the merest shadow of a lie, even when she had refused to explain herself, and that in the days following his recovery, when he was still deluding himself about an impossible reconciliation, she had told him: "Everything is over between us. What I have decided and accepted concerning my own future is my secret, and you do not have the right to question me."

'Yes, yes, you're right,' Laurent exclaimed. 'I was unjust, this fatal curiosity I have is a torment it was truly criminal to force on you as well. Yes, poor Thérèse, I subjected you to humiliating interrogations, you who owed me nothing. Oblivion was my only due, yet you grant me a generous pardon! I turn things round: I put you on trial, when I am the guilty party, the one condemned! I raise an ungodly hand to rip away the veil of modesty in which your soul has the right and no doubt the duty to conceal its relations with Palmer! Well, I thank you for your proud silence! My regard for you is all the higher. It proves to me that you have never let Palmer interrogate you concerning the mysteries of our own griefs and joys. And I understand the point now: a woman does not owe her lover these confidences; but not only that, she owes it to herself to refuse them. The man who demands them debases the thing he loves. He is asking her to behave badly, whilst at the same time thinking ill of her by associating her with all the fantasies plaguing his mind. Yes, Thérèse, you are right: if you have an ideal before you, it is your job to work to preserve its purity; and I spend all my time profaning it and expelling it from the temple I had built for it!'

After such explanations, and when Laurent said he was ready to signal it with his blood and his tears, it seemed that calm must descend and happiness begin. Nothing of the sort happened. Laurent, eaten up with a secret rage, returned next day to his questions, his insults, his sarcasms. Whole nights were spent in deplorable arguments, in which he seemed to have an absolute need to exercise his own genius by use of the lash, injuring it, torturing it, to make it produce with horrific eloquence a rich stream of invective, and to bring Thérèse and himself to the outer limits of despair. After these storms, there seemed nothing left to do but commit suicide together. Thérèse was expecting it at any time and held herself ready, for she now felt a horror at living; but no such idea had yet entered Laurent's head. Overcome with fatigue, he fell asleep, and his guardian angel seemed to come down and watch over his slumbers, sketching on his features the divine smile of heavenly visions.

The invariable rule with this strange temperament, as absolute as it was extraordinary, decreed that sleep reversed all his resolutions. If he went to bed with his heart full of tenderness, he woke with his mind eager for combat and murder, and equally, if he had gone home cursing the previous night, he hurried round the next morning to bless.

Three times Thérèse left him and fled far away from Paris; three times he ran after her and forced her to forgive his despairing behaviour, for as soon as he had lost her, he adored her and began once more to beg her with all the tears of an impassioned repentance.

In this hell into which she had again plunged, eyes closed and sacrificing her own life, Thérèse was simultaneously wretched and sublime. She took her devotion to such self-destructive lengths that her friends trembled for her; and it earned her the condemnation, almost the contempt, of those proud and wise people who do not know what it is to love.

And besides, this love Thérèse had for Laurent was incomprehensible even to herself. There was nothing sensual in it. Laurent had resumed his old dissolute habits, in an attempt to kill off a love he could not destroy by force of will; and having thus defiled himself, he had become for her an object of disgust more repulsive than a corpse. She no longer had any caresses to give him, and he no longer dared seek any from her. She was no longer defeated and dominated by the charm of his eloquence and by the childlike appeal of his many repentances. She could no longer believe in the future; and the wonderful melting tenderness of their reconciliations which had brought them back together so many times before was now, for her, no more than the dreaded symptom of tempest and shipwreck.

What kept her attached to him was the pity which becomes an unconquerable habit with people one has forgiven, and forgiven so much. It seems that forgiveness engenders forgiveness to the point of satiation, even to the point of idiotic weakness. When a mother has concluded that her child is incorrigible, and that he must either die or bring death, there is no other choice but to abandon him or to accept everything.

Thérèse had been in error every time she had thought to cure Laurent through abandoning him. It is perfectly true that he then became better, but it was conditional on the hope of receiving her forgiveness. When he no longer hoped for that, he relapsed helplessly into idleness and disorder. She then came back to rescue him, and she succeeded in making him work for a few days. But what a price she paid for the little good she managed to do him! When his distaste for normal life overcame him again, he could scarcely find strong enough terms to blame her for trying to turn him into "what her *patron Thérèse Levasseur* had made Jean-Jacques", in other words, according to him, "an idiot and a maniac".

And yet, in Thérèse's pity, for which he begged so ardently only to fling it back in her face once given, there was an enthusiastic and even slightly fanatical respect for the genius of the artist. This woman, whom he accused of being bourgeois and unintelligent when he saw her working with artless persistence for his well-being, was a great artist herself, in her love at least, since she accepted Laurent's tyranny as a divine right and sacrificed her own pride to it, her own work, and what any other less devoted woman would perhaps have called her own glory.

And he, luckless wretch, he could see and appreciate this devotion, and when he became aware of his own ingratitude, he was overwhelmed by a destructive remorse. What he would have needed was a robust and carefree mistress who would have laughed at both his anger and his repentances, and suffered not a jot on his account provided she could still hold sway over him. Thérèse was not such a woman. Weariness and grief were killing her, and seeing her perish before his eyes,

Laurent sought in the suicide of his intelligence, in the poison of drink, momentary forgetfulness of his own tears.

XIII

One evening, he engaged her in such a long and incomprehensible argument that she could no longer follow it and fell into a doze in her armchair. After a few moments a light rustling made her open her eyes. Laurent immediately threw on to the floor some gleaming object: it was a dagger. Thérèse smiled and closed her eyes again. She understood, feebly and as if through the veil of a dream, that he had thought of killing her. By that point it was entirely a matter of indifference to Thérèse. To be able to retreat from living and thinking, whether through sleep or death, she would leave the choice to fate

It was death she felt such contempt for. Laurent believed it was himself, and in a fit of self-contempt, he finally left her.

Three days afterwards Thérèse went to the flower market. She had decided to take out a loan (this life of upsets and squalls was killing her work and ruining her existence) which would enable her to go on a serious journey and be absent for a long time. She bought a white rose bush and sent it to Laurent without giving the porter her name. It was her farewell. When she got home she found a white rose bush, sent anonymously: it was a farewell from Laurent too. They were both leaving; both of them stayed. The coincidence of the rose bushes moved

Laurent to tears. He rushed to Thérèse's house and found her finishing her packing. Her seat was booked for the six o'clock mail coach that evening. Laurent's seat was booked for the same vehicle. They had both had the same idea of going back to see more of Italy, without the other.

'Well, let's go together!' he exclaimed.

'No, I'm not going now,' she replied.

'Thérèse,' he said, 'it's no use our trying, this terrible bond that ties us will never be broken! It's folly to think it still might. My love has withstood everything that can destroy a feeling, everything that can kill a soul. You must love me as I am, or we must die together. Will you love me?'

'I would be willing myself in vain, I can't do it any more,' Thérèse said. 'My heart is exhausted: I think it is dead.'

'Well then! Will you die?'

'I don't care if I do die; you know that; but I don't want anything to do with you in life or in death.'

'Ah, yes! You believe the self is eternal! You don't want to meet me in the other life! Poor martyred creature, I can understand that!'

'We shall not meet each other, Laurent, I am certain of that. Each soul goes towards its natural home. I am called towards rest and peace, and you, wherever you are, you will always be attracted by the tempest.'

'You mean you don't deserve to go to hell!'

'Nor do you. You'll go to a different heaven, that's all!'

'What's left for me in this world, if you leave me?'

'Glory, once you stop looking for love.'

Laurent became pensive. He said to himself many times over: "Glory!" like an automaton, then he knelt before the hearth and poked the fire, as was his habit when he wanted to be alone with his thoughts. Thérèse left the room to cancel the arrangements for her departure. She knew very well Laurent would have followed her.

When she returned she found Laurent quite calm and good-humoured.

'This world,' he told her, 'is no better than a limp comedy; but why should we want to raise ourselves above it since we don't know what exists on a higher plane, or even if anything does? Glory, which you secretly laugh at, as I'm all too aware...'

'I don't laugh at other people's glory...'

'What other people?'

'The ones who believe in it and love it.'

'God knows whether I believe in it, Thérèse, or think it's just a farce and mock it! But you can certainly love a thing you know has little value. You love a stumbling old horse that breaks your neck, and tobacco that poisons you, and a bad play that makes you laugh, and glory, which is just a masquerade! Glory! What is that for a living artist? Articles in the papers which slate you and get your name talked about, and then praises that no one reads, because the public only enjoy bad reviews; and when someone goes into raptures over their particular idol, he doesn't take a bit of notice. And then groups all pressing round a piece of painted canvas then moving off and being succeeded by other groups. And then monumental commissions which send you into transports of joy and ambition and leave you half dead from exhaustion with your great idea still unrealised... and then... the Institute... a collection of people who detest you, and who themselves...'

Here Laurent gave vent to the bitterest sarcasms, and concluded his tirade by saying:

'It doesn't matter! That is what glory consists of in this world! We spit on it but we can't do without it, since there isn't anything better!'

They talked on until it was almost evening, mocking, philosophical, and gradually becoming entirely impersonal. One would have said, to hear and see them, they were two peaceable old friends who had never exchanged a cross word. This strange situation had arisen several times during the worst period of their great crisis: for when their hearts kept quiet, their minds still suited and understood each other.

Laurent felt hungry and asked to dine with Thérèse.

'Aren't you leaving?' she said. 'It's almost time.'

'Well, you're not leaving!'

'I shall leave if you stay.'

'Right, I'll leave, Thérèse! Farewell!'

He strode briskly from the room and was back after an hour.

'I missed the mail coach,' he said. 'I'll go on tomorrow's. Haven't you eaten yet?'

Thérèse, preoccupied, had forgotten the meal before her on the table.

'My dear Thérèse,' he said, 'grant me this one last favour: come and have dinner with me somewhere, and let's go to a show together afterwards. I want to become your friend again, nothing more than that, your friend. That will mark my recovery and the salvation of both of us. Test me out. I shan't be jealous any more, or demanding, or even amorous. Listen, I have to tell you, I have another mistress, a pretty little

241

society woman, slight as a fawn, white and delicate as a sprig of lily of the valley. She's a married woman, I'm a friend of her lover and this is all behind his back. I have two rivals, two chances of a fatal duel every time I see her on her own. It's very exciting, and that's the whole secret of this affair. So, my senses and my imagination are satisfied in that direction; it's my heart pure and simple and the exchanging of my ideas with yours, that's what I'm offering you.'

'I refuse them,' Thérèse said.

'What! You're vain enough to be jealous of a person you no longer love?'

'Certainly not! I'm not giving my whole life over to anyone again, and I can't conceive of the sort of friendship you are asking for without that kind of exclusive devotion. Come and see me as my other friends do, I'd like that; but don't ask me for any more private intimacy, or even the appearance of it.'

'I understand, Thérèse; you have another lover!'

Thérèse shrugged her shoulders and said nothing. He was dying for her to match his boast with a similar claim of her own. Weakened and demoralised, he was beginning to feel his strength return and he needed a battle. He waited anxiously for her to rise to his challenge so that he could heap reproaches and disdain on her head, and inform her perhaps that he had invented this mistress to force her to betray herself. He did not understand the power of Thérèse's inertia. He preferred to believe he was a man hated and deceived rather than some irksome visitor in whom she had no interest.

Her silence wore him down.

'Good evening then,' he said. 'I'm going out to dine, and

after that, to the ball at the Opéra, if I'm not too tipsy.'

Thérèse, left alone, sought inside herself for the hundredth time to understand the workings of his mysterious destiny. What was missing that prevented his from being one of the most splendid of human destinies? Reason.

"But what does reason amount to then?" Thérèse asked herself. "And how can genius exist without it? Is it because genius is such a powerful force it can kill reason and yet live on? Or is reason only an isolated faculty, and its combination with the other faculties not always necessary?"

She fell into a sort of metaphysical reverie. It had always seemed to her that reason was a gathering of ideas and not a discrete item. All the faculties of a well-organised being both lent it something and borrowed from it. It was both the means and the end, and no masterpiece could escape its laws, and no man could have any real value after he had determinedly trampled it underfoot.

She reviewed in her mind the old masters, and also considered the contemporary artists. Everywhere she could see the rule of truth allied to the rule of beauty, yet everywhere there were exceptions, startling anomalies, figures at once dazzling and damaged like Laurent. Aspiring to the sublime was even a malady of the age and the milieu in which Thérèse found herself. It was a kind of fever which gripped the young and made them scorn the conditions of conventional happiness and at the same time the duties of ordinary life. Through the force of events, Thérèse found herself, without having desired or foreseen it, cast into this fatal circle of the human inferno. She had become the companion, the intellectual half of one of those sublime madmen, one of those extravagant geniuses; she was on hand to witness the perpetual agony of Prometheus, the continual furious outbursts of Orestes; she suffered the repercussions of these inexpressible afflictions without understanding their cause, without being able to find their remedy.

God was still present in these rebellious and tortured souls, however, since there were times when the good and enthusiastic side of Laurent would re-emerge, since the pure source of holy inspiration had not run dry; his was not an exhausted talent, and he was perhaps still a man with a great future. Was it right to let him slide into the grip of delirium and wear himself into a stupor?

Thérèse had, as we have said, come too close to the edge of this precipice not to have experienced at times the vertigo it provoked. Her own talent, and her own character, had nearly brought her unwittingly into this same desperate situation. She had known that heightened suffering which makes one see life's miseries on the grand scale, and which floats between the limits of the real and the imaginary. But her spirit now, through a natural reaction, turned towards what is true: which is neither the one nor the other, neither the uncontrolled ideal nor the unpoetically material. She felt this was where beauty lay, and that one needed to seek a material life that was simple and dignified in order to return to the intended life of the soul. She reproached herself heavily for having been untrue to her principles for so long: then a moment later she reproached herself no less heavily for being too preoccupied with her own fate in the presence of the extreme peril that threatened Laurent's.

In all its many voices, that of friendship as much as that

of opinion, the world was calling on her to stand tall again and master herself. That was indeed where duty lay according to the world, whose name in such cases invokes general good order, the interests of society: "Follow the right path, leave those who wander from it to perish." And official religion added: "For the wise and the good, eternal bliss; for the blind and the rebellious, hell!" Is it therefore of small importance to the wise that the crazed should perish?

Thérèse revolted against that conclusion.

"The day I believe myself to be the most perfect, most precious and most excellent being on earth," she said to herself, "I will allow the death penalty on all the others. But if ever the day comes when that is what I believe, will I not be more mad than all the other madmen? Get thee behind me then, folly of vanity, mother of egotism! Better to carry on suffering for someone other than myself!"

It was close to midnight when she rose from the armchair into which she had dropped, inert and shattered four hours previously. Someone had just rung at the door. A porter had brought a box and a note. The box contained a cloak and mask in black satin. The note contained these few words in Laurent's hand: *Senza veder, senza parlar*.

Without seeing, without speaking... what did this puzzle mean? Did he want her to come to the masked ball and thereby afford him the banal adventure of discovering her identity? Did he want to try to love her through a disguise? Was it a poet's fantasy or a libertine's insult?

Thérèse sent the box away and fell back into her chair; but her anxiety left her no time for further speculation. Was it not her duty to do everything she could to draw this victim away from his hell-bent path?

"I shall go," she said. "I shall follow his every step. I shall see and hear what his life is like when he is not with me. I shall know how much truth there is in the base goings-on he tells me about, to what extent his love of evil is innocent or affected, whether he really has depraved tastes or if he is only looking for ways to numb an over-excited mind. When I know all the things about him I wanted not to know, about this unsavoury world, all the things conjured by his recollections and my imagination that I kept at arm's length, I shall perhaps discover some agent, some device that might pull him back from the brink."

She remembered the hooded cloak Laurent had just sent her, although she had hardly given it a glance. It was in satin. She sent out for one in coarse Naples cloth, put on a mask, carefully hid her hair, attached ribbons and bows in varied colours so as to change how she looked should Laurent come to suspect her in that costume, and calling for a carriage, she made her way, alone and resolute, to the Opéra ball.

She had never set foot in the place before. She found the mask intolerable to wear, stifling. She had never tried to alter her voice and did not want anyone to guess her identity. She slipped silently along the corridors, looking for deserted corners when she was tired of walking, not lingering if she saw anyone approaching her, seeming always to be on her way somewhere else, and succeeding more easily than she had hoped in remaining completely alone and free in this swirling crush of people.

It was the period when dancing was not permitted at the Opéra ball, and when the only permitted disguise was the black cloak and hood. So it was a serious and sombre-looking crowd from the outside. It may have been intent on intrigues as disreputable as the bacchanalian proceedings at other gatherings of this kind, but seen from the upper levels, as a whole, it had an imposing aspect. Then suddenly, from time to time, a braying orchestra played wild quadrilles, as if the management, waging war with the police, had wished to incite the crowd to break their prohibition; but no one seemed to think of doing so. The black ant-hill continued its slow march and its whispering in the midst of the din, which was rounded off by a pistol shot, a bizarre, fantastical finale which seemed powerless to disturb the lugubrious character of this festive occasion.

For a while Thérèse was so struck by the spectacle that she forgot where she was and imagined herself in the land of sad dreams. She looked for Laurent, and failed to find him.

She risked going down to the foyer, where, maskless and hidden under no disguise, the men known to all of Paris stood in groups. She made a circuit and was on the point of retreating when she heard someone in a corner speak her name. She turned round and saw the man she had so intensely loved sitting between two young women in masks. Their voices and accents had a quality of limpness and acidity all in one, the tones that betray a weariness of the senses and a bitterness of the spirit.

'Well!' one of them was saying, 'have you given her up at last, that famous Thérèse of yours? I hear she cheated on you when you were down in Italy, and that you didn't want to believe it?'

'He began to suspect,' the other went on, 'the minute he

succeeded in sending the happy rival packing.'

Thérèse was mortally wounded to see the painful story of her life given over to such interpretations, but still more so to see Laurent smile, tell these girls they didn't know what they were saying, and to speak to them of other things with no show of indignation and as if without memory or concern for what he had just heard. Thérèse would never have believed he was not even her friend. Now she was sure of it! She remained where she was, still listening; she could feel a cold sweat stick her mask to her face.

Laurent was saying nothing to these girls, however, that could not be heard by anyone. He chattered, enjoyed their gossip, responding in an easy, companionable manner. They had no great wit, and two or three times he yawned, only half suppressing it. Nevertheless he remained there, unconcerned at being seen by everyone in that company, letting people come up to him and pay court, yawning with fatigue and not real boredom, gentle, absentminded, but friendly, and speaking to these newly-met women as if they had been women from the best circles of society, almost as good and serious friends, sharers in fond memories of pleasures one could freely discuss.

All this continued for a good quarter of an hour. Thérèse stayed where she was. Laurent had his back turned to her. The bench he was sitting on was positioned in the embrasure of a glazed door, its closed and unsilvered panes facing him. When groups of people strolling in the outer corridors stopped beside this door, their suits and cloaks made an opaque background and the window became a black mirror. Multiple reflections of Thérèse appeared in it without her being aware of them. Laurent saw them at intervals without thinking of her; but gradually the immobility of that masked figure began to worry him, and he said to his companions, indicating it in the dark mirror:

'That mask, don't you find it frightening?'

'Do we frighten you, then?'

'No, not you: I can tell the shape of your nose under that scrap of satin. But a face you can't see, that you don't know, and that stares at you with those intense eyes... I'm getting away from here, I've had enough of it.'

'You mean,' they said, 'you've had enough of us?'

'No,' he replied, 'enough of the ball. You can't breathe here. Do you want to come and watch the snow fall? I'm going to the Bois de Boulogne.'

'But you'd catch your death of cold, surely?'

'Why yes, certainly! Shall we go and die? Are you coming?'

'Gracious, no!'

'Who wants to come out in their cloaks and hoods to the Bois de Boulogne with me?' he called, raising his voice.

A group of black figures jostled round him like a flurry of bats.

'What's it worth?' said one.

'Will you do my portrait?' said another.

'Driving or on foot?' said a third.

'A hundred francs a head,' he replied, 'just to kick your feet through the snow by the light of the moon. I shall be following you at a distance. I want to see the effect... how many of you are there?' he added after a few moments. 'Ten! Hardly enough. Never mind, let's start walking!'

Three stayed where they were, saying: 'He hasn't a penny

on him. He'll make us all catch pneumonia, and that'll be all.'

'You're not coming?' he continued. 'That leaves seven! Bravo, a special number, the seven deadly sins! Three cheers for God! I was worried I was going to be bored, but here's an invention that saves me.'

'Listen to that,' Thérèse said, 'an artist's fancy…! He remembers he's a painter. All is not lost.'

She followed this strange company out to the entrance porch to confirm that the fanciful idea was indeed put into practice; but the most determined of the women recoiled in the face of the cold, and Laurent allowed himself to be persuaded to abandon the idea. They wanted him to change their party into a supper for all.

'Good Lord, no!' he said. 'A scared and selfish lot like you? You're absolutely no different from honest women! I go about in better company. Hard luck!'

But they pulled him back into the foyer, and there sprang up between them, various young friends of his, and a troop of shameless females a general discourse so animated and full of exotic propositions that Thérèse, overcome with disgust, withdrew, telling herself it was too late. Laurent loved vice: there was nothing more she could do for him.

Did Laurent love vice, really? No, the slave does not love the yoke and the whip. But when he is a slave through his own fault, when he has allowed his liberty to be taken from him, for want of the courage or prudence to make a stand, he becomes used to the servile state and all the miseries it brings: he justifies the profound remark that has come down to us from antiquity, that when Jupiter reduces a man to that state, he robs him of half his soul.

When enslavement of the body was the terrible fruit of victory, heaven acted thus out of pity for the defeated; but when it is the soul which itself seeks the deadly embrace of debauchery, the punishment is already there in its entirety. And henceforth Laurent deserved it, that punishment. He had been given the chance to redeem himself; Thérèse had risked, in the enterprise, half her own soul: he had failed to take advantage.

As she was getting into the carriage to return home, a wild-eyed man rushed up alongside. It was Laurent. He had recognised her just as she was leaving the foyer, from an involuntary gesture of horror she had made without even being aware of it.

'Thérèse,' he said, 'let's go back into the ball. I want to say to all those men: "You are brutes!" and to all those women: "You are disgusting!" I want to shout your name, your sacred name, before that imbecile crowd, grovel at your feet, eat the dirt, calling down on myself every manner of contempt, insult and shame! I want to make my confession out loud before that whole assembled masquerade, as the first Christians made their confessions in the pagan temples, purified all at once by the tears of penitence and cleansed by the blood of the martyrs...'

This state of exaltation endured until Thérèse had taken him back to his own door. She no longer understood at all how and why this man, unprompted by drink, so much the master of himself and so much the pleasant chatterbox amidst the women of the masked ball, became impassioned to an extravagant degree the moment she appeared.

'I am the one who turns you into a madman,' she said to him. 'Just now they were talking to you about me as if I was a dreadful woman, and even that did not rouse you. I have

251

become like some vengeful spectre for you. That is not what I intended. So let us part, since I can no longer do you anything but harm.'

XIV

They saw each other the following day, however. He begged her to give him one last day of brotherly conversation and a friendly, calm, *bourgeois* outing. They went together to the Jardin des Plantes, sat beneath the great cedar, and climbed up to the maze. The weather was mild, all traces of snow gone. A pale sun peered through pinkish clouds. The buds on the plants were already swollen with sap. Laurent that day was a poet, nothing but a poet and contemplative artist: a deep calm, never previously present, no remorse, no desires or hopes; some innocent good cheer at moments still. For Thérèse, who was observing him with astonishment, it was barely believable that all was broken between them.

The storm returned the next day, with no cause, with no pretext, and exactly as storms form in summer skies, for the mere reason that the previous day has been fine.

Then each day everything turned darker; and it was like the end of the world, like continuous thunderclaps in the heart of darkness.

One night, he walked into her house very late, in a state of complete bemusement, and without knowing where he was, without saying a word to her, he let himself collapse asleep on the sitting room sofa.

Thérèse went up to her studio, and prayed God, ardently and desperately, to release her from this torture. She had lost all heart; this was her limit. She wept and prayed all night.

Daylight was showing when she heard a ring at her doorbell. Catherine was asleep, and Thérèse thought some late passer-by had come to the wrong house. The bell rang again; it rang for a third time. Thérèse went to look through the staircase window which gave a view over the front door. She saw a boy of ten or twelve, whose clothes suggested easy circumstances and whose face, when he looked up, seemed to her angelic.

'What is it, my little friend?' she asked him. 'Are you lost in this quarter?'

'No,' he replied. 'Someone brought me here. I'm looking for a lady called Mlle Jacques.'

Thérèse went downstairs, opened the door and looked at the child with unusual emotion. It seemed to her that she had seen him before, or that he resembled someone she knew but whose name escaped her. The child, too, seemed troubled and uncertain.

She led him into the garden to question him, but instead of giving her any reply:

'Are you,' he said, trembling all over, 'Mlle Thérèse then?'

'I am, my child. What do you want from me? What can I do for you?'

'You have to take me with you and keep me if you want me!'

'Who are you then?'

'I am the son of Count ***.'

Thérèse held back a cry, and her first impulse was to push the child away. But suddenly she was struck by how his face resembled one she had recently painted by looking in a mirror, meaning to send the portrait to her mother, and that face was her own.

'Wait!' she exclaimed, suddenly putting her arms round the boy. 'What is your name?'

'Manoël.'

'Oh, my God! So who is your mother?'

'She's… they advised me very strongly not to tell you straightaway! My mother… was at first the Countess of ***, who lives back there, in Havana. She didn't love me and she often told me: "You are not my son, I am not obliged to love you." But my father loved me, he often told me: "You only have me, you don't have a mother." And then he died eighteen months ago, and the Countess said: "You're mine now and you're going to stay with me." It was because my father had left her some money, provided she passed me off as the son of both of them. But she kept on not loving me, and I got very tired of living with her, and then a gentleman from the United States called M. Richard Palmer suddenly came and asked for me. The Countess said: "No, I refuse." Then M. Palmer said to me: "Do you want me to take you back to your real mother, who believes that you are dead, and who will be very pleased to see you again?" I said: "Yes, of course!" So M. Palmer came at night, in a boat, because we lived beside the sea; and me, I got up very, very quietly and we both sailed out to where a big ship was waiting, and then we crossed the great wide sea, and here we are.'

'Here you are!' said Thérèse, who had knelt to hug the

child to her breast, trembling with excitement, holding him tenderly and pressing on him a long and ardent kiss as he was speaking. 'Where is he? Palmer?'

'I don't know,' the boy said. 'He brought me to the door, he said: *Ring!* And then I didn't see him any more.'

'Let's go and look for him,' said Thérèse, getting up. 'He can't be far away!'

And running with the child, she found Palmer standing in the road a little way off, waiting to be certain that the child was recognised by his mother.

'Richard! Richard!' Thérèse cried, throwing herself at his feet in the middle of the still deserted street, although she would have done just the same if it had been crowded with people. 'Is this an act of God? What have you done for me?'

That was all she could say. Choked by tears of joy, she thought she must lose her mind.

Palmer led her to a bench under the trees on the Champs-Elysées and made her sit down. It took her at least an hour before she could calm down and gather her wits, and manage to hug her son without danger of suffocating him.

'Now I have repaid my debt,' Palmer told her. 'You gave me times of hope and happiness, and I did not want to remain a debtor. I am handing you back a whole lifetime of tenderness and consolation, because this child is an angel, and it costs me something to part from him. I have deprived him of his inheritance and I owe him one in exchange. You cannot oppose me in this; I have made my arrangements and all his own interests are settled. He has in his pocket a wallet which will guarantee his immediate needs and his future. Farewell, Thérèse! You may count on me as your friend in life and in death.'

Palmer walked away happy; he had performed a good action. Thérèse did not wish to set foot again in the house where Laurent was sleeping. She took a cab, after having sent a messenger to Catherine with her instructions, which she wrote from a small café where she took breakfast with her son. They spent the day criss-crossing Paris together, gathering what they would need for a long journey. In the evening, Catherine came to join them with the luggage she had packed during the day, and Thérèse departed to hide her child, her happiness, her peace of mind, her work, her joy, her life, deep in Germany. Her happiness was entirely for herself: she no longer thought about what would become of Laurent without her. She was a mother, and the mother had put an irrevocable end to the mistress.

Laurent slept all day long and woke to find himself alone. He got up, cursing Thérèse for having gone out without thinking of leaving him anything for supper. He was astonished to discover Catherine was nowhere to be seen, told the house it could go to the devil, and walked out.

It was only after some days had passed that he understood what was happening to him. When he saw Thérèse's house sub-let, the furniture packed away or sold, and when he then waited weeks and months without receiving a single word from her, hope evaporated and he could only think of deadening his senses in the familiar way.

It was only after a full year that he found the means to get a letter to Thérèse. He declared himself the author of all his unhappiness and sought a return to their former friendship; then, coming back to their old passion, he concluded like this:

"I know I cannot even claim to deserve that, because I have cursed you, and in my despair at having lost you, I have acted like a desperate man to try to get over my feelings. Yes, I have forced myself to misrepresent your character and your behaviour in my own eyes; I have spoken ill of you with those who hate you, and I have taken pleasure in hearing ill said of you to those who do not know you. I have treated you in your absence the way I used to treat you when you were here! And why are you no longer here? If I am going mad, it is your fault; you should not have abandoned me... oh, wretch that I am, I feel that I hate you at the same time as I adore you! I feel that my whole life will be spent loving you and cursing you... and I can see plainly enough that you hate me! And I would like to kill you! And if you were here, I would fall at your feet! Thérèse, Thérèse, have you then become a monster, do you know no pity any more? Oh! What a terrible punishment it is, this incurable love alongside this unappeased anger! What have I done then, my God, to be condemned to lose everything, even the freedom to love or to hate?"

Thérèse wrote in reply:

"Farewell for ever! But know that there is nothing you have done against me which I have not forgiven, and nothing you can do in the future which I will not still forgive. God condemns certain men of genius to wander in the storm and to create in pain. I have studied you closely enough in your darkness and your light, in your grandeur and your frailty, to know that you are the victim of a preordained destiny, and that you must not be weighed in the same balance as the majority of other men. Your sufferings and your doubts, what you call your punishment, are perhaps the necessary condition of your glory. Learn therefore to endure it. You have strained with all your might towards the ideal of happiness, and you have only grasped it in your dreams. Well! Your dreams, my child, are what reality is for you, they are your talent, they are your life; are you not an artist?

"Be at peace, go your way, God will forgive you for not having been able to love! He condemned you to this insatiable yearning in order that your youth should not be claimed by any woman. The women of the future, the ones who will contemplate your work from century to century, those are your sisters and your lovers."

Dedalus Celebrating Women's Literature 2018–2028

In 2018 Dedalus began celebrating the centenary of women getting the vote in the UK with a programme of women's fiction. In 1918, Parliament passed an act granting the vote to women over the age of 30 who were householders, the wives of householders, occupiers of property with an annual rent of £5 or graduates of British universities. About 8.4 million women gained the vote. It was a big step forward but it was not until the Equal Franchise Act of 1928 that women over 21 were able to vote and women finally achieved the same voting rights as men. This act increased the number of women eligible to vote to 15 million. Dedalus' aim is to publish 6 titles each year, most of which will be translations from other European languages, for the next 10 years as we commemorate this important milestone.

Titles published so far:

The Prepper Room by Karen Duve
Take Six: Six Portuguese Women Writers edited by Margaret Jull Costa
Slav Sisters: The Dedalus Book of Russian Women's Literature edited by Natasha Perova
Baltic Belles: The Dedalus Book of Estonian Women's Literature edited by Elle-Mari Talivee
The Madwoman of Serrano by Dina Salústio
Cleopatra goes to Prison by Claudia Durastanti
The Price of Dreams by Margherita Giacobino
Primordial Soup by Christine Leunens

The Girl from the Sea and Other Stories by Sophia de Mello Breyner Andresen
The Medusa Child by Sylvie Germain
Venice Noir by Isabella Panfido
Chasing the Dream by Liane de Pougy
A Woman's Affair by Liane de Pougy
La Madre (The Woman and the Priest) by Grazia Deledda
Co-Wives, Co-Widows by Adrienne Yabouza
Catalogue of a Private Life by Najwa Bin Shatwan
Take Six: Six Spanish Women Writers edited by Simon Deefholt and Kathryn Phillips-Miles
Days of Anger by Sylvie Germain
Fair Trade Heroin by Rachael McGill
This was the Man by Louise Colet
This Man, This Woman by George Sand

Forthcoming titles include:

Baltic Belles: The Dedalus Book of Latvian Women's Literature edited by Eva Eglaja
Take Six: Six Latvian Women Writers edited by Jayde Will
Take Six: Six Balkan Women Writers edited by Will Firth
Eddo's Souls by Stella Gaitano
The Father's House by Karmele Jaio
Cry Baby by Ros Franey
The Scaler of the Peaks by Karin Erlandsson
The Victor by Karin Erlandsson
The Queen of Darkness (and other stories) by Grazie Deledda
The Christmas Present (and other stories) by Grazie Deledda
Marianna Sirca by Grazie Deledda

For further information please contact Dedalus at
info@dedalusbooks.com

This was the Man by Louise Colet

The middle-aged and dissolute poet Albert de Lincel pursues Stéphanie, marquise de Rostan who, although attracted, continually rebuffs him. What is the problem? Is it Albert's notorious affair twenty years previously with the celebrated writer Antonia Black?

Set as a story within a story, the desperate Albert recounts the true tale of his stormy relationship with Antonia, hoping to set the record straight. But Stéphanie's reluctance, moved though she is, has another cause. She has given her heart to a man far away, toiling at the great novel which will make his name.

Louise Colet (1810-1876), a successful poet, was the mistress of Gustave Flaubert when he wrote *Madame Bovary*. Her brilliantly complex roman à clé sets the impassioned affair between Alfred de Musset (Albert) and George Sand (Antonia) against her own experience of loving two men of towering but contrasting literary reputations.

£11.99   ISBN 978 1 912868 80 3   416p   B. Format

A Woman's Affair by Liane de Pougy

Despite her beauty and her riches, Annhine de Lys, one of the most notorious courtesans of 1890s Paris, is bored and restless. Into her life bursts Flossie, a young American woman, and everything changes. The love she offers Annhine is dangerous, perverse and hard to resist

'*A Woman's Affair* is melodrama at full pelt... Beneath the melodrama is something more interesting: a straightforward acceptance of same-sex love that in 1901 could perhaps only have been expressed in Paris... It is worth noting that *A Woman's Affair* was nearly thirty years before Radclyffe Hall's much milder allusion (to lesbian love) prompted a British court to brand *The Well of Loneliness* (1928) obscene... The more thoughtful feminism glimpsed beneath (the frou-frou and silliness in *A Woman's Affair*) is illuminating on the choices facing women in the early 1900s, and on the dangers of sex work. Anderson does justice to both registers – silly and serious – in a lively translation that captures Pougy's effervescence as well as her uneven style.'

Miranda France in *The Times Literary Supplement*

£9.99   ISBN 978 1 912868 48 3   314p   B. Format

Chasing the Dream by Liane de Pougy

'Pougy's debut novel, *Chasing the Dream* was published in 1898. Admirably pragmatic, Anderson describes it as "a kind of half-time report on her career to date". It opens with the heroine Josiane horizontal on a chaise longue in her negligee. Suddenly a stranger arrives – her old lover, Jean, who declares his undying love, then politely enquires what she has been up to. It is a long story, so Josiane proposes a correspondence in which she will relate the details. The letters that follow chart Josiane's ascent through the Parisian demimonde via assorted aristocrats, politicians and businessmen.'

Miranda France in *The Times Literary Supplement*

'*Chasing the Dream* is a light piece of entertainment, but it is cleverly done. Managing to indulge in the most typical romance-tropes but also upending many of the expectations one has from this kind of story, de Pougy shows a fine touch in this, her first novel.'

M.A.Orthofer in *The Complete Review*

£9.99   ISBN 978 1 912868 56 8   176p   B. Format

Days of Anger by Sylvie Germain

'A murdered woman, lying buried in the forests of the Morvan, is the still beating heart of *Days of Anger*. A rich, eventful saga of blood, angels, obsession and revenge, this marvellous novel is a compulsive, magical read, passionate and spell binding.'

James Friel in *Time Out*

'It reads like Thomas Hardy rewritten by some hectic surrealist and it plants in its rural glades a medieval vitality.'

Robert Winder in *The Independent*

'Germain's creations are strong such as Hubert Cordebugler, the despised village knicker-thief who recycles lingerie in his secret love-chamber, and Fat Ginnie, a voluptuous, towering sherry trifle of a woman who gives birth to a strapping son every Feast of Assumption. An icon for women of substance everywhere.'
Geraldine Brennan in *The Observer*

£9.99   978 1 912868 71 1   238p   B. Format

The Medusa Child by Sylvie Germain

'Sylvie Germain's *The Medusa Child* beautifully translated from the French by Liz Nash, tells a heartbreaking and violent story about sin and redemption in fantastical language; a myth from la France profonde.'

Books of the Year in *The Independent on Sunday*

'Germain's language is redolent with decay, rich with religious torment and ecstasy, and filled with the decadence so loved by this publisher.'   *Time Out*

'*The Medusa Child* is her most accessible novel, and my favourite. A coherent pattern of metaphor depicts an enchanted country childhood. Lucie explores the marshes around her home and studies the stars. But when she is given a room of her own, an ogre starts to pay her nocturnal visits. Helpless and alone, Lucie decides to fight back by turning herself into a monster. This is a superb and compassionate study of damage and resistance.'   Michele Roberts in *Mslexia*

'The ascetic sex scenes between the eight-year-old and the 'blond ogre', and omnipresent sense of sin and salvation, show what a good writer Germain can be.'

Carole Morin in *The New Statesman*

£9.99   978 912868 30 8   247p   B. Format

Dedalus European Classics 1984–2022

The Dedalus European Classics series exists to rescue neglected authors and publish authors who have yet to be translated into English, as we widen what constitutes a classic to include the bizarre and the fantastic from the late 19th century to the middle of the 20th century and work from the small linguistic areas of Europe.

Many of the authors we have published in this series were not felt to be classic authors at the time but we have in most cases made them so. We also like to produce a body of work so a reader can judge an oeuvre and not just a book. We have established or re-established the reputation in English of J.-K. Huysmans, Giovanni Verga, Octave Mirbeau, Gustav Meyrink, Johann Grimmelshausen and Eça de Queiroz by having new translations made of their work and for the first time having a whole oeuvre available in English.

In our thirty-eighth year we are trying to get as many titles as possible back into print so our readers can enjoy nearly all the titles in the Dedalus European Classics list in a print edition. Some titles will remain as ebooks only and some will not be available in the foreseeable future. We have put an estimated publication date for titles which will shortly be reprinted or printed for the first time.

Dedalus European Classics by author: